Breakfast at Cannibal Joe's

Breakfast at Cannibal Joe's

Jay Spencer Green

ISBN: 1514377659
ISBN 13: 9781514377659

Praise for Jay Spencer Green

"Irrepressibly funny, savagely indignant, and immensely readable."

Olibhéir Ó Fearraigh, writer and broadcaster

"Funny, shocking. Demands to be read."

Arthur Smith, comedian, writer, and broadcaster

"I first encountered Jay Spencer Green's inimitable voice on his blog and became an immediate fan. His was the pitch of screamingly funny we all wanted to reach. He's read everything and has byways in his mind you just want to linger in and poke around, watching his neurons spark. His particular blend of the philosophical and the absurd is wholly original, and his masterful narrative skill is strong enough to bind the deliciously anarchic and farcical elements of his stories into a rollicking whole. He writes, we delight. He's the real deal. He also happens to be a thoroughly lovely man."

Sami Zahringer, columnist, blogger, breeder of domestic long-haired Americans.

"Any time I read Jay's work I expect my funny bone to be taken on a trip in a fast car that is then driven off a cliff."

Donagh Brennan, editor, *Irish Left Review*

"Too clever by half. Too funny by three and five-eighths."

Niamh Greene, author, *The Secret Diary of a Demented Housewife, Coco's Secret, Letters to a Love Rat, Rules for a Perfect Life* (Penguin)

"A higgledy-piggledy hodge-podge of style which makes Swiftian use of Burroughs and Burroughsian use of Vonnegut. Set in an archetypal dystopia that may never have existed … or will it? A *Catcher in the Rye* for the Wi-Fi generation."

Carlton B. Morgan, novelist, cartoonist, musician

"Savagely funny and deftly anarchic, Jay Spencer Green's writing is as exquisite as it is deliciously dangerous."

Lisa McInerney, author, *The Glorious Heresies* (John Murray)

"A number of things struck me while I was reading Jay Green's book, but I was laughing so hard I only felt the pain once I'd finished."

Richard McAleavey, blogger, Cunning Hired Knaves

"This book is a fat man standing on an air bed in a pool of over-ripe peaches."

John Hyatt, author of *Navigating the Terror* (Ellipsis), artist, lead singer of the Three Johns, Renaissance man, quiet genius

"Witty, acerbic, and wired to words."

William Wall, author, *This is the Country, Ghost Estate, No Paradiso*

"Jay Spencer Green is the most exciting voice to pretend to come out of Ireland since the leprechaun in *Leprechaun.*"

Oliver Jones, animation rigging supervisor, Laika Inc. (*The Corpse Bride, Boxtrolls, Coraline, Paranorman, Fantastic Mr. Fox*)

"I pride myself on having read Jay Green's work without being physically sick."

Caitriona Lally, author, *Eggshells* (Liberties Press)

"As they say round our way, that guy knows how to hold a pen."

Lorcan McGrane, comedian and writer, Monaghan Arts Network

"I was there at the start of Jay Green's writing career, and I hope I'm there at the end."

Niall Quinn, broadcaster, columnist, Republic of Ireland soccer legend

"The comic writing of Jay Spencer Green always makes me laugh out loud."

Karl Whitney, author, *Hidden City: Adventures and Explorations in Dublin* (Penguin)

"Scathing, scabrous, scatalogical, scary."

Daphne Wayne-Bough, blogger and bonne vivante.

For Mom and Dad
who are without blame for the contents

There is no document of civilization which is not at the same time a document of barbarism.

Walter Benjamin

If at first you don't succeed, fuck it.

Lenny the Bruce

THE END

How long have I been in the dark? Days? Could be longer. I can't move a muscle and it feels like there's an anvil on my chest. Barely breathe. Something's broken.

Me.

Another bomb? Is that it? The stench of sweat, of death. The wetness of blood.

Dust, dirt in my mouth.

Wait. Voices. Mumbling and scrabbling above me. *I'm down here!*

Piece it together. The party at the ambassador's residence. The crucifix. The hooker. I showed her how to masturbate like an Iranian.

Ronald Reagan. He's involved in all this.

Ronald Reagan. Ronald Reagan. Ronald Reagan. His lungs are in a hotel room in Thailand.

Focus, Dammit!

Bovril is the German word for bolt gun.

Chambers. My name is Chambers.

My wrists are stuck. What was in that Scotch?

Sounds like sniggering. *Down HERE you bastards!*

There is a tapeworm. His name is Steve. He is the high priest of a Wiccan coven at a U.S. Army base. He is fucking my wife.

Was fucking. He's dead now. Stone ground brown bread. What's my wife's name?

Come on! I'm here!

Sinéad? That sounds right. Sinéad.

No. Not Sinéad.

Get. A. Grip!

My legs are laughing at me. I don't even know what that means. I must be concussed.

It mussion be concussion.

They're getting closer.

Come on, you bastards. Here I am!

I'm waiting for you!

Wearing a pedometer will tell you precisely how many fucking miles you've walked around Paris.

A cool dad never eats fruit.

They're nearly here. Thank Christ for that.

Over here! Come and get me! Come on, you bastards. Come. ON!

They're here. They're here. Thank you, Jesus. Thank you.

Thank you, thank you, thank you.

THE BEGINNING

No. 75
The Trotsky Surprise

6 oz. Mexican Tequila
6 oz. Russian Vodka
No ice
Serve unexpectedly from behind

I had COITUS on the phone today. Paula Layton, Chief of International Trade (United States). Only briefly, mind you. She doesn't go in for foreplay.

She was ringing to tell me that head office had looked benignly on Niamh Collins's teleworking proposal. An assistant editor in the Political and Economic Science database, Niamh lives out in the wilds beyond Lucan and spends close to four hours a day traveling to and from the office, which makes it difficult—and expensive—to mind her two young kids properly. What if, she inquired, she was to work from home? The job is perfectly made for it: there's no face time with the public, all communication is done via email, and any meetings can be held using conference calls. She had the whole thing worked out. Documentation, sample teleworking contract, the lot. On the plus side for the company, there'd be reduced heating, lighting, and electricity bills, she could use her own computer (with appropriate antivirus software), and the research shows that teleworking leads to reduced turnover of staff. She'd done her homework. Graduates have been coming to us to receive training before jumping ship for one of the better-paying multinationals down the road in Sandyford that promised them career advancement, hot meals, and the kind of half-decent wage that spoilt Southside dimwits find hard to refuse. Niamh had the sense to point out how teleworking would facilitate any staff member thinking about starting a family, not only by giving them more time at home but also by enabling them to move out of Dublin to places where the crap wage we paid them could stretch to things like diapers, food, and heating. She made a pretty good case. And New York is always on my back to get the bills down.

"We've done the math here, Joe, had the accountants run through Niamh's proposal, and we'd like you to get this up and running as soon as you can."

I hid my surprise behind clenched teeth. Whetstone usually has the turning circle of a beached whale.

"Encourage as many of your staff as possible to take up the option. If you can clear out a couple of the floors in the building, we'll be able to sublet them and recoup some of the outlay from the original lease."

"Sure."

"I'm amazed you never thought of this option sooner. You're our man on the ground there, Joe. We need you to spot these possibilities, the potential to cut costs, increase productivity. We aren't paying you to sit on your ass all day."

Jeez, cut me some slack, Jack. For one thing, that's exactly why you're paying me. For another, I never claimed I was suited to this desk-jockey, office-politics shit. Your every-day, run-of-the-mill unscrupulous boss would have instinctively known that Niamh's idea was a good one and that he should pass it off as his own. Me, I give credit where it's due. I don't count that as a failing.

"See if you can make other savings, too. Is there any scope for freelancers?"

"Freelancers?"

"There must be dozens of former staff over there who're out of work now and looking for extra cash. Have Sinéad go through the personnel files, ask around after some of the losers who quit and re-applied for vacancies later. Surely *some* ex-staff have quit the firm and regretted it."

"Must be." I winked at Sinéad, who'd been remarkably restrained up to this point. "I'll get on it this afternoon."

"Be diplomatic in your approach. A lot of these kids today resent having to admit you were right all along, and they don't appreciate you rubbing their noses in it. Phrase it like they'd be doing you a favor, not the other way round."

"Will do. Although a lot of the ingrates have fucked off to Canada, to be honest, Paula. The ones who're still here are either sponging off their wealthy folks or can't leave because their kids are in school and they have negative equity."

"Start with the latter. The spongers will be spoilt, lazy fucks. The ones with kids in school will bite the bullet. They'll even give you a smile and doff their cap."

"Nice. I often feel there isn't enough cap doffing these days. I may make it compulsory."

"You do that. And meanwhile, start shifting the staff out the office. It'll be an easy sell. And check how we're fixed for sublets. Get that ball rolling too."

"Anything you say."

After COITUS, all animals are sad.

Delia called round after work and offered to drag me down to Toner's, one of the few establishments on Baggot Street that still serves reasonably priced alcohol and where you can sit outside for a smoke if the sun's out. Seeing as how he was paying, I accepted his offer graciously, optimistically stuffing a couple of Cohibas into my jacket pocket before leaving the apartment and heading down Herbert Place. This used to be a beautiful part of Dublin. Herbert Place is the last intact stretch of Georgian houses along the Grand Canal. There aren't many Irish who can afford to live here these days, though, and the businesses that once kept the terrace respectable have long since gone belly-up. The horse-drawn carriages still come along late at night, and sometimes they're even showing tourists round, but more likely they're carrying punters cruising for sex. The girls stand on the canal side of the road, the driver pulls up when requested by his fare, and the lucky winner climbs aboard. The driver discreetly pulls over the hood once the transaction has been negotiated and lets them get down to business—I guess the driver takes a commission or gets freebies. Few are the American hibernophiles cooing over Patrick Kavanagh's statue as they trot by on a Sunday morning who know that only the night before the driver was cleaning jizz off the seats like Travis Bickle.

Before the powers of the Dáil were reduced to censuring blasphemers and we moved to the perfect post-democracy of European bank dictatorship, this place used to turn into Little Saigon whenever the party conferences came to town. According to a pilot friend of mine, the seats on Leeds/Bradford flights into Dublin would be occupied exclusively by acne-ridden hookers knocking back brandy and black-currants or whiskey and limes to fortify themselves prior to meeting their "regulars," pillars of the rural community, up for the Ard Fheis or the rugby. Other girls, of course, came to Dublin purely on spec, because "you have to go where the work is."

I had a Guinness in Toner's to start with, to be polite, while Delia ordered a quinine. Because it was a bit nippy outside, and to avoid looking conspicuous, we took our glasses downstairs to the cellar bar, which is only ever frequented by spies, rats, pimps, students, and TDs. In descending order of respectability.

"Did you hear the one about the dead epileptic who wouldn't fit in his coffin?" I took his query as an expression of concern.

"No. Was it someone at the tennis club?"

"You prick, Joe. It's a joke." He slurped on his quinine. "Wasted on you."

"Sorry. I wasn't concentrating."

"It's what's known as gallows humor, Joe, Gallows being a small town in Scotland where Methodists go for their annual comedy festival." I was reminded of the futility of attempting sensible conversation with Delia. And why I enjoy his company.

A small group of screenagers clattered down the stairs and asked the barman to turn on the TV above the counter. I pondered how they might look with their innards splashed across the Bushmills mirror behind the bar by machine gun fire and was surprised by how much it cheered me up.

"It's no wonder you live alone, you sad bastard," I said to Delia after he'd bought the next round and sat back down, taking off his jacket. "No woman could ever take you seriously."

"They don't want serious, Joe. Women love a sense of humor. I'm beating them off with a shinty stick. It's murder. Why do you think Wilde pretended to be gay?"

I muttered skepticism. Delia pulled out a new bag of salmiak, that appalling salt licorice shit he uses to stave off the nicotine cravings, and started chomping.

"Believe me, Joe, I'd much prefer the kind of life you have."

"What do you mean, *my* kind of life?"

"You know...Indifferent. Chaste. Sexless."

"You cheeky son of a bitch." I put down my pint. "I'll have you know I'm horny as a lizard and three times the size. You *do* realize that there are no legs on this table. I'm holding it up with my boner."

Delia laughed and thumped the tabletop. Beermats jumped with fright. A ball of gum clung for dear life to the underside.

"Ow!" I feigned agony, and we both chuckled. Then supped.

"Have you heard this one, Joe? What's the difference between a Christmas pudding and a Buddhist?" I shook my head, glass at my lips.

"You put out the flames on a Christmas pudding."

Hah. Delia makes living in Dublin almost bearable. And not just for his sense of humor and his willingness to buy drinks. He pretends to find me likeable, too.

"By the way, Joe, before I forget. I'm going to have something for you next week, after I've seen my cousin. Seems like he's come up trumps."

The training kicked in and I was able to stifle my elation by using mental displacement and deep-breathing techniques. I only responded once I'd climbed down off the chandelier.

"That's a fine fucking family you belong to, Delia. What did you say the name was again?"

"I didn't, Joe," he smiled. "I didn't. Remember: A rolling stone gathers no rosebuds."

"That's very true," I said. "Just wrinkles."

"Nice one. You're learning. Listen. I'll give you a ring for a tennis match. You'll probably want to rent a van or an estate. Keep your boot empty."

"My boot?"

"Your trunk, I mean. Your trunk. You can fill your boots after."

"Thanks, Del," I said. "Chances are, I will."

No. 54

The Road to Basra

3 oz. Araqi Date Liquor

6 oz. Sandeman Sherry

Use the Sandeman as an Araqi chaser

Stopping on the way home at lunchtime to contemplate the significance of a dead zebra on Northumberland Road cost me the news. I only managed to catch the end of the final item:

…and eventually he was cut free from the device by sniggering firemen.

Shit.

Nuala Malone will be here next with the weather, but that's all from me until this evening. Have a good afternoon.

Good afternoon.

There was a shooting in the Phoenix Park, and given the people I hang around with, there's always a chance I'll know those involved. Back when I lived in Athens, I was always getting shot at. Islamic fundamentalists, Marxist revolutionaries, anarchist insurrectionists, disgruntled neo-Platonists. Dublin, not so much. When was the last time you saw video footage of a kidnapped U.S. citizen denouncing his country's use of Shannon airport for rendition flights or America's continued deployment of tourist buses along Nassau Street or its creeping cultural imperialism? Never, right? The Irish are such pussies.

It wasn't an impromptu trip home. I was heading back to the apartment for lunch anyway. The Whetstone office is full of grudge-bearing, self-regarding smart alecks who, simply because they have to work in silence all day, get their jollies during the lunch hour by trying to "rip the piss" out of their stupid Yank boss. My apartment is only a ten-minute walk away, so the temptation is always there to sneak out and hope nobody's noticed. I come home, turn on the TV, and make myself a ham and tomato sandwich. Listen to the news and look out my study window down at the canal. Used to be that the canal bank opposite was sprinkled with nubile office workers enjoying their Taytos and sushi, which afforded me the chance to knock one out while leering at them from behind my bedroom curtains, but they've all gone now. The only bodies reclining on the canal bank these days are those of sullen, purple-nosed, cauliflower-eared winos, and you can't pull yourself off looking at them. Trust me.

These canals were once the pride of the city. One city councilor even proposed changing the city's coat of arms to include a dead dog and a shopping cart. These days, like the councilor, the canals are just full of shite. Not many people know this, but from time to time the Irish army engages in what's described as "brown propaganda," driving around the city-center streets late at night and spraying sewage over the homeless as they sleep in the doorways and under bridges. The idea, as I understand it, is to arouse the disgust of passers-by on their way to work in the morning. "Somebody," they're meant to say to themselves, "some shallow-thinking do-gooder is feeding those feckers. And then they sit around getting pissed all day and shit in the doorways." It prepares the public psychologically for persecution, obviously, but it's also a stroke of neo-Keynesian economic genius. Paying the army to spray crap everywhere creates a whole bunch of sanitation jobs and generates demand for industrial-strength cleaning products.

At 4.30 every morning, while you, dear blessed and upright citizen reader, are still fingering yourself in your pit, the city's streets teem with JobBridge interns equipped with hoses and jet sprays and organized into battalions of street cleaners, window wipers, park hooverers, and traffic-light polishers, all charged with the task of making this city look less distressed than it really is. When the tourists staying in the B&Bs in Malahide and the few remaining businessmen who stay at the Shelbourne or the Hilton step out onto the sidewalk, they see nothing but a nice, bright, shiny Dublin—a limpid Liffey, a buffed Ballsbridge, a sanitary Santry. They fly home thinking what a polite, well-mannered, well-manicured, and prosperous place Dublin is. "I can't see what all the fuss is about," they tell their spouses, lovers, mistresses, servants, ladyboy concubines when they get home. "Ireland's flourishing under austerity."

I can't claim to be flourishing, exactly—my complexion is flour-ish and that's about it—but I'm surviving, and things could be a lot worse. After the events-that-will-not-be-named in Athens, I half-expected to be fed to the wolves. Or worse, the Gray Wolves. Fortunately, I'd accumulated enough intel from my fieldwork over the previous two and half decades to warrant rescuing. Not forgiveness, but rescuing. "The Company looks after its own, Joe," they told me. "You've no need to worry. We'll see you right."

They couldn't fire me, you see. I had too much upstairs—and too much on those upstairs—for them to take that risk. Instead, they Farmed me out, the Farm being the CIA's training facility in Virginia. That's where I was expected to impart my extensive, expensively acquired expertise to new recruits in the clandestine services. Then, when they'd milked that particular intellectual teat, and before any investigative journos from the *Nation,* the *Guardian* or Z-Net could come sniffing around, they retrained me in library information services and business management before smuggling me into Dublin. Which is how I come to be running a publishing house full of grudge-bearing self-regarding smart alecks who get their kicks from winding up their stupid Yank boss every lunchtime.

Head office pretty much leaves me to get on with things, which is how I like it, although I have to liaise once a week with New York and meet up on a regular basis with Frank Prendergast, the CIA Chief of Station at the embassy and an old friend of mine from more reckless times in Los Fresnos. Frank has a real hands-on attitude to his own work, which means he's too busy to bother himself with my activities. And that's how I like it. How I like it is to spend my afternoons playing tennis over at Lansdowne rather than plow my way through reams of quality stats and invoices, and so that's exactly what I do, given half a chance. And I know Frank wouldn't be seen dead in a tennis club. "If I've got to watch two lesbians grunting and squealing, I expect at least one of them to be wearing a strap-on," he says.

I suppose the government has to have somewhere to send people like me and Frank: the detritus, the embarrassments, the forgotten men. Somewhere that no one pays any attention to and where all sins are either forgiven or of no consequence. It used to be the Senate. Now it's Ireland.

According to its marketing spiel, Whetstone Publishing "specializes in the production of comprehensive and concise online databases geared toward facilitating the rapid retrieval of the most up-to-date, relevant, and readily understandable information for research purposes." Or, to summarize, we summarize. We summarize millions upon millions of magazine and journal articles to help researchers in schools, colleges, libraries, and prisons around the world do their job more efficiently. You name it, we distil it. We are the Diageo of knowledge. The Whetstone offices here in Dublin are staffed by a "dedicated team of 'professional' writers, editors, indexers, and abstracters"—most of them recent college grads, so they're cheap—who spend all their waking hours reading shit like *Geophysics Today, The Lancet, The Nairobi News, Oil & Gas Journal, Cosmopolitan, Field & Stream,* and *Traction Engine Buyers' Guide,* and then summarizing the articles for inclusion in our online databases.

Perhaps this isn't the sort of thing you'd expect from a CIA front company. In the turbulent minds and byzantine imaginations of conspiracy theorists, we should be running guns, printing counterfeit renminbi, secretly funding boy bands. They forget that the CIA is all about collecting information. Information for other people to act on. If you join the CIA expecting a life of laser guns, ju-jitsu, and exotic STDs, bear in mind that your only contact with them may come through the pages of *The Lancet* and *Popular Mechanics*.

You get the idea. Information is knowledge, knowledge is power, power is the ultimate aphrodisiac. Thus, I am the king of sexy.

Sexy isn't what it used to be.

Everything we produce at Whetstone, the collected wisdom of the world's wordsmiths, is delivered straight back to Langley for analysis, safekeeping, and possible retrieval should it ever become necessary to check, say, the Dalai Lama's views on the Turin Shroud, the role of koala bears in Gothic architecture, or whether the price of steam rollers in Kenya was affected by rumors about Charlize Theron.

Times being tight, however, and because the CIA is such a cheapskate catchpenny organization, we're also expected to make a profit from what we do, which means selling our products—after they've been suitably diluted and shorn of detail—on the open market to private enterprise and academia. Front or no front, business is business, a truism that provides me with a raison d'être, a moral code, and a pain in the ass.

The staff working at Whetstone don't know they're working for the CIA, but why would they? After spending the entire day trawling through *Die Welt, Asahi Shimbun,* and *Business Mexico,* the poor saps could be forgiven for not knowing what country they're in, let alone who they work for. It's the one piece of information that never crosses their desks. Knowledge is power, ignorance is bliss. Besides, the way I see it, Whetstone is providing a social service by allowing dozens of overeducated postgrads to do what they do best—sit around all day, read, smoke, moan, drink coffee, write one-paragraph essays—and get paid for it. It's like university, except without the cheap beer and bad sex.

I was educated at the university of real life but I was kicked out. Now, I'm practicing at the bar.

My job, as Managing Director–Europe (MDE), involves taking overall responsibility for the productivity and profitability of the various departments, making sure the whole Dublin operation runs smoothly and cheaply, and identifying priority news items for immediate dispatch to Paula in New York.

Smoothly and cheaply are the difficult bits. The last part of the job, identifying priority news items, was made much easier for me by the recruitment—at New York's instigation—of Sinéad O'Shea as my assistant. I say "at New York's instigation," but I don't know precisely who in New York made the decision or what selection criteria were used. All I know is she turned up for an interview I had been told would be a formality and which I should treat as a getting-to-know-you meeting. So I shaved, stuck on a tie, cleaned my hair, combed my teeth. Sinéad breezed in 35 minutes late. Breezed in like a Kerry-born tsunami, with an ant-stomping gait and fetus-choking hips.

"Surry-um-laite-now," she said, "Only uh dornt normally getup until…two-in-the-aftuh noooon."

The hell is *this*?

"You wornt believe wut a time ahad trarn-tuh-find displayuss." She shed her canvas jacket to reveal a green and yellow GAA shirt and willowy pink arms spritzed with moles like chocolate confetti. "Uv not seen inside unufficebuilding since Nine Eleven happunnd. An' even *dat* wuz on duh-teeeveeee."

This announcement was delivered with such a cheery, sing-song lilt from smiling, big-pillow lips that the content barely registered. She could have been telling me I'd got cancer of the head and I'd have thought I'd won the lottery. How New York ever managed to find her I have never been able to fathom. Maybe their Skype has subtitles. Suffice to say that there were more than a few misunderstandings in the early days, not helped by the fact that I'd never encountered the name Sinéad written down before. I assumed it was a typo in the memo, and for our first three months together, she answered to the name Sinbad.

"Why didn't you tell me sooner?" I asked when she finally put me straight during post-work drinks in O'Neill's.

"You wuh my new borss. Uh thought it might be some kind uv tayest."

Of course, I've gotten used to the accent since our first encounter, and she now sounds like a perfectly normal human being, no different from you or me. She got her own back, too. Overhearing me on the phone refer to her as "my factotum," she now calls me her "fatscrotum."

Disrespectful and grounds for sexual harassment, some may say, but I take it as a compliment.

For the sake of appearance and to satisfy the lawyers, I had to interview several candidates, but she must have been tipped off, too, that our meeting was only a formality.

Me: *Can I ask what you see as your particular strengths with regard to this position that might set you apart from the competition, Ms O'Shea?*

Her: *Well, I'm cheap, which is important nowadays. Although you've got to be prepared to pay for quality, haven't you? Pay peanuts, you get elephants. Also, I'm a bit older than all those spotty-faced losers out in the hall. Even if they have better qualifications, they won't have my sense of responsibility or the capacity to destroy colleagues for the sake of their own career advancement.*

Me: *Hmm. And how would you define 'sense of responsibility'?*

She: *Oh, that's easy. Recognizing when you've been caught red-handed.*

Me: *Interesting. And what would you regard as your particular weaknesses? With regard to the job, I mean.*

She: *I'm supposed to say here that I'm a perfectionist, aren't I? But I won't lie to you. I'm not. And it's not that I <u>can't</u> lie. If anything, my biggest weakness is my lack of honesty. And my willingness to plámás to get what I want.*

Me: *That's not a term I'm familiar with.*

She: *Oh, my apologies. It means to flatter someone in pursuit of an ulterior motive. You'll soon pick up these Irish terms.*

You're clearly an intelligent and perceptive man. Not to mention devastatingly attractive.

Me: *Thank you very much. Would you regard yourself as having strong interpersonal skills?*

She: *Yes, I'm very much a "people person," as you can see from my past work as a traffic warden and airport security guard, so I know what vermin people can be. If a job requires me to knock a few heads together, give someone the bullet, I have no problem with that.*

Me: *I see. It's not the kind of thing one relishes though.*

She: *Of course not. It's always better to let someone else do it and look bad.*

Me: *And let me ask you, what kind of tasks do you find the hardest, or the most tiring?*

She: *Anything involving independent thought. I think I'm at my best when I know what I'm supposed to be doing. That way, I can do what I'm told, get paid, go home, and forget about work. There's a reason why it's called a job.*

Me: *Sorry?*

She: *Like in the Bible. The Book of Job. Suffer in silence. Don't ask questions. Keep the faith.*

Me: *Ah. I see (takes notes). Finally. If I were to ask you to sum yourself up in one word, what would that one word be?*

She: *Prone to elaboration.*

Me: *That's three words.*

She: *Yes, I know, but I always feel that a one-word description doesn't provide me with the opportunity to fully account for myself. One-word answers are inevitably ambiguous, open to interpretation, liable to mislead. Even if it means answering the question in a way that transgresses the rules, I think it's worth it for the sake of clarity. Which doesn't mean that I can't follow rules, only that I believe that they are worth bending on occasion if the outcome warrants it.*

Me: *Thank you, Ms O'Shea. Your answer tells me a great deal. Now, do you have any questions for me?*

(Pause)

She: *Only one. If I get this position—and I'm fairly confident I will—where do I plug in my foot spa?*

Yeah, I thought she was joking, too.

To be fair to her, she's done okay, notwithstanding her unorthodox interpretation of Human Resources. We work well as a team. In addition to flagging up items for dispatch to New York, she also picks out "the funnies," articles that have cropped up during the day that she thinks will give me a laugh. It's a considerate gesture that brightens my day and takes my mind off the fact that I'm treading water in a neo-colonial outpost with no prospect of career progress just because of one lousy indiscretion eight years ago with a bottle of Metaxa, a tub of Starbucks Java ice cream, and the spouse of a European leader.

Here is today's batch:

The *Florida Senior Gazette* reports with some glee the case of St. Petersburg widower Irving Binzz, who decided to advertise in a rival newspaper for someone to share his retirement activities with. After five unsatisfactory meetings with potential new buddies—"Like nothing I'd encountered during 35 years in the army"—Binzz's disappointment was explained with searing clarity when he double-checked his advertisement and saw that his hobbies had been listed as "golf, wildlife conservation, and coarse fisting."

The *Daily Mail* has an advert for a Quasi-modular course in French bell ringing by distance learning at the University of Notre Dame.

I'm not entirely sure what's funny about that one. In fact, I might phone the contact number and find out more about it. Maybe there are classes online.

The *Evening Herald* reports that troops have shot dead fifteen Travelers in a two-hour gun battle near Kells. Three of the Travelers were dressed as Cossacks.

Headline in the *Drogheda Leader*: Pro-fracking TD Says Nothing Wrong with Drinking Water.

Yeah, right. If you're a fish.

No. 22
The JFK

1 oz. Green Spot Irish Whiskey
8 oz. Tomato Juice
4 oz. Cuban Rum
Three slugs of Harvey's

As it turned out, nobody interesting was shot in the Phoenix Park. I caught the *6.01 News* and it said some fat German tourist got a cap in his ass while he was bent over tying up his Timberlands. The shooter thought he was a Rhodesian Ridgeback. Easy mistake.

Whenever there's a storm imminent, a tight, vise-like humidity descends on Dublin, so tight it makes you want to barf. All clammy and close and sweaty and liable to bring you out in hives. Tempers fray. Argument becomes the usual mode of discourse. Fighting and wife beating cease to be privileges reserved for members of An Garda Síochána: Anyone can do it. The brain of Damo the average Dub swells up like a sponge. His propensity to violence multiplies. To provide a more socially acceptable outlet than spousal abuse, the government encourages him to shoot dogs. Indeed, some people believe that the government was behind the last rabies outbreak in Ireland, that it deliberately channeled Damo's frustrations with a life ill lived into a project that could be claimed to serve some community interest. Sooner he shoot dogs than start wiping out the homeless.

That's the army's job.

Sadly, nobody warned the government how addictive cruelty to animals could be. Who'd have thought there'd be gun junkies queuing up to unload their Uzis and Kalashnikovs into unsuspecting poodles gamboling nervously across the gauze? Sometimes the Phoenix Park is littered with red, quivering objects more at home in a David Cronenberg movie. It isn't pretty.

The unpredictable nature of the indigenous population is one of the reasons why CIA operatives are discouraged from making friends outside of work. What passes for polite and discreet conversation among civilized American citizens may be treated as a deliberate attempt at gossip-mongering among lesser tribes, and even the best-trained, strictest disciplined, and most circumspect of us is not immune from offering up a significant morsel of information during a relaxed and convivial conversation, say, or at the moment of orgasm, and you never know who might be listening, even if you think you're alone. I should say, however, that I regard this anti-fraternization imposition as no longer binding on me. For one thing, I'm no longer technically a career CIA operative. For another, while it might be a tolerable restriction if you're being moved from assignment to assignment, when you've been stuck in one place for years on end, neglected and disparaged except when annual accounts are due, it becomes an insufferable and unreasonable demand. It is only inevitable that you will do what you can to make the best of your lot. You will make friends with people who, ordinarily, you'd buy a mobile home to avoid.

Which is not to say that Delia is uglier or meaner than any other Irishman. Only that they shoot Travelers, don't they?

Derek is his real name, by the way. Everyone calls him Del. Delia is my nickname for him, a term of ironic affection, after Delia Smith, the British equivalent of Julia Child. Ironic because of the alarm provoked in him by kitchen utensils. Delia can't cook for shite. Never eat his pork chops.

There is an Irish equivalent of Julia Child, but he's a bloke from Cavan, which is a joke in its own right. Besides, you wouldn't think that Delia was Irish, what with his stocky build and the kind of swarthy Latin looks that once made Che Guevara such a catch for the Bolivian military. Apparently, his physique is not uncommon among Galwegians. There used to be a lot of trade between Spain and Galway—and obviously not just trade, although money probably changed hands. Once upon a time, Delia was a lecturer in computer studies at UCD, but when all the software firms upped sticks and left Ireland and the department shut down, he had to turn his hand to whatever he could find, not easy for a nerd with attitude. He gives some private tuition and does upgrades and a bit of web design for people who still have broadband, but there isn't much call for that sort of thing anymore. Most of his income he gets from importing coke and fags on the sly. This can be quite a delicate operation and a risky one to boot. There's a lot of competition, and the market is dominated by some real nasty characters. Delia's strictly low-key and small fry, making a few bob where he can, but I do worry for him sometimes.

His dubious origins and black-economy instincts probably explain his exotic relationship with the English language. At the best of times, the Irish are masters of obtuseness. Delia approaches English side on, like a winking crab sketched by a drunken Picasso. He's forever coming out with these sayings—I assume they're poorly translated ancient Irish proverbs—like "People who live in glass houses shouldn't throw parties," or "You can't make an omelet without breaking wind." Both of which, curiously, are true.

We'd arranged to meet at Lansdowne Tennis Club on Londonbridge Road in the afternoon. It's quiet then. I'd hired a car like he'd told me to, for a couple of days, from the rental place on Haddington Road. Not having driven for 18 months, I decided to take it out on the roads of Dublin for a spin, to familiarize myself with its operation, before heading down to the tennis club. The last thing I wanted was to be rear-ended driving away from the club with a trunk full of contraband.

Not the most inspired of ideas. Much of the grass that used to grow out of the cracks in the road around Stephen's Green has been dealt with, but the potholes are less visible; if anything, the grass used to give drivers some idea where the uneven parts of the road were. I managed to negotiate the road with only a couple of jolts before heading down Dawson Street, where things were even more chaotic: clapped-out buses that could barely roll down the street under their own steam, struggling along like emphysematic pensioners, pausing to lean against the curb to pick up passengers while catching their breath, and the odd government Merc zig-zagging between the detritus, carrying its precious cargo to Leinster House or Buswell's bar.

Round onto Nassau Street to Dublin's American Quarter, past the gewgaw shops on the right-hand side and the tourist coaches on the left, parked crocodile fashion along the boundary wall of Trinity College, not so much a seat of learning as a butt of academic jokes. I prayed for German tourists to step out between the coaches, expecting the traffic to halt for them the way Europe's economy has, then headed past the old dental hospital and round in front of the Davenport Hotel, stopping at the traffic lights, the only set of lights in the city center that works, outside Oscar Wilde's old family home, before turning onto Merrion Square. Of a weekend here, you can see hundreds of paint-by-numbers landscapes on the railings, hanging there like vampires to suck out the contents of gullible Americans' wallets. And from Merrion Square directly to a million Illinois garage sales. Something to threaten the grandchildren with: Behave or you'll get *that* in my will.

Past Holles Street Maternity "Hospital," along Blood Transfusion Street, formerly Mount Street, past the Tattooed Bourgeois, one of my favorite pubs, the old Refugee Applications Center on the opposite side, closed now, and down Northumberland Road, where most of the foreign embassies can still be found because no one else can afford the rents.

I turned left at the junction with Haddington Road, past the Beggar's Bush pub and the former museum of labor history, now the Museum of Public Safety, over onto Londonbridge Road, enduring the speed bumps that can only have been left in place as a joke, and into the tennis club car park, empty save for the presence of Delia, sitting on the hood of his Prius, his sports bag on the gravel.

He dropped to his feet as I parked the car and made for the clubhouse door, glancing around to ensure we were alone. I followed him up the dingy stairs, saying nothing, tense with anticipation, to the changing room, where he proceeded to put his kit on, indicating that we were going to have to go through all the formalities of actually playing a match first.

"Need to sweat out the Dublin toxins," he explained, the bastard. He knew he had me on tenterhooks.

Delia has all the latest Wilson gear, no doubt thanks to another dodgy cousin of his, so he looks the part, especially with his Latin coloring and his wristbands. I had my lucky funeral shirt (it's a Lacoste, so it doubles up for tennis), my Nike shorts, cheap Moore Street socks (35 euros for 6 pairs), and 5-year-old Dunlops. He plays with two Head Platinum X4 Supa-lite Extensors, whereas I come out onto court with my trusty second-hand Wilson Sledge Hammer. Needless to say, I always win.

On this occasion, though, there was too much at stake. Conscious that he'd done me a major favor and possibly even taken one or two risks, I let him win the second set before taking the third with two breaks of serve.

"I think your shots were actually harder in the third set than in the previous two," I told him in consolation as we were leaving the court. "Either your stamina's improving or your rackets need a restring."

He didn't know if it was a compliment or not. That's what tennis players do. Snide.

He's right about the toxins, though. They leave a dark sheen on the skin that looks like a tan. I was tempted not to shower afterwards, but Delia always does, so it would have been unseemly not to. Then he insisted on dragging me into the bar, overlooking Courts 1 and 2, where all the poseurs usually play. A bunch of old farts were playing doubles on Court 2, so we sat at the table in the panoramic window and sneered.

"Did you see that documentary about Michael Jackson the other night?" he asked. Brian the barman arrived with two ersatz coffees.

"Who?" I was distracted by a particularly vicious spin serve from a doddery geezer in a bandana. A sort of geriatric Agassi.

"Jackson." He said it an offhand manner, as though preoccupied with loftier thoughts. He often does that. "Michael Jackson."

"No. Any good?"

"Excellent." He opened up a brand-new packet of salmiak. Like they're going out of fashion. "Want some?" I waved the offer away.

"Apparently, by the end of his career, he was living entirely on a diet of mephedrone and kiwi and banana yogurt."

"Is that so?"

The receiver of Agassi's serve had lobbed Agassi's partner, a gangly coffin-dodger standing inert and semi-conscious at the net, leaving a panicked Agassi, who had optimistically followed in behind his serve, to backpedal, a frantic dash of spraying sweat, gammy leg, and wobbly paunch.

"According to the documentary, yes. Only, I don't think they had mephedrone around when Jackson was alive."

"Probably made it up. Don't get me started on documentaries."

"Yeah." He gnawed on a piece of licorice. I realized that I'd left my Nicorettes back at the apartment.

"Besides, I don't think there's any such thing as kiwi and banana yogurt. Kiwis are a protected species."

Agassi made a desperate lunge for the lob and miraculously succeeded in putting up a lob of his own into the stratosphere. His opponents looked nervously at each other and shuffled around the court. Neither of them wanted to take the smash for fear of busting their corset. Looked like we'd have a few minutes before the ball came down.

"Do you have any change on you, Del? I want to get some nuts."

"Sure." He fumbled in his tracksuit bottoms. "Are you certain you won't...?" He proffered the salmiak again. I configured my facial features in such a way as to suggest unmitigated horror. He handed over some shrapnel and I stood up to go to the bar. The ball on Court 2 came down and bounced once. One of the old farts was lining up to take the smash. I stayed for the denouement.

He netted it.

"Dick," said Delia.

Agassi and his partner high-fived like pros.

"Did you ever see Jackson?" I asked, upon my return from the bar with a bag of dry roast nuts and no change. Delia shook his head. "I think he played Dublin, didn't he? Before he died."

He looked up from the spot where his change was supposed to be and frowned.

"Yes, Joe. Before he died. That would have been the optimal time to play."

Smartass.

"Not that I wouldn't have gone to a posthumous gig," he continued. "It would have had an entertainment value all its own. Think of *Thriller,* but with added realism. Or a Madonna gig with less."

A 15 mph ace from Agassi.

"By the way, Joe. Any holidays arranged?"

"Holidays? Can't, Del. There's a major gig on at the ambassador's residence that I'm expected to attend. Won't get away before then."

"That's tough." He shrugged sympathetically. "Work related, is it?"

"Yup. I have to represent Whetstone. Maintain the company profile, that sort of thing. Not really my scene, but it's free booze and a day out of the office."

"Cool. An all-dayer, so."

"I don't *really* have to go until the evening. The reception and the fireworks. Prior to that it's all formal stuff."

"Will you be able to let your hair down"—He tossed another piece of licorice into his mouth without interrupting his flow—"or are you expected to behave?"

I snorted.

"Like I give a shit."

"Really? There'll be some pretty important people there, I imagine."

"The few remaining Americans and a smattering of Irish politicians. It's an occasion for schmoozing. Schmoozing and boozing."

"I don't think I could stick it, Joe, mixing with those feckers. How do you put up with all the fakery and insincerity?"

"I'm the master of fakery and insincerity, Del. I paste on a smile and remind myself I'll be dead one day."

"It was your fakery and insincerity I was referring to. If you ask me, I'd rather top myself."

"You can't drink when you're dead."

He took the hint and knocked back the coffee.

"You're not wrong, Joe. Why don't we go downstairs and check out my car?"

The rest, as they say, is unalloyed happiness. I pulled my rental up beside the Prius, opened my trunk, and inspected the contents of his.

Few are the moments in a man's life that can genuinely make his heart flutter. The time he reads the letter telling him he's been accepted by the CIA. The first time he sets eyes on his first wife. The first time his mistress sits on his face.

This was one of those moments. Inside Delia's trunk were 16—count them—16 bottles of Glenmorangie. Standing to attention in their russet glory, waiting to be carried away, swept off their feet by me. What a fine, wonderful, dear man Delia is. I would have kissed him there and then if my head hadn't been swimming, if my mouth hadn't been so dry from hyperventilation, if he'd bothered to pop that zit on his chin.

"How the fuck did you manage this?"

He tapped his nose and put his forefinger to his lips.

"Sssshhhh, Joe. Don't look a gift horse in the bush."

"You are the love of my life. Have I told you that?" I was being excessively effusive, but what else could I do?

"Bet you say that to all the girls, Joe. I haven't finished yet." He reached into a Woodie's DIY canvas sack and pulled out a box of twenty-four Romeo No. 1s. Not the best cigars in the world, admittedly, but who am I to complain? I know when to be gracious.

"Delia, I don't know what to say. I'm flabbergasted."

He was chuckling merrily.

"Don't say a word. To anyone. Conserve your energy for carrying this lot up the stairs to your place."

"What do I owe you?" I'd have happily donated an organ. One of the spare ones. A kidney. My brain. My dick. Anything except the next tennis match. I do have limits.

"Leave it with me, Joe. I'll get back to you. You wouldn't be interested in any of this, would you?"

I hadn't even noticed that the bag from which he had extracted the cigars also appeared to contain, what, a hundred and fifty, maybe two hundred grand's worth of coke. Cellophane packed, sellotape wrapped, plastic bagged, nose bound. I balked.

"Not really my scene, Del. I wouldn't know what to do with it."

"Fair enough. No harm, no foul. I've got to try to shift it one way or another. Can't sniff the lot myself."

A black SUV pulled into the car park and Delia slammed the trunk.

"How do you normally get rid of it?" He scowled at my failure to change the topic of conversation. I copped on. "I'll get you a pint at the Schoolhouse. A box of chocolates from Bewley's. Something to tide you over."

He gave a perfunctory nod and made to depart. Three racket-waving kids leapt out of the back door of the SUV and raced to the clubhouse door.

"Get us again, Joe. I've gotta shoot. Phone us for another game."

"You betcha."

He climbed into the driver's seat of the Prius. "And remember the old saying: Many a true word is spoken. Ingest."

"I will, Del. I will. As soon as I get home."

National Geographic Magazine for Kids presents surprising facts about giraffes.

- The word "giraffe" means "sees a long way" in Kikuyu.
- The first snooker rests were made from giraffes' femurs (with their horns on the end).
- Giraffes shed their tails every six months. Giraffe's tail soup is a delicacy in China believed to have anti-depressant properties.
- Giraffes have an attention span of thirty-five and a half minutes.
- In Malian literature, giraffes are frequently portrayed as telepathic.
- Unlike leopards, giraffes can change their spots by holding their breath for two minutes while blinking rapidly.
- A giraffe features on the coat of arms of Peru.
- Giraffe meat tastes like sour apple Altoids, but you'd be advised not to try it, because it causes cancer.
- A kick from a mother giraffe defending its young can send three acrobats on a penny farthing into a skip of lard sixty feet away.
- If you shave all the hair off a giraffe, it loses four feet in height and three tons in weight.
- Most of a giraffe's nutrition is acquired from moonlight and cold tea.
- Giraffes thrive in zoos, except in France, where they all die of baguette poisoning.

No. 62
The Cuban Invader

2 oz. of Bay Rum
2 oz. Pig's Nose Scotch Whisky
Serve up on a plate

Sinéad came into my office around noon, looking for clothes to be donated to PACS, some local ecumenical organization that does charity work in the corporation blocks—the projects—around the office. The way I understand it, the name stands for Protestants and Catholics in Solidarity (it's meant to sound like Pax), and they're a bunch of concerned religious trying to reclaim the moral high ground from secular materialism, socialism, capitalism, and Islam, creeds that it regards as having usurped Christianity's rightful place as the ultimate arbiter of social justice in Ireland. That usurpation happened, if you remember, after all the hypocrisy and child fucking the church was doing. What was it the Jesuits used to say? "Give me a child when he is six and I'll show him my man."

I had a garbage bag full of old gear to give to Sinéad that should keep them happy for a while. I say old clothes, but really it was stuff I wasn't going to wear anymore, stuff Ellie, my wife, bought me. There was some pretty cool gear in there: a Thierry Mugler sweater, a red leather Pierre Balmain jacket, a Shanghai Tang suit. The idea of some dosser squatting in the gutter in designer gear Ellie'd spent a fortune on amused me. At least someone might benefit from our marriage.

Not that I'm the sort of guy to bear a grudge for long. I forgave Ellie years ago for what happened between us. I never told her I'd forgiven her, of course, and I think she still holds herself accountable.

I fucking hope so.

I don't like explaining to people that my wife ran off with a wizard, because generally their first response is to laugh, and their second is to tell their mates that my wife is screwing Harry Potter. But it's the truth. Ellie and I were living in Fort Hood, where I was working as a liaison officer and she was part of EXFOR, the Experimental Force, which tested out ideas, weapons, and technology for use in the field. They have this Open Circle thing there, a Wiccan coven, and Ellie joined—I didn't see any harm in it. She ended up falling in love with Steve the high priest or top druid or whatever the fuck he called himself, and one night 12 years ago they disappeared without so much as a puff of smoke.

Some people have marriages made in heaven. Ours was made in Taiwan.

After Sinéad left, I got a visit from Frank, sporting the same perverse air that enamored him to me 20 years ago. We were pen pushers back then in Los Fresnos, not far from home for me. I used to take him out, show him a good time, pay for his whores, that sort of thing, generating and solidifying the sense of indebtedness he's had toward me ever since. We got split up for a while when Frank was sent over to Indonesia while I got the Eurobeat, but with him being so skilled in low-intensity conflict, it was inevitable that he'd end up in Ireland at some point. He'd been angling for this position for a while because he knew he'd be left to his own devices—of which he has many, some homemade—but he'd also been angling for it because of his interest in, well, angling, which explains the monthly weekends away in Mayo. It meant making a move to the Western Hemisphere division, but somehow he managed it without screwing up his pension in the process. He must have some family connections. Or electrical connections.

I arrived in Ireland a couple of months after Frank, a little wiser and a lot colder—"You get used to the damp, it's the smell that never leaves you"—whereas he hadn't changed at all. He was chafing at the lack of any competent drinking partners and at the fact that what constituted a night's competent drinking could set you back a few hundred euros, but he'd kept his pecker up, managed to somehow consume as much booze as before, and was screwing around probably more than ever, even though most of the hookers in Dublin give every impression that the last time they saw an antibiotic, it was growing on the dishcloth they use to wipe the spunk off their belly.

When Frank and I got together again, we resumed where we'd left off. Staggering around Leeson Street at six in morning trying to find somewhere to sleep; stomping round Smithfield, loudly declaring our desperation at not being able to find the brothel on Thomas Street we'd been told about; gatecrashing parties in obscure, sleazy apartment blocks full of students with no alcohol; engaging in hopeless, half-hearted arguments and brawls with the natives. The only difference between the Frank Prendergast of five years ago and the Frank Prendergast of today is that he now sports a scar on his left bicep from the night we indulged in a spot of empty-headed combat on Arran Quay with two Scottish matelots over here for the Tall Ships Race. I don't recall what the fight was about, but it was Frank who pulled the knife, a kitchen knife at that, to scare the fuckers off, only he was so smashed that in his act of wielding it he tripped, managing to push the knife, ever so neatly, into one of the matelots' stomachs.

"Fuck…I'm sorry about that. I didn't mean to hurt you," Frank said as he got up from the floor, sounding almost sober.

The matelot, I'll never forget, there was something unnaturally androgynous and depraved about him, like a balding Christina Ricci, stood his ground and contemplated the knife for a moment before turning to Frank and shrugging.

"Nay problem, pal. I've plenty of scars on my belly. Ship's doctor took out my appendix with something like this."

With barely a grimace or a strain, he bent forward, pulled the knife from his own stomach, and lunged for Frank. A swipe that would have taken off a puppy's head zipped by Frank's bicep before sending the matelot off balance and onto the sidewalk, where he proceeded to hemorrhage without concern for public probity. I don't think Frank realized that he'd been slashed. The three of us who were still vertical stood there for a minute or so in silent contemplation of the moribund body before us.

"Better look after your friend, I reckon," I finally said to the other matelot, coming to my senses and not really wanting to be implicated in any new misdemeanors. I grabbed Frank's other arm and off we dashed to my place to inspect his wound and down a bottle of fucking Jack Daniel's. I'll always remember that night. It was the last bottle I had.

Frank was fine the next day. His arm hurt a darn sight less than his head, probably because I'd been kicking it repeatedly as he slept for finishing off the bottle while I was taking a wizz. We went to the embassy doc, who knows better than to ask any daft questions, and Frank got bandaged up. Then we hit the bars again.

He likes his work here because he's undisturbed—though many would disagree. As for me, I've been put out to pasture. So long as I'm here, I'm not drawing attention to myself. After the fiasco in Athens, there wasn't much they could do with me, although Turkey wanted me as a national hero. It wasn't until my predecessor here kicked the bucket that there was somewhere to get me away from the public gaze. Who the fuck knows where Dublin is? Ask any American sophomore to point to it on a map and they'll get it wrong. Even on a map of Dublin.

Bitter? No, I'm not bitter. I've got my health, my looks, a job with good pay. I have carved from the soapstone of futility a meaningful modus vivendi, cultivated my very own not-quite-fecund but furtively festive amateur miniature ecosystem, featuring osmosis, symbiosis, apoptosis, and psychosis. It is finely unbalanced. I even have friends who would die for me.

Okay, not die for me. Kill for me. And only because they enjoy it. But it still counts.

So anyway, Frank popped in to my office and, I kid you not, he was wearing this chunky crucifix thing around his neck. What a great sense of humor. As a devout agnostic, Frank doesn't believe in anything, one of the reasons why he's so good at his job. I assumed that the crucifix was a fashion statement.

"What's with the homunculus, Frank?"

Frank fingered Christ in an unseemly manner.

"What? This old thing?" There was a gruffness to his voice. He was hoarse again from all the shouting at work. "I've had it years."

Maybe he had. It was hard to remember. It usually is after so much booze. That's why I drink. To forget. I can't remember what it is I'm drinking to forget, or even if I *am* drinking to forget, but I'm sure that if I stop drinking I'll remember the reason why I've been drinking to forget what it is I've forgotten. Besides, alcoholism is good for you. What is it Delia always says? The road of excess leads to the palace of Westminster. Something like that.

"What is it? Some kind of memento?" Frank looked at me like I was stupid. He tried to raise his voice but it clearly hurt.

"Memento? Christ died over two thousand years ago. I wasn't even born then."

Frank isn't easily annoyed unless it's something trivial. He's as cool as an Eskimo's fart when it comes to taking lives. That's what makes him one of Western Europe's finest torturers. And that's not just my say-so. Babes in arms spit in the street at the mention of his name, and he gets fan mail from all over. Two years ago, he won the Interrogator of the Year award from *Intelligence Quarterly*. Quite an honor, I thought, but it went in the trashcan with all the other awards. "Fuck 'em. Reflected glory is all they're after," he said.

He may get easily annoyed about trivial things, but he's still a very tolerant man. He can't stand intolerance. He thinks intolerant people should be taken out and shot. He's one of the most intolerant people I know. But he's fair. He's intolerant of everyone to an equal degree. Except for himself. He hates himself more than he hates other people. Except for intolerant people. "There are no strangers," he once said to me, "only friends you haven't alienated yet."

Easily annoyed, intolerant, and promiscuous. The man with the Velcro fly, Frank will fuck anything that's stationary for more than two minutes. I have wheels on my office chair. At the moment, he's fucking Margot Scheisskopf, the cultural attaché at the embassy. I don't have conclusive evidence of this, but last Christmas Frank was her Secret Santa in the office draw, and he bought her a pair of "tingling knicks"—panties with a vibrating pad sewn into the lining with a speed control to "suit your own personal requirements." Straight away, she knew it was Frank who'd bought them. She was tickled pink.

You might think it peculiar that Lucy doesn't mind Frank's promiscuity, but it isn't *that* peculiar when you consider that she's only nine months old, the latest addition to the Prendergast family. It's his wife, Janet, who should be bothered, but she's not all that fussed now that online divorce has been recognized in Ireland. She'll get the house in Dalkey, which is, let's be honest, all anyone wants these days. They don't shoot stray dogs in Dalkey. They don't *have* stray dogs in Dalkey. They have to import dogs from Shankill and then hire someone to go out and do the shooting for them.

Under his close-cropped hair that reminds me of the back yard that my old man never let me play in, Frank has two, hard, deep-set, black marble eyes that remind me of the black marbles my old man would never let me buy so that I couldn't go out into the back yard and not play with them. Eyes. Windows of the soul. Frank's are bricked up.

"So why are you wearing a crucifix, Frank?"

Frank fingered Christ again, and my own words came back at me, a little tinny, but indisputably mine. He could tell I was impressed. I shifted my buttocks in my chair. Not that I was uncomfortable. I like shifting my buttocks in my chair. And fondling my scrotum through my trouser pocket.

"Pretty neat, huh? Amazing what they can do with nanotechnology these days."

He undid the chain at the back of his close-cropped, back-yard head and laid the crucifix on my desk, flipping it open to reveal a micro recorder encased within.

"I'm beta-testing it for R&D. Plausibly disguised, easy to carry, holds two terabytes, and available in three different colors. Simple to operate, too. Just flick the two nails in his hands—there—that one's record, that one's playback. Course, you'd need a magnifying glass to see it all properly."

He clipped it back together and refastened it round his neck while nonchalantly eyeing the papers on my desk.

"What'll they think of next?" I mused, at which point he plugged his earring into my laptop and showed me film of him fishing the Moy.

—

Here's something cool that Sinéad spotted and put on my desk at lunch:

Julbo Trail ($150)

The superbendy lenses in these 28-gram sunglasses are made of a material called NXT, which was developed for the U.S. Army to withstand the stress of combat. This means they are plenty durable should your mark put up resistance and throw a couple of punches, and any debris that might get kicked up, like teeth or fingernails, won't damage the scratch-resistant lenses. These were worn by advance snipers during Desert Storm and lasted throughout the campaign. The photochromatic lenses lighten when you're knifing someone in a dark alleyway and darken when you're taking someone out from a rooftop on a summer's day with a sniper rifle. They're also easy-clean, making them perfect for wet jobs that threaten to get a little messy.

Rudy Project Sportmask SX ($160)

Some wraparound sunglasses can take on an imposing sci-fi look, swallowing your face and tipping your victim off prematurely to your intentions. This isn't the case with the new scaled-down Sportmask SX, which has all the UV protection you need in a 24-gram design that's perfect for smaller faces. You can customize the nosepiece to fit your face and choose from gray, brown, or olive-green polycarbonate lenses. Operatives who like to look inconspicuous and carry out hits at close range using silencers or hunting knives will appreciate the Sportsmask's understated silhouette.

Nike Impel Swift ($159)

Slip on a pair of the 18-gram Swifts, and your target becomes sharper, brighter, and much, much easier to take out. Without any spare weight in the design, these shades feel invisible and clarifying, allowing you to focus on putting one right through the neck or temple instead of fidgeting with fit. The adjustable nose bridge is comfortable, and the flying lens design provides plenty of coverage and antifog venting for those humid nights in the woods or along the canal when you have to dispose of the bodies.

Under Armour Draft ($150)

With polycarbonate lenses, titanium, rubber, and thermoplastic frames, these sunglasses are as tough as they are light (24 grams). Their compelling design features a slightly off-center lens that delivers crisp peripheral vision so that you can see cops, troopers, or other malefactors trying to sneak up on you. Under Armour completes the package with ratcheting temples for a custom fit so that they'll stay on no matter how frantic the getaway. The large lenses also help to conceal the face and disguise your features, ideal for those jobs when you need to put the frighteners on a mark.

Zeal Optics Lift ($110)

Forget migraines, brain freezes, and the stress-related headaches you've been having since you had to strangle those children. Sometimes just stepping out into the summer sun can be a nightmare. The Lift's rosy-brown lenses relax the eyes and amplify colors while blocking UV rays. And the streamlined design makes these 19-gram shades feel even lighter. Classy-looking but also functional, these are the glasses worn by federal officers and Secret Service details from May to September, so if you're planning on a high-profile hit or need to impersonate agents in order to infiltrate and bomb a government installation, these are ideal. The lenses also feature a polarizing filter that reduces glare, so there'll be no need to squint when you pump those bad boys into that journalist; one less thing for you to worry about.

Reviews of sunglasses from the July issue of *Professional Hitman* magazine.

No. 25
The March on Moscow

6 oz. Napoleon Brandy
1 oz. Russian Vodka
Serve warm, in a large, optimistic glass

"Take a look at these abstracts, Joe. Tell me if anything strikes you as unusual."

Sinéad had spent all morning going through the quality stats of the staff who'd signed up for the teleworking scheme and had done a random sampling of work by each one to make sure they could be left unsupervised. She had a sheaf of papers under her arm as she walked past the conference room, where I was about to begin my umpteenth rant on the speakerphone to the management company about the frayed carpets in the foyer, the dodgy wiring on the hand dryers in the jax, and the knackered strip lighting at the far end of the conference room that had left it so dim I'd twice caught abstracters hiding there.

She didn't knock. She strode in and tossed a couple of pages onto the table in front of me. I picked up the abstract on the top. I'm perverse like that.

> New findings indicate that a cure for AIDS may be around the corner. Experts at Carnegie-Mellon University's Simian Research Laboratory (SiReLab) report a breakthrough in the production of a vaccine

> to combat SIV, the simian equivalent of HIV. Vernon van Yelling's staff have been trying to develop such a vaccine to generate cellular immune responses by employing an SIV-infected baboon model. Every significant part of the cell-mediated immune response consists of cytotoxic T-lymphocytes (CTLs). Researchers believe that CTLs are central to controlling HIV and SIV. What has restricted our understanding of CTL effectiveness to date has been the fact that most standard immunological assays do not measure antiviral activity directly. Overcoming this obstacle has meant developing a new neutralization assay that quantifies the ability of virus-specific CTL populations to control viral growth. Rendering the antiviral activity of CTL of different specificities measurable will identify those CTL most effective against SIV. Knowledge of this sort will probably shape the design of all future HIV vaccines.

"Is this a trick question?" I said. She shook her head.

"Nothing obvious, Joe?"

I ummed and aahed for a minute to make it look like I was giving the matter serious consideration, but I might as well have been looking at Rorschach blots. I tried to bluff it.

"Well, the hook strikes me as redundant. The abstract could start with the findings."

She moued, her face Apache'd by the bands of light from the venetian blind.

"Anything else?"

"Hmm. I'm not sure. Hey, look at the bloody coffee rings on this table."

"Don't change the subject. Think about it."

When I first got this job, the Company made me run through the training package given to abstracters so that I could bullshit my way through conversations with the minions. It wasn't helping.

"Ah! There's no need to use the abbreviation for the laboratory. It doesn't appear again in the abstract, so it's of no use."

She gave the smallest of nods.

"We'll come back to that one. What about this?"

> Several performers at the Donmar Warehouse in London have taken to wearing masks in protest at pollution caused by construction work in the adjoining buildings. Masks range from those used in Kabuki theater to superhero masks to surgery masks. Often the masks are worn during rehearsals only, but more militant performers are also wearing them during shows. Kabuki masks in particular can seem out of place when worn, for example, during plays set in Victorian England or pre-war France. Even union representatives are embarrassed by some of the actors' intransigence. Donmar officials insist that they can do nothing about the construction taking place. Only audience forbearance and curiosity has prevented this from spilling over

> into a full-blown dispute. Performers at the Donmar say they are not being deliberately awkward and that the pollution affects their capacity to speak their lines. Even those with non-speaking parts have taken to wearing gasmasks, however.

"Thoughts?"

"Certainly conjures up some amusing imagery."

"The abstract, Joe. Look more closely." I squinted.

"Quite a lot of repetition of the word 'mask.'"

"Yes, Joe. Well done. You've spotted that it's about masks. What else?"

"Structurally, it's not great. A little disjointed. Here, for example, in the second half. Union representatives... Donmar officials...Audience forbearance...Performers." The tone of my voice told her that even I didn't believe it.

"You haven't got a clue, have you? Check the first letter of each sentence. Spell them out for me."

"S-M-O-K-E-D-O-P-E. Smoke Dope."

"Yes, Joe. Well done. And the other one."

"N-E-V-E-R-W-O-R-K."

"Never Work. The old Situationist slogan. This is the tip of the iceberg. I have hundreds of them. SMOKEDOPE. NEVERWORK. HELPIMTRAPPED. KILLMENOW. IWANTBEER. Hundreds."

I twirled an imaginary moustache. "Who's doing it? I bet it's that Dermot Morris in Geology. He's a bong sucker if ever I saw one. The B.O. The hair. The heavy metal T-shirts."

"It's all of them, Joe. They're all at it."

"All of them? Are you sure? What the hell are they up to?"

"They're bored is my guess. And it's not just the writers. The editors must be in on it too for the redundant hooks to get through."

"COITUS doesn't know, though, right?" She traced a line with her forefinger along the chipped edge of the tabletop.

"Not as far as I'm aware. And the abstracts are probably too dispersed among the databases for clients to spot them. I suspect you're talking about a few hundred, maybe a couple of thousand, out of millions. Precisely the sort of infantile gesture of defiance you'd expect from this lot, to be honest. Pathetic, really."

"I imagine it makes their sniveling excuse for a life more bearable to put one over on The Man like this. Mitigates the endless genuflections we demand of them." She nodded cursorily.

"So, what do you want to do about it?"

I puffed my cheeks. "Nothing, I guess. It isn't affecting productivity and nobody else has cottoned on. Keep an eye on it in the regular audits to make sure there's no sudden increase in frequency."

She picked up the first two pages before handing me a third. "That sounds eminently sensible."

I *am* eminently sensible.

Journalists working for the Italian magazine *Oggi* are holding a series of presentations at its HQ in Bergamo to familiarize law-enforcement agencies with the problems caused by celebrities. *Oggi* magazine has been involved in a number of high-profile legal cases in recent years brought on behalf of film stars and musicians objecting to invasions of privacy. Every case, say the journalists, involved celebrities whose agents had previously contacted the magazine with stories. Such hypocrisy has typically been tolerated by the police and the courts, they argue. Understanding the pressures placed on journalists and paparazzi would reduce the harassment journalists face and, in turn, reduce the underhand methods they are sometimes forced to resort to. Celebrities who court publicity while craving secrecy should appreciate the role of journalists, said Gabriella Conte, representing the staff. Knowing that journalists are vital to the creation of a celebrity's profile should mean something. Some do already appreciate this. Conte cited a number of film stars who set a good example. Of those cited, however, few were willing to discuss the issue. Conte argues that this demonstrates the stigma still attached to celebrity journalism. Knotty though the issue is, she expressed confidence that the presentations would help. She really did.

"Sack the lot."

Ten minutes before lunch, Feargal at the hospital phoned to tell me my medication had come in. I let Sinéad know I'd be out of the office for the afternoon and went about getting to Dun Laoghaire. I'd handed the rental car back in, so I'd have to take the bus. It isn't worth having a car in Dublin because a) everywhere important, with the exception of the hospital, is within walking distance; b) the roads are so potholed and obstacle-strewn that it's quicker and more comfortable to walk anyway; and c) the cost of gas, even with expenses, renders car use uneconomical. Frank says the wheel is man's greatest invention, only he doesn't mean for transportation, he means for torture.

The National Rehabilitation Hospital performs a number of functions, such as serving as a base for the military and home to a number of interrogation units. Once upon a time, it was the place where car-crash victims learned to walk again. Today, it's more usual for people to arrive here having the use of their legs and to leave on crutches. Statistical evidence alone should be enough to deter you from going to hospitals. More people die there than in any other social institution. That includes marriage.

Frank spends a lot of his time at the NRH, you won't be surprised to learn. It's where he conducts his "therapy." This is the hospital, he never tires of explaining, where people suffering from the psychiatric disorder of dissidence come to get analized. That's not a typo.

The hospital also functions as a link in the country's food chain. Ever since Ireland gained "independence" back in the 1920s, meat has been essential to the nation's sense of its own identity, proof of its capacity to thrive once the yoke of empire had been cast off. So when the meat industry collapsed a few years ago, some ingenuity was called for if the nation was to retain its self-respect—what self-respect it could still muster, I mean. *E. Coli* and the various poultry flus coming in from Asia had already devastated the poultry industry, and what beef we had was inedible, what with the BSE, TB, foot and mouth, the monkeypox epidemic, and all those antibiotic-resistant viruses.

It might have been okay if the economy had been prospering, but we'd had the crashes of 2009 and 2012, with nobody stepping up to shoulder the blame and eat the sins. Consequently, the government did what governments usually do when it can't get away with blaming the people for its own fuckups. It pointed the finger at outsiders. The unreliable ones. The suspect classes. Bloody immigrants, bloody unemployed, bloody homeless, bloody Travelers, bloody circuses. The people living at the margins, about whom no one gave a proverbial.

And let's not forget the Jap encephalitis.

That was a real low blow. It was the Jap encephalitis that destroyed Ireland's pig population. The outbreak began in Longford and soon crossed over a few borders, not just between counties; between species as well. The government reintroduced the Emergency Powers Act so that a cull could be initiated whether the pharmers liked it or not, and soon all that was left of the country's pig population was a couple of hundred sows and a lot of redundant pharmhands. Ireland's always been full of one-horse towns, but one horse doesn't go all that far, even if you eat the glue.

Fortunately, some lateral-thinking civil servant, a vegetarian with a philosophy degree, I wouldn't wonder, drew his line manager's attention to the opportunities presented by xenotransplantation, where you take the organs from one species and use them in another. For years, pigs' organs had been used to keep human patients alive. Why not the reverse? Who's going to miss a few winos and Travelers so long as there's bacon on the plate of a Sunday morning?

China showed us the way years ago, executing criminals to order. Hospitals paid upfront for the organs they required and told the authorities when the recipient was prepped for surgery. This being Ireland, there is more red tape than in China, but the process is pretty much the same: straight from the cells, sorry, I mean wards, in the hospital here, out to the firing squad, and off to surgery. And ultimately, I suppose, onto your plate, if you accept that the pigs bred for food are at least partly composed of flesh and blood provided by their parents.

It's a bona fide 21st-century Irish entrepreneurial success story. We should all be very proud.

I passed through the various security cordons around the hospital by flashing the quasi-legit embassy ID that Frank had obtained for me. At the main entrance to the building—a brown, functional, unimaginative 1930s brick of a place—dried blood stubbornly polka-dotted the tarmac, marking where patients had been dragged in by their legs, their heads banging on the steps.

The lights inside the foyer seemed to have been robbed from watchtowers: huge spotlights squatting in the corners or hanging awkwardly from the ceilings along the corridors. People in rags milled around, unsure of their exact purpose. But that's doctors for you. The patients lay around on the floor, also covered in rags but distinguishable from the staff by their groans. Nurses paced back and forth, trying to look too busy to care. Old women in black headscarves carrying baskets of flowers muttered to themselves about God. Alkies in overcoats spewed up across the marble, and barefoot children skimble-skambled tohu bohu, laughing and splashing through the puke. One kid in mauve pajamas was wealthy enough to have flip-flops. They slapped against his heels rather than the floor, so that the soundtrack to his cavorting was out of sync. Casual as I could, I pushed my way to the front of what I took to be a queue, where a nurse was expertly ignoring a middle-aged couple with a little boy clamped to the father's thigh. The kid had an electric toothbrush stuck up his nose. I offered the nurse my ID and she blanched, the way jobsworths often do when confronted with unimpeachable fake credentials.

"Joe Chambers, U.S. embassy. Here to receive a consignment on the embassy's behalf. You phoned me this morning."

"Not me, Mr. Chambers," she said with an air of attempted formality, though I could tell she was intimidated, if not positively moistened, by my good looks and authoritative mien.

"No, not you specifically, but you should have been notified." She made a play of turning over a couple of stapled sheets on the counter.

"Er...no...no, I wasn't. Could you hang on a moment, while I check?"

I was going to say "Do I have a choice?" but she had already shifted her attention to a terminal on the adjoining desk and was clicking through screens with a mouse. I amused myself for a minute or two by imagining her in civvies. Then in skivvies. Then in a privy.

Eventually, without looking up to admit that there was no system to the filing, she said, "I have no mention of an appointment here." She turned away from me to open a metal drawer and pulled out a large olive-colored folder, playing for time. She placed the folder on the counter between us, opened it, and scanned the names. I sighed. Out of nowhere, a spider ran across the back of her left hand. Without batting an eyelid, she squashed it dead with the palm of her right.

"Got it," she said, decisively.

"Oh good," I said.

"I meant the spider." Her look said she wished it had been me.

"Now, Mr. Chambers, if that is your name, I can't find any details of your appointment, but you're welcome to pop down to the pharmacy to see if they have any record of you there. Do you know your way?"

I nodded cheerfully, she flicked her head as much as to say, "Off you fuck then," and off I fucked, but you know how hospitals have those signs at every junction that point you in the direction of the various wards, and how they also have those color-coded lines inlaid into the floor that you're meant to follow so you'll be led to your desired location—red for oncology, blue for maternity, green for outpatients, yellow for obstetrics—so there are two schemes to enable you to find your way to the right ward, in case you don't grasp the principles of one of them, or if, I suppose, you're illiterate or color-blind? Well, the National Rehabilitation Hospital doesn't have any of those. It would rather you wander around fruitlessly. I'm surprised there isn't a sign outside the front door that says "Get Lost." Which is what I did. For 45 minutes. Even though I'd been to the pharmacy several times before. Maybe the hospital was constructed like this to deter pirates.

When I eventually found the pharmacy, after asking some geezer dragging his catheter behind him, I saw yet another queue I'd have to jump. Fortunately, Feargal, my contact, was manfully manning the counter and spotted me from a distance. Motioning to me to come round to the side door next to the counter, he unlocked it, came out, and shook my hand.

"You made it then, Joe," he said, his jelly-wobble voice making me laugh inside.

"Eventually. This place is a fucking madhouse."

"You say that every time you come. We *could* deliver this stuff round to your home, you know. For a few quid, like."

"And miss a delightful day out of the office?" He had reached under the counter and pulled up a shoebox-sized package. He turned it over and over, looking for the label.

"Let's see. Codeine. Pariet. Arofil. Destolit. Emadine. All present and correct. Here y'go."

"Niclosamide."

"Which?"

"Niclosamide. There should be a course in there. It's on the prescription."

He turned the box over again and unsealed it. "Ah yeah. It is, so. That's a different one. They must have put it in special for yuz." He handed the box over. "Sign here."

"Cheers, Ferg. Appreciate it. You must come round one of the nights and we'll have a bevvy or two."

"No worries. Though as you can see, I'm run off me feet, so it won't be for a while."

"I see it okay. What's the story?" A wee urchin ran between me and the counter, a dancing streamer of snot in his wake.

"Staff cuts. Same all over. You know, I had to perform six enemas this morning before breakfast."

"Jesus. Probably a good job you hadn't eaten."

"Eaten? No. I mean before I *made* the breakfast. I'm working shifts in the kitchens of the staff canteen. I do the hash browns."

"How ridiculous."

"Tell me about it. We have cardiologists cooking the fry-ups and gynecologists stirring the porridge."

"Do the podiatrists make the corn flakes?"
"Don't be daft, Joe."
"Sorry."
"They're in charge of the jam."

From *Astrology Today* magazine, readers' superstitions for the 21st century:

- It's bad luck to use the same razor to shave your balls as you use for your face.
- It's bad luck backstage at the *X Factor* to mention Susan Boyle. She is to be referred to as "The Scottish Singer."
- If you press channel 13, 13 times, on your remote, whoever appears on the screen will be dead within the year. Unless they're already dead, in which case YOU will die.
- If your ears are burning, your iPod's on fire.
- Premature ejaculate should be flicked over your left shoulder.
- Never open a packet of cigarettes indoors.
- It's bad luck if a soldier's funeral cortege passes you in the street; to lift the curse you must turn your back and spit on the ground.
- If two Jehovah's Witnesses come to your door and you manage to kill one but the other gets away, that's bad luck.

- Tread on a crack, sue the council.
- Sign up with Sky for their Entertainment package and you'll have 18 months of bad luck.
- When your laptop crashes, somewhere in America a programmer dies.
- To wish someone good luck before they play an online video game, you should say, "Break a wrist."
- It's bad luck to find a horseshoe still attached to the hoof.
- If you see a priest being beaten up, make a wish!

Ireland's first trillionaire has appeared on the Forbes list of the world's richest people, according to *Irish Business Week.* Pharmaceutical giant Heinrich Fallon puts his success down to his strong work ethic. "I work through lunch four days out of five and often stay in the office until well after the cleaning staff have gone home. Even on the golf course in the morning I have my mobile turned on, and all of my yachts are fully Internet-enabled so that I can keep an eye on Ukrainian chemical futures." When asked whether he believes others can attain the same dizzying heights of financial success, Fallon says, "Of course. As an entrepreneur, I expect people to work as hard for me as I do. Most of my job is really about management of people. Give them a vision and clear goals and they can join you on your journey without you having to micro-manage or waste money on HR, surveillance, and control. They get the chance to fly beneath your wings until they learn to soar too. I see myself as an enabler." Well known for his love of science fiction and fantasy, Fallon has said, "I always regarded Mr. Spock's benediction, 'Live long and prosper,' as an instruction. I tell all my employees that they, too, may prosper, if they live long enough."

No. 26
The Retreat from Moscow
6 oz. Russian Vodka
1 oz. Napoleon Brandy
Lots of Ice
Serve outdoors in a chill wind

Tom in the IT department has been pulling all-nighters configuring the servers to deal with the new teleworking system. It's difficult to tell whether he's happy about the new system.

"You know, Joe," he said, "in theory I could also telework once the servers are set up right. I'd only need to come in for electrical faults or hardware upgrades. Everything else I'd be able to do from Enniskerry."

"Yeah," I said, "but you'd miss my smiling face, wouldn't you? And you'd be scraping banana, breast milk, and baby spit off your monitor every morning with a spatula."

He gurned a grin.

"There is that," he said.

Tom doesn't have any kids. Just an unusual diet.

Strange the designs fate has in store for us. I never imagined in my wildest dreams when I landed in Glyfada that I would be destined to spend most of my career in a run-down, shit-stained, disease-infested dump that few people had heard of, let alone care about. I don't mean Athens, of course. I mean this place. Dublin. It's all the fault of Mrs. Papadopoulos. If she hadn't kicked the bucket when she did, I could still be living it up in Psychico as Henry Kendall, Ontario kitchenware manufacturer.

Athens is a great place. As much booze as you can drink, all the pussy you can eat, and every other refined and delicate privilege that goes along with being a certified defender of the world's number one democracy. The weather was incomparable and the workload fairly acceptable, providing you didn't get stuck on the Middle East desk. The only drawback to the place is that it's in Greece, and the Greeks hate Americans more than they hate the Turks or the Krauts. Don't ask me why. Something to do with military dictatorships way back when. Still, if you were able to pass yourself off as Irish or, better yet, Canadian, nobody gave a flying *fassolaki*.

Athens was where I first met Seymour Stiveley. *Colonel* Seymour Stiveley, as he never tired of reminding everyone. Stiveley was running MI6's Greek operation and having the time of his life. Athens was his ideal posting. A former student of St. Andrews University in Scotland, he'd graduated with firsts in archaeology and Mesopotamian, so as an expert in dead cultures he was perfectly suited to a career in "Six." He was one of the few field operatives responsible for pulling more bodies out of the earth than he put in.

Typical English officer class, Stiveley, the sort of asshole you see in photos surrendering Singapore to the

Japs. Abnormally tall and skinny. Angular features. Pipe-smoker since he was five. The usual hauteur, the detached demeanor, largely indifferent to the existence of others: he was eight before he discovered he was a Siamese twin. After he and his sibling were separated, Seymour went to some obscure boarding school, whence he was expelled for emotional instability, a remarkable achievement given that emotional instability is the purpose of boarding school. And killing a boy for putting down "qiviut" during a game of Scrabble seems a not unreasonable response, in my opinion. After that, Seymour kept a low profile, stuck to his studies, and, unable to find a proper job, went into academia. Two years after taking a seat at Durham, he came out of the closet and was promptly recruited by British Intelligence.

Most people assume that spooks spend all their time planning assassinations, eavesdropping on the Russkies and the Chinese, and taking photos of documents with miniature cameras. The reality is that only 95 percent of their time is spent doing that. The other 5 percent is devoted to trying to incriminate rival services. It's important to monopolize the reliable sources of information in any given geographical location, and this means trying to eliminate the competition by getting them deported. So, in my defense, I was only doing my job. Quite how those Bronze Age artifacts from the Benáki Museum found their way into the trunk of Stiveley's Bentley are beyond me. Those weren't my fingerprints on them. They were his. And I should know. I put them there.

Stiveley claimed diplomatic immunity and never saw the inside of a Greek prison—much to his disappointment—but he was still booted out the country. I thought that was the last of him, but then Mrs. Papadopoulos came over all tight chested and cemetery-minded with my cock still inside her, and the next thing I know I'm in Dublin, followed six months later by bloody Stiveley, apparently still none the wiser about my part in his departure from Greece. When he came looking for me I thought my number was up, but he said he was merely looking up old friends; the Benáki artifacts didn't merit a mention. Lately, though, I'm beginning to think he's worked it out.

Incidentally, before we go any further, I should probably own up to my drink problem. My drink problem is that there's nothing left to drink. With the taxes and the price hikes and the social charges and the bed-wetting nanny state trying to shut down all avenues of pleasure so that we never have to avail of the health service, alcohol is all but unaffordable these days. There's the Jack Daniel's that I can occasionally wangle off staff at the American Embassy, but I fucking hate Jack Daniel's with a vengeance that would almost tempt me to join ISIS. I have to rely on Delia to do me favors or on Frank to bring me something back when he flies off to "give advice" to security forces in Saudi, Bahrain, or one of them other liquor-loving states.

And I hate having to ration the Glenmorangie. It's the sort of drink you want to throw back in a lusty declaration of the magnificence of life, accompanied by a cry of joy and tears of melancholia, recognition that we are all of us so fortunate to live in times of glory, abundance, and affirmation.

I realize we don't, but if you drink enough Glenmorangie, sometimes it feels like we do.

As it is, I have to resign myself to a ritualistic sup on special occasions—the Fourth of July, Veterans Day, Memorial Day, 22nd of November—and even then I have to drink it back at the apartment so I don't have to share with anyone. If I run out, it's Jack Daniel's or my own urine, and I only opt for the former because it gives me less of a hangover.

The Glenmorangie is kept under lock and key, so nobody can get at it. By nobody, I'm thinking particularly of Stiveley, who has a nasty habit of breaking into my apartment and taking a bottle or two for no other reason than spite. He doesn't drink the Scotch. He kidnaps it, holds it hostage. This is why I think he's sussed Athens out. A couple of days after the break-in, I'll get a ransom note from him or a mocked-up photo of a blindfolded bottle with a gun to its head. I really need to put a stop to it.

As sublimation, a form of therapy, if you will, I have been compiling for my own amusement a compendium of cocktail recipes that it is my resolute intention of mixing and imbibing, every single one, the day I receive the news that my pension has come through and I can say goodbye to the Company forever. The experience may kill me, but not if the Company, boredom, or Stiveley doesn't kill me first. All being well, I will publish it upon my retirement in the hope that it will be read and enjoyed by those of an empathic or dypsomaniacal disposition. Part of me is rather fond of a fantasy in which college students take the book to heart in the way they have movies like *Withnail and I* and the *Big Lebowski*. It has, after all, the right degree of adolescent insouciance, and the content is so uniform that it allows for a drinking game that has only one rule: Every time a drink is mentioned, you have to drink it. Even college students can follow that.

News from Sinéad:

According to *Nuneaton World Management* magazine, 17 mourners at a funeral in Solihull died after eating the dead man's dog. His widow and two of his children were among those who perished.

Remember that Quasi-modular course in French bell ringing that I saw in the *Daily Mail*? Turns out it was an April Fool's joke. I still don't get it.

The *San Jose Mercury* reports that in order to drum up some interest and demonstrate the continued relevance of space exploration, NASA has announced that the crew of the first mission to Mars will be all-nude.

And I see from recently liberated government documents that Michael O'Leary complained to our ambassador about CIA rendition flights receiving government funding and thereby undercutting Ryanair. I don't think we have a case to answer. At least with rendition flights you have some idea what country you'll end up in.

Lost one and a half pounds.

No. 121
The Syriza Sling
Small Greek Beer
A lot of Red Bull

New words to learn today: mentulate – having a large penis; gland-monkey (sl.) – someone who engages in excessive ingestion of hormones; moinous – given to investigating orifices; ecdysiast – a stripper; vagile – able to move about freely; cucumiform – shaped like a cucumber; callipygian – being in possession of shapely buttocks; symplegma – statuettes of entwined figures; luagh – to break wind quietly; stiction – the force necessary to make one body that is in contact with another move; keruff – artificial flavoring used in nutraceuticals.

Why are so many members of the judiciary so keen on rectal probing? Was David Icke right after all? Are they aliens from the eighth dimension? If it isn't the ritual humiliation of suspects forced to bend over in countless Garda stations around the country so that the cracked and greasy digit of the officer on duty can slide in easily, it's the penetration of high court judges by large-breasted women wearing unfeasibly large strap-ons. It's a perennial (and perineal) question that has plagued psychologists ever since *Psychopathia Sexualis* was withdrawn from the shelves of Irish libraries by De Valera's League of Public Decency. Even in these inegalitarian times, it's rare to find a social scientist with the cojones, the imagination, or the funding to explore the differences between the classes when it comes to sexual preference. One has to rely on unreliable anecdotal sources such as the *Daily Star,* Twitter, or stories relayed by brothel keepers on a Friday evening in Sandycove. Much of the time, they're stories you'd rather not hear.

Frank's colleague, rival, and opposite number at the Spanish embassy, Manuel Estímulo, believes that the answer to my opening question lies in judges' sense of fair play and decency. Rather than satisfying some sado-masochistic desire to be punished, he says, they feel the need to be on the receiving end of the punishments they mete out purely from a sense of professionalism and moral obligation. If they are sentencing a single mother to be stripped naked and birched for failing to pay her water charge, he argues, they are able to pass such a sentence with the necessary equanimity and good faith only because they can point to their own personal experience. "I've been stripped naked and birched on many an occasion and frankly it isn't the unpleasant ordeal that the ignoramuses in the media and civil liberties organizations imagine." Similarly, if he is condemning an adolescent to 20 years in Mountjoy for possession of skunk, His Honor needs to know what it feels like to have his ass stretched by a priapic overweight prison officer on a regular basis (hence the reason for the myth that judges have a large-breast fetish; the large breasts simply mimic the officer's stomach). This is also why, Estímulo says, brothels such as his are so rarely raided by police. They understand the role that brothels play in upholding Ireland's judicial system and making it possible for judges to sleep soundly in their beds after a particularly difficult day of hangings. Judges' wives in particular should be especially grateful, he feels.

I don't know that I buy this argument, not least because so many high court judges appear to relish punishing offenders; it isn't like they need any encouragement. My own view is that they're so decrepit, so incapable of feeling, both emotionally and physically, that the only way they know they're having sex is if it involves laceration, bruising, or the tearing of delicate tissue. Their butts are so calloused by years on the bench, their hides so leathery and tanned by port, Stilton, and Montecristos, that they need sensations of such intensity to feel alive, and the only options are extreme pain or Class A drugs. And Class A drugs rarely reach high court judges because customs officers get first pick.

You'd think the head of Spanish intelligence in Ireland would have better things to do than run a brothel in Dun Laoghaire. Spying on Spanish students clogging up Dame Street every summer, say, or sending death threats to his compatriots who seem to be behind every worthwhile protest movement in Ireland. Well that's conspiracy talk, my friend. Besides, there *is* no worthwhile Irish protest movement. It's a much better use of his time to run a knocking shop wherein the influential and powerful are provided with services which, were they made public, would result in resignations, scandal, a change of government, a couple of faked suicides, and a run on the euro. Given the pressure they're under, all TDs need to let their hair down now and then, and what better place to do it than one that won't show up in expense claims and which promises discretion, decorum, and deception?

Why deception? Because it goes without saying that Señor Estímulo does not advertise the fact that his fine premises are home to the two oldest professions. Instead, the establishment is run by two very efficient and respectable middle-aged madams named Miss Whipcream and Jane Bondage. The way I heard it, these two professional ladies of the evening contacted Estímulo personally, figuring that a Spanish ultra-Catholic fascist would be the perfect cover for their establishment while also providing the necessary security (not muscular security—he's barely five feet tall, after all—but political) should the Chief of Police turn up on their doorstep looking for something other than an Indian helmet massage.

Having spent many years in the high-end escort business, the ladies had cultivated a regular clientele of the powerful and influential by blowing bigwigs, felching financiers, fellating fat cats, bumming bankers, masturbating magnates, milking moguls, cockvaulting carpetbaggers, muckdiving mugwumps, tugging tyros, tromboning tycoons, chandeliering chancers, and pissing on politicians. Much of which they have on film, I suspect. And they prefer not to have their highly profitable business (or the associated website) troubled by God-bothering pinch-faced epicaricacious spinsters from Roscommon with nothing better to do than write letters to the *Indo* complaining about lax public morals.

A brothel isn't primarily a place for blackmail, although it can serve that purpose too. It's a place for gathering intelligence, a first-rate source of information. You'd be surprised at the names that some TDs shout out when they come. It isn't always "Mommy."

What has all this to do with the production of abstracts? Very little, to be honest, other than that both whores and abstracters are in the information game. My familiarity with Jane and Miss Whipcream is entirely above board and work related. I know them only through Frank's dealings with Señor Estímulo; Frank and I travel out to Dun Laoghaire every other Sunday for lunch and stop off on the way back into town, the way one would visit the in-laws. Yes, it is true that I have visited Knockmerry House on a number of occasions and enjoyed the odd dalliance over a sherry or two with Jane while Frank and Manuel have disappeared into the dimly lit and bead-curtain-concealed backrooms to discuss operational matters. I have even been offered a tour of the facilities by Miss Whipcream, but sadly had been forewarned against it by Frank, his knowledge of the 24-hour surveillance system in operation beyond the Reception being unnervingly detailed. It's one thing for judges, solicitors, and politicians to be caught on film or tape—they've usually concocted an alibi or have their back covered by someone—quite another for a working stiff like you and me, who get fed to the sharks at the most opportune of moments and find ourselves spread-eagled on the front of the *Star*. Besides, I get all the gossip I want from Jane, who is careful to stimulate only my curiosity, and Frank isn't exactly tight lipped on the car journeys home. I think he finds the conversation cleansing. Cathartic. Spending more than a couple of hours with a Francoist dwarf complaining that he has to read the Koran to train in "the new girl" because some rich cunt wants to shoot his load over a niqab wouldn't be my idea of a languid Sunday afternoon either.

—

Another card from Stiveley, this time with a photograph of a bottle of Jameson on the front. On the back, he's written, "I will kill you." What a prick.

—

When I arrived into the office on Monday morning, Sinéad was sitting at her desk wearing a pair of shades.

"Very sophisticated," I said. "Rough night, was it?"

She dismissed my concern with a brusque wave.

"Screen."

I frowned my incomprehension. "I've got the brightness on the screen turned up full to help the grass grow."

A tilt of her head toward the monitor directed my attention to two small pots of, well, pot, strategically positioned to derive the maximum value from the glare.

"Is that strictly legal, Shin?"

"It's for workplace morale. I don't know anything about the legality of it, but we need something to keep people's spirits up."

"Why so?" I dropped my case to the floor and pulled up the back of a chair to rest against.

"The chat going round the office is that the teleworking is bad news. That the company's cutting costs because it has financial problems."

"Fuck's sake. You do people a favor and they still find a reason to moan."

"People don't like change. They get suspicious."

"They'd rather be bored and writing sardonic acrostics than working from home and grateful."

"They'd rather be working from home *and* writing sardonic acrostics. You're never going to get gratitude, Joe. Don't expect it."

I scanned the office. One of the problems with a workplace run like a monastery is that every conversation is overheard, every raised voice becomes cause for speculation. I lowered my voice.

"We're getting squeezed all round. High costs here and low sales out there. It would help if the firm had more than one sales rep for the whole of Southeast Asia and she wasn't based in Sydney—"

"The model's dying on its arse though, too. You can't charge for information that people can get for free. Subscription databases have got to offer something customers can't get elsewhere. What's our USP?"

"Our USP? Isn't it abstracts that spell out WE'RE DOOMED?"

"There's a dwindling market for overqualified begrudgers, I'm afraid. You're competing against open-access providers like Scielo and the DOAJ. Until there's some kind of primitive accumulation on the Internet, some Enclosure movement that shuts down access to freely circulating information, you're going to struggle to monetize your knowledge."

"I got about half of that."

She leaned back from the desk and made circles with her shoulders the way we're all trained to do but nobody does. Let me take a break to do it now.

"Make hay while the sun shines, Joe." She reached for the vase next to her printer and lifted out the flowers. "Wanna drink?"

"No thanks. We have a cooler for that."

"Not for this you don't. It's vodka."

Fake flowers. How did I miss that?

"I'll get my mug."

DUBLIN, Ireland (AP): Irish atheists are celebrating as a "natural miracle" the discovery of a pomegranate which, when cut open, revealed the phrase "There is no God," spelled out in seeds. The pomegranate was bought by local resident Aoife O'Sullivan from a greengrocers in Ranelagh, South Dublin.

Andrew Cox of the Irish Association of Atheists commented that, "It only tells us what we've known for a long time, but while we discount divine intervention in the physical universe as an explanation for material phenomena, it's comforting to know that Nature is even handed in the arbitrary messages She conveys."

Leaders of the country's Muslim community have been less impressed. A spokesman said, "The pomegranate is a fruit through which Allah has traditionally spoken to Muslims. I have no doubt that this discovery is one of a series, the other members of which will complete the phrase with the words "but Allah, and Mohammed is his prophet."

Followers have been instructed to buy up all available stocks of pomegranates in Ireland in order to locate the missing text. They can expect tough competition from the Irish Nietzschean Society, however, who anticipate finding the entire text of *Thus Spake Zarathustra* in a pomegranate-seed format.

And more proof of the Endtimes, this time from the *Offaly Herald*:

The home of Mr. Michael Flynn was hit overnight by a storm of fully assembled heavy industrial lifting machinery. His entire property bears evidence of a highly localized storm, possibly a by-product of Hurricane Bisto, which ravaged Cuba last month. A large derrick, two cranes, an automatic digger, a forklift truck, and two tractors were carried by winds of over 500 mph and deposited on Mr. Flynn's house and grounds. The damage caused was substantial. Mr. Flynn, a security guard for an ice-cream firm, said, "I was out at the time."

No. 61
Profumo Punch

4 oz. Stolichnaya Vodka
4 oz. Beefeater Gin
Some Schnapps
Drink blindfolded

MI6's finest, Seymour Stiveley, has broken into my apartment again, the dick. He always waits until I'm out. He must be watching from across the road, from Percy Place. I'll have to take a closer look at the winos who congregate on the benches over there of an evening. They always look nervous, act furtively, but it never occurred to me that one of them might be Stiveley. He should be easy to spot. You don't see that many winos smoking pipes.

He must have gotten in when one of the downstairs tenants was going out, then picked the locks on the internal door and shorted the alarm. He knows where the drinks cabinet is, but I've hidden the Glenmorangie in a steel cage in the attic. He couldn't break the code on the lock of the cabinet, so he used a jigsaw and went in through the side. I'm going to have to booby-trap that panel.

It looks like he took all the full bottles: a bottle of Haig, a bottle of Teachers, and the Absolut Mandarin. What a sucker. As if I'd buy them to drink! There's supping whiskey, and there's stealing whiskey. What he got there was my stealing whiskey. He fell for it. I escaped intact.

Because he's not a drinker, he lacks the necessary connoisseurship. He's not au fait with the merchandise. He'll rob anything he imagines I get pissed on. I must check if he's nabbed the shoe polish.

This is all about trying to scare me, trying to show me how vulnerable I am, that he could take me any time he wanted. The fucker even left a note behind, composed using letters cut out from the papers. Very punk rock. It says, "Give Up." Which shows how little he knows me. I gave up a long time ago.

I took my first Niclosamide capsule this evening. At last, a chance to be rid of Steve. That's the name I've given to this unwelcome guest who's been lazing around, living off my dinner money, eating half my food for the last six months. He's like the friend you never knew you had, who's also called Steve and who suddenly turns up on your doorstep on a regular basis to pick your wife up and take her to covens, and you're such a trusting soul, and so pleased your wife finally has a hobby that doesn't involve maxing the Visa, that you hardly check his credentials; you're convinced your wife adores you, and you find it reassuring that she has taken to exploring her spiritual side. She seems so happy these days that sometimes you think you should encourage her to get out and about even more. And now and then you invite the guy into your home and you put up with him drinking your beer and pinching your chair in front of the fire and sharing comments with your wife in front of you that you *know* are disparaging but which you can't prove and which they'd deny in any case. And then one day she doesn't come home at all and you find out she's been screwing the bastard rotten and everyone knew but you, you fucking retard social outcast.

So what do you do for revenge? You do what any sane, cuckolded, jealous, desperate imbecile would do. You name your tapeworm after him. That'll teach him.

Oh yeah, the tapeworm. Thanks, Delia. The only time I ever eat meat round your place—pork, of course, which you had no idea how to cook—and I come home with a tapeworm. A secret sharer. My intimate, my confidant. Mon frère.

I've been able to live with the sporadic indigestion he gives me, and I've lost a bit of weight, which was no harm. It's the Jane Fonda method. I've been going to Weight Watchers of a Wednesday evening after work to keep track of my progress, although my ulterior motive has been to meet nicely curved women who congratulate me every other week on my willpower and my success at sticking with the program. "What's your secret, Joe?" they demand, eager for me to demand theirs in return.

"I don't have any secrets," I tell them. "Unless you mean my history of undercover work for the CIA." Bless, how they laugh, the jiggling gigglers.

I won't miss Steve when he disappears round the U-bend, but he's done me no real harm, in fairness, and he never spent Sunday afternoons fucking my wife. Perhaps if I'd fucked her myself I wouldn't have needed

Weight Watchers, but the indigestion would have been worse.

Sinéad reliable as always. The top smartphone apps downloaded in Northern Ireland this month:

1: Ubisim: A GPS app that locates the nearest monkey.
2: Fangora: Start times and release dates of all vampire-related TV shows, films, books, and church deconsecrations.
3: JisSum: Popular sperm count app. Just yack your barley over the touchscreen.
4: Speciiii: Lost or broken your glasses? Enter the speckifications and dimensions into this app and place your phone on the bridge of your nose. (Pronounced "specky four eyes.")
5: NutTeller: Indispensable journey planner that takes into account the movements of local weirdoes so you don't get on the wrong bus or have to cross the road.
6: Gaydoh: Have all the homophobic jokes from the Simpsons ready to hand.
7: CuntBusters: Details of the venues, dates, and times of all showings of movies featuring Phil Collins, so you can avoid them.
8: MapMap: Provides directions to the nearest town center map. Map included.

9: BodyCount: Enables you to use your iPhone as a rectal thermometer.
10: Podcast: Gives off a high-pitched scream when hoodies lob your iPhone into the canal.
11: Sticki: Pictures of twigs.
12: Crossword: Invent new swearwords for any occasion, you ferominal spuntjucker.
13: BlackFace: Organizes your Facebook friends in ascending order of skin pigmentation.
14: Cappit: A virtual lens cap app for your iPhone's camera. Don't forget to remove it before taking any photos.
15: Kartoonize: Turn your life into a caricaturish parody of the real thing simply by using your iPhone all day.
16: Status Quo: A GPS-based app that tells you precisely where you are without enabling you to get anywhere else.
17: Momus: Set it when you go to bed, this alarm app will go off at random intervals during the night and tell you how long you've been asleep.
18: Hot Stuff: Overheats your iPhone so you can use it to keep your hands warm in cold weather.
19: Scofflaw: Updates on any forthcoming funerals of individuals employed in the legal profession.
20: Ghost: Hide your iPhone in your kids' bedroom and it will emit eerie whispers and the occasional moan during the night. Upgrade promises to knock over lamps.

No. 70
The Vatican Banker
4 oz. Ambrosia Creamed Rice
3 oz. Benedictine
6 oz. Trappist Beer
4 oz. Dominican Rum
Drink under a bridge to swing music

No shades for Sinéad today. She's been busy organizing the electricians on the third and fourth floors for their subletting to a company of architects, a task that required eye contact. I spent half my weekend in the office shifting furniture down to the first and second floors, having drawn up a plan to reorganize the layout in light of our unmitigated success at promoting the teleworking scheme. More than half of all the writing staff have opted in. A couple of the junior editors even took demotions in order to qualify rather than stay on in the office as editors. Are we really such poor company? Or is it that they feel a desperate need to talk to someone—anyone—during their working day, even if it's only a toddler? "I read a fascinating article this morning on the Russian Orthodox church's involvement in copyright infringement, Lucy. Please take Daddy's highlighter out of the cat's bottom."

Sinéad's taken to carrying a stress ball with her around the office, which she clenches like she wishes it was my goolies. "Are you working out some suppressed rage?" I asked in my usual, concerned-sarcastic tone the first time I saw it, the day after she got back from a long weekend in Chicago. The fleetest of fugues flamed through her eyes. "My taser was confiscated at customs." Concern for the welfare of my staff abated slightly at the news. "Still," she said, dipping into her bag, "They did let me bring this through." She plonked her latest executive toy on her desk. It was a mini guillotine.

My man bits are in danger.

Not just my man bits, if Sinéad's reading of matters is accurate. We had another conference call with COITUS this afternoon (morning New York time) to report on the progress of the teleworking scheme and to be appraised of the latest developments.

"The board is very impressed by the changes going on over there, Joe. I've no doubt that we'll soon be seeing a real difference in the balance sheet for the Dublin operation. The board has asked me to see if we can pursue this approach in other areas of the company and maybe follow through by carrying its implications forward via alternative strategies."

I didn't like the sound of that. I didn't understand it, for one thing, and when you don't understand something management says, it's usually a sign of bullshit. When they want to be understood, they'll be candid. When they don't, they'll slather the shit in more shit. Deep, dark, dirty, bad bullshit coated in bland, blurry, buttery, banal bullshit. The Milky Bar Skid Mark.

"What sort of alternative strategies?" Sinéad didn't like the sound of it any more than I did.

"Well, we've been beta-testing a new model using software produced by a company down in Alabama that generates abstracts using optical character recognition, word frequency, Bayesian probability, and a simple semantic mapping tool to see if it can produce cost-effective products capable of standing in for their naturally generated equivalents."

More bullshit. I shot Sinéad a knowing smirk, but she was fuming. Clearly, I was missing something.

"You're talking about replacing staff with software."

"Merely testing at the moment, Sinéad, to explore the financial parameters of such a move. Naturally, the impact your end will be minimal. We'd expect that the software-generated abstracts would still need to be edited, after all. There has to be a quality audit process of some sort to ensure that there is no decline in quality, or at least a managed decline so that it stays within the boundaries of customer tolerance. That's something else we're investigating too, as you'd expect."

"You mean it's the only the writers who need to be worried."

There was no immediate response. The no immediate response of shame. Eventually,

"That's right."

Sinéad's nails were digging deep into the squeezy ball as COITUS continued. "We're also in discussion with a number of companies in India, Israel, and the Philippines. We've shipped over a few sample documents to see if their content-generating staff can meet our levels of performance."

"You're talking about outsourcing."

"They've a large pool of English-speaking graduates—much larger than Ireland, especially now that so many Irish have emigrated—who cost substantially less, and while we don't know what sort of standard we'll see, I re-iterate that you have a high-quality editorial staff there that will be able to knock the discounted work into shape."

"It'll mean taking on more editorial staff here if the quality of the written abstracts deteriorates significantly."

"Well, we'll look at that once we've got a better idea of the kind of deterioration we're talking about. I'm really only giving you a heads-up so that you don't put any of the probationary staff on full-time contracts in the immediate future or take on any new writers unnecessarily. You've managed a massive reduction in staff turnover, which is super, well done, guys. But if there are any vacancies that come up in the next few months, try to make do with what you have…use freelancers to fill in. Don't be hasty in making long-term calls. The usual stuff."

"The usual stuff," Sinéad repeated to me after COITUS had rung off. "That's such crap." I tried to placate her.

"She *did* say it was only beta-testing. You know how often flags like these get run up the pole and nobody salutes. I can guarantee you nothing will come of it."

"Can you?"

"Sure. We're going great guns here with the teleworking. Saving them a fortune on bills and overhead. And with the subletting. We're golden. We can do no wrong. You watch. These abstracts will come back from Alabama and the Philippines and they'll be useless. Accounts will look at the cost of having to take on new editors to deal with the quality deficiencies and decide it's a non-starter." Sinéad didn't look convinced. "It happens all the time."

"I hope you're right. But bear this in mind. If they have to increase editorial staff, their next step, logically, will be to try to find cheaper editors. And woe betide you if they start looking to do that, because you won't have anyone left here to manage."

I hadn't thought of that.

"For you to compete with these feckers cost wise, you're going to have to get the editors out of the office."

"What do you mean?"

"It's your only option. If they start looking for cheaper editors, you're going to have to make your editors cheaper simply to stay in the game. Put the editors on the tele-working scheme and sublet the ground and first floors. Otherwise, there's nothing to stop them transferring the whole operation to Mumbai."

"I've never been to Mumbai."

"You won't be going. They'll have people already in place. I expect you'll be out of a job."

Was it my imagination or did she take pleasure in saying that? Surely she'd be out of a job too. What use is a Human Resources manager when there are no Human Resources?

It was reasonable point to make, but I didn't dare make it. Not the way that squeezy ball was bulging.

"You have a case. I think we know what we have to do."

"We do," she said. "I'll book the flights."

"Right," I said. "Wait. What?"

"The flights. I'll get the taser back from customs. We'll track down COITUS at home, paralyze her, you deal with the body."

I recoiled. "You're messing, right?"

Nothing.

"Right?"

"Of course I am. You nob."

Thank fuck for that.

"They'd see us coming a mile away. What we need is a hitman."

"A hitman."

"Or woman."

"Who we'll pay with what? Sarcastic abstracts? Sinéad, the Venn diagram of hitmen and disaffected librarians is an empty set."

"I understand they'll take payment in hard drugs. Do you have access to hard drugs?"

"Of course not. You?"

"Some amyl nitrate. Poppers. Not much. Not enough."

My raised eyebrow went unnoticed.

"Although I think they prefer unmarked notes or Bitcoin these days. I read an abstract about it last week."

"Been researching it, have you?"

Her gaze settled on my tie.

"I don't know about you, Joe, but I love this job. I'm not about to give it up because a beancounter in New

York wants to farm it out to some backwater Beijing bonzery."

"No. Yeah. Right. Me too."

"This is business, Joe. Don't rule out any options."

—

"Let me tell you a story. I am a humble, not very well-known, diminutive Spanish man born in Madrid, 1953. *Just there.* My father, in contrast, was a notorious brave airman in the Spanish air force, while my mother rode horses all the time. *Down a bit.* My early years were estatically happy, even though I had a slightly older brother, Hornolo, who was not bullying me all that much but who was undoubtedly my father's favorite as he was the first-born son. Fortunately, we were not seeing my father that very often because of his important air force work. *Slow.* Hornolo was explain to me back then that the Spanish air force was in its entirety three airplanes, two hot air balloons, and a squadron of gryphons, which are animals that have the body of a lion and the head and wings of an eagle; he tell me that the pilots climbed on the back of the gryphons with their revolvers drawn and their bombs strapped to them, which they then drop from a great height on Basques, Communist demonstrators, the Camp Nou, and so on. *Slower, slower.* It made me very proud of my father, although I have since checked up in books and discovered that Hornolo was lying about some of this. I never find out why. I think he does this because older brothers can. I am not bearing him any grudges. And anyway I have got my revenge."

I'm back at Knockmerry House, and I think I'm supposed to feel grateful to Frank for allowing me to meet Manuel Estímulo. An Audience with Kylie Minogue it ain't. We were making our weekly visit to Miss Whipcream and Jane Bondage's house of dubious moral standards a day early, which meant the head honcho was free. Ish. Why Frank thought he was doing me a favor is beyond me. It can't have been pity or a desire for me to share in his good fortune. He's always been a little miffed that Spanish intelligence got into the escort business ahead of the Company, particularly because there aren't enough good-looking Irish hookers to go round. Perhaps he's considering going into business for himself and wants me to have a look at the model before he commits. Anyway, for the moment, Miss Whipcream's establishment is the main conduit for intel that can't be acquired by ECHELON, break-in, or blowing the admiral of the fleet, unless you want to do it yourself, and although Frank's always been very hands-on, he draws the line at being lips-round.

Whatever the reason, I'm forced to spend my Saturday afternoon with Jane Bondage and Frank, imitating Frank's feigned fascination while this Falangist sleazebag, reclining like a miniature Jabba the Hutt on a 17th-century chaise longue that's still too long for him, rabbits on incoherently and a teenage Croatian whose name I didn't catch timidly polishes his cock.

"Two years after I was born, it was then the turn of my sister, Candelaría. She was my younger sister. *Tighter.* The first few years playing with her was very good fun, because now I was able to torment her in the same way that Hornolo had torment me, escept with the added bonus that Candelaría was a girl, which meant there were different things on her to examine. *Use your teeth. Yes.* In those days, we—Candelaría and myself—we invent acupuncture and colonic irrigation, independent of both the Chinese and Lady Diana. Not that I am condone scientific experimentation as a way to discover fundamental truths about the world, you understand. *Lick my balls!* Sadly, I must tell you, our relationship soured when I reach the age of eight and Candelaría was six. One summer's day, while my mother was upstairs in the house sacking one of the maids, we were outside playing naked around the pool, I cannot remember the name of the game what it was. *Attend to the perineum.* And I push Candelaría into the pool and then I run into the house and hide in the cloakroom, especting her to come chase after me with a fork, her favorite implement of distressing me. *Yes, that's it. Now the head.* What I was not aware, however, was that, as she is falling in the pool, Candelaría bang her head on the side and she knock herself unconscious. While I am hiding in the cloakroom naked, smelling everyone's coats, she is at the bottom of the pool with nobody noticing. *Grip it with two fingers. Yes. All the way.* It was only when she was not forking me for a long time that I go out to look for her and locate her at the bottom of the pool. She did not hear my screams and shouts to wake up, and she was not move either when I drop rocks at her, but fortunately one of the garden staff hears me, and he dive in to retrieve Candelaría while I run in to tell my mother to call the ambulance. We still had to fire the gardener for negligence, but I think you will agree he got off lightly."

Jane has heard this a thousand times before but is an expert at faking a look of concern. She does it for all the johns who come in here.

"Candelaría is lazing at the pool bottom for eight minutes altogether but she is not dead at all, only brain damage. She is made into a kind of vegetable, which kind I am not sure; the doctor at the hospital was not specific. At the time, because I was small, I thought it was a mong bean, but afterwards I realize that this was because of things the boys at school was saying when they tease me about her and were also chasing me with a fork. I found out later when I talk to Hornolo that she is not a mong at all, which is something completely different. *Pull the skin right back.*

After this point, of course, things change a lot. My mother is blaming herself very much for leaving me unsupervised, but she is able to soften the pain of this responsibility by using large quantities of gin, which she had specially flown in from London by the air force. My father also help with softening the pain for her by blaming me, holding me from that day accountable for all my actions and emphasizing to me the importance of guilt and responsibility and shame and the necessity of begging for forgiveness from God and Jesus. He tells me to specially make sure I demonstrate my guilt and sorriness whenever my mother is in the room. *Both at the same time. Suck and use your fingers.*

My father continue to be absent whenever he can, but this circumstance was not lasting forever, and when I get to 12 years old and Hornolo is 14, my mother say to my father that she has had enough of having to look after us—specially at weekends, when we come home from boarding school, which was also when she receive guests and must therefore to remain sober—so from that point my father is doing all the boy-raising. A good deal of my manly education take place now, which was, I am embarrass to admit, rather late for a young Spanish boy of the bourgeoisie. However, also, my father was very much a man of the world, with more important things to do than raise children, and he tell us that he is not going to change his routine one jot in order to accommodate us. It is time, he say, for us to become men, like him, and therefore he was allow us to tag along behind with him when he visit the barbershop, the Bernabeu, to go to casinos, to make visits to various brothels, to do other gambling, to visit the corrida, to attend the illegal dogfights, to do the small bit of smuggling, and attacking negroes. All of this esperience was very educational. *Yes, faster now. Move your tongue.* Was because of my father's decision to educate us this way that I lose my virginity, but also gain much insight into the world, at the age of 13, in a well-known whoring house near Salamanca with a very nice middle-age lady with one eye, some teeth, and big tummy, who have pleasant maternal technique but without the smell of gin. *Keep going.* We have a lovely shower together, during which she make my small young penis extremely hard—this had happended before, of course, but only when playing with my sister or the dogs—sometimes using her mouth, sometimes her breasts. *Yes, deeper. Get ready.* Then she make me squat down with her in a shower cubicle, so that we hug one another very tight while she insert my penis inside her. Was very nice. *All the way.* She then use her vaginal muscles to milk the puppy fat out of me but also, at the same time, she use the shower head on full power to spray up into my, how you say, bottom, causing my sphincter muscle to go into uncontrollable spasms. Yes. *Yes. Is coming.* As you can imagine, this was incredibly invigorating esperience for me. I have the most famous orgasm ever and I shit myself at the same time!"

I wasn't sure if I was meant to be impressed, horrified, or to clap. Perhaps all three. Estímulo pushed the Croatian girl from his lap, giving her a tissue to wipe his come from her lips. He rolled over to one side to reach for a digestif of Cardenal Mendoza and re-lit his Cohiba.

"If I remember correctly, this weekend of significant joy and passage of rites was spoilt entirely by the discovery, when Hornolo and I get home, that my mother and Candelaría have managed to gas themselves to death. Silly stupid idiots!"

He leaned back and exhaled Cuban smoke.

"You know, to this day, I am so very, very annoyed that I never was able to tell my mother about my esperience with the whore. Typical fucking women, eh?'

"Indeed, Manuel," said Frank. "Typical." Estímulo eyed him suspiciously.

"Anyway, enough of memory lanes. I am sure I have bore you no end. And clearly you are distract. I will leave you in Jane's capable hands. I have accounts to attend to." He turned to me. "You understand, my friend, I am sure. Unending Spanish bureaucracy."

"Kuh," I said, agreeing. He took it for sympathy and rose from the chaise, covering his wet cock with his gown.

"Si. Mi casta es su casta. We are the same breed, you and I. I can tell. I hope we will see more of you…"

"Joe," said Frank helpfully. Estímulo pointed at him, then me, as if to say "Yes, that" and also "It's too much effort for me to say it myself."

It was only when he had departed that I realized the timid Croatian teenager had gone too. How discrete. A Ninja whore. Maybe she hid under his gown.

In other news:

From August's *Entertainment Weekly*.

...and now that the director has finally bagged that elusive Oscar, he will return to another back-burner project, an all-adult cast remake of *Bugsy Malone*. Scorsese said, "With all respect to Alan (Parker), I felt he took liberties with his actualization. The main themes have never been examined in great detail, and we've been waiting 20 years for the chance to do them justice."

Principal photography will begin in Rome in the fall of next year, and the cast is believed to include Robert De Niro, Ray Liotta, and Jodie Foster.

Also:

The mystery behind one of Harry Houdini's lesser-known tricks may have been solved. Often performed at private parties, Houdini would have his hands cuffed behind his back, be stripped naked, and have a hessian sack secured over his head and shoulders, having already swallowed the key to the handcuffs. He would then be locked in a bathroom for 15 minutes before emerging with key and cuffs but with the sack still secure on his head.

It is now believed the trick was achieved by Houdini digesting a skeleton key and laxatives sometime prior to the performance, excreting the key into his well-placed hands and then washing the evidence off in a shower which he had his audience leave running, supposedly to cover the noise of the escape.

Don't try that at home.

No. 103
The Litvinenko Stinger
8 oz. of Sloe Berry Tincture
Serve in a hot teapot

Can you believe the imbeciles they have on *The Weakest Link*? Listen to these answers from today's show:

Q: The occupation of the character Figaro is given in the name of the opera in which he appears. What is it? A: *The Italian Job*

Q: Red Admiral and Cabbage White are types of what? A: Paint

Q: What was the name of Robin Hood's sweetheart? A: Trudy Glenn

Q: Which European island do Maltese terriers come from? A: The Isle of Dogs

Q: What 'S' would you be likely to catch while fly-fishing in Scotland? A: Syphilis

Q: A human being's sex depends on possession of X and Y chromosomes. Which sex has a Y? A: Doggy

Q: Which organization has the motto, "Higher, Faster, Stronger"? A: Narcotics Anonymous.

Q: Alanis Morrissette had a hit with her album entitled *Jagged Little* what? A: *Shit*

and

Q: Which Mick is the lead singer of the Rolling Stones?
A: Bono

I know for a fact that at least one of these is wrong.

So, what did I learn this weekend from my chats with Jane Bondage that might be more edifying than a sex show with a dwarf? Not a great deal, it must be said. A few bits and pieces that Frank had already divulged on various occasions when pissed, such as the fact that all guns brought into Ireland come through a disused fish factory near the mouth of the Boyne outside Drogheda; that three government ministers like to dress up as German frauleins and be pelted with butter while hanging upside down from a climbing frame; that Jedward are triplets and the third one had all the talent but was kept locked in a cellar by Louis Walsh. All these things are common knowledge among the Irish political elite. I did *not* know that Manuel Estímulo does not allow clients to bring drink or drugs into the premises for recreational use with members of staff. Which seems a little narrow minded, particularly for someone running a brothel, but then he is a Catholic fascist; narrow minded is his middle name (actually, I think it's Ramon, which is less apt, being almost an anagram of normal). Not that this information has much use value. Or exchange value, for that matter. It couldn't be made into an abstract, for instance. To sum up, she and I made polite chit-chat and danced casually to Tom Jones while Frank disappeared into the anterooms to carry out his usual business.

"How's the training of the new girl coming along?"

"Your guess is good as mine, Hun. We hardly ever get to see her." I don't know why she calls me Hun. I'm more of a Vandal.

"Would this be unusual?" I jerked my hips from side to side and raised my hands like a cat about to pounce.

"Yeah. *That* would be."

"Not this. This is my Tom Jones move. It's not unusual." Her eyes demurred. I continued. "I meant is it unusual that you don't get to see the new girl? I'd have thought you and Miss Whipcream would have taken charge of her induction."

She walked over to the laptop in time to the beat, high heels lending her strut a drunken vulnerability. She checked the playlist before turning the sound up a notch.

"Manuel's looked after the whole thing. And we never see the client. A towncar pulls up outside the front door at noon on a Saturday, she's there waiting at the bottom of the steps, jumps in, and off they go." I clicked my fingers.

"Diplomatic plates?"

"Hire car. Traceable but bound to be a pseudonym and cash payment." She shimmied. I shimmied back.

"Curiouser and more curiouser."

"I know, Hun. And get this. The client asked for an Iranian. Specifically, an Iranian. What do you make of that?"

Jazz hands.

"I've no idea. Perhaps he has a thing for Shi'ites." Jane chuckled.

"I hope not. Manuel couldn't get an Iranian. He got an Iraqi instead. Hoped the client wouldn't notice. They're pretty similar, right?"

"Sure. Right next door to each other." I boogied, span round, and froze, looking cool. A small fleck of spittle carried on, hitting the drinks cabinet. It dribbled. "I'm sure Manuel's got her up to speed, anyway. Taught her how to be Iranian. All the Iranian sex tricks, the way they hold a cock differently, all that sort of stuff." I imitated a choo-choo train with my arms. Tom Jones was working on a railroad. Apparently.

Her forehead furrowed. You could have held the national plowing championships on it.

"What do you know about Iranian cock-holding, Hun?"

"Only what I've read in books. And to be honest, what I've read may only apply to gay Iranians."

Damn you, William Burroughs. "The Green, Green Grass of Home" came on. A chance to take a breather. Jane motioned to the sofa.

"Still, you'll have to show me. It's a part of my job to know these things."

"Of course I will, Jane. As a favor. But let them bury Tom first."

"The cloaca-munching gobsheen that churned out this monkey-sucking dick splatter should be forced to headfuck heifers for the rest of his unnatural existence, the fetus-shitting snaggleshaft."

COITUS had passed on the results of some of the beta-testing, and Sinéad was singularly unimpressed. We'd hunkered down in the conference room to trawl through samples of computer-generated illiteracy, which we were comparing against abstracts produced by our own employees and by similar, but more eager, rice-fueled drones in Southeast Asia.

"Is that from the Philippines or Alabama?"

"I'll read it out to you and you try to guess: Manila or machine?"

She straightened her back, pulled herself to her full height, and cleared her throat, either to enhance her delivery or to convey to me the gravity of the moment. Maybe both.

"Business interests have argued for the implementation of the higher minimum wage to be introduced over a period of ten years or more—full stop—But—comma—for now—comma—the ballot initiative lingers in the background while the council debates matters of law—full stop. A Woman—capital double-you—holds a sign calling for Philadelphia to introduce a $12 an hour, not hyphenated, minimum wage during a May Day rally—full stop. The only socialist city councilor in the United States is torn—full stop. A group of minority-owned businesses wrote to Kempton saying the increase would hit immigrant workers hard—full stop. Another study came to a similar conclusion about a large increase in the minimum wage in Pittsbrugh. That's P-I-T-T-S-B-R-U-G-H. No full stop."

"You've started me with a toughie," I protested. "It sounds like proper sentences but there's something skew-whiff about it. Not to mention Pittsbrugh."

"It's horseshit. There's no hook, no context. Look at the original article. There, on the desk in front of you. The line about the woman holding a sign is the caption underneath the photo. Can you see? It's like lines have been picked out of the article at random. And a sentence beginning with a conjunction? Appalling."

Indeed.

"I'll plump for the software," I said and she nodded. "Even a Filipino knows not to do that."

"Try this one then."

More throat-clearing noises.

"English and technology are a sine qua non—no italics, comma—for teeny tyros growing up in Vietnam—full stop. A Communist state with a fiercely capitalist system—comma—citizens are imbued with the Asian values that put the success of the young generation first—full stop. The streets of Hanoi are full of women on bicycles—full stop. May 12—comma—2015—comma—New York Times—unitalicized, full stop. You can order a copy of this story here—full stop. SHare—capital 's', capital 'h'—this page—full stop. ORder—capital 'o', capital 'r'—reprints—full stop. Today's—full stop. Subscription—capital 's'—rates—full stop."

"Has to be software. It's even incorporated the web site's hyperlinks. Bloody useless."

"Ya think? Even though the initial letters of the sentences spell EAT MY SHORTS?"

"You're kidding. You mean it's one of ours? That's indefensible."

She screwed up the page and binned it.

"Worse. It's the software. They must have fed samples from our databases into their system and it's able to produce acrostics. It's still gibberish, but if software can do that, we should be worried. It's only a matter of time before it becomes fully conscious."

"Fuck. Let's hope it turns out to be as indolent as our lot."

From the *Perth Gazette*:

The craze currently sweeping Australian high schools of snorting crushed genital crabs is believed to originate in the urban myth that the crabs reprocess THC contained in the blood of marijuana users. Jean Corley, headmistress of Wollamura High School said, "There is a worrying trend among some of our students for cultivating crabs on their bodies as if they were pubic farms. On the bright side, unwanted pregnancies have dropped by 50% this year."

No. 88
The Yeltsin Sunset
6 oz. Scotch Whisky
6 oz. London Gin
6 oz. Russian Vodka
6 oz. Cuban Rum
6 oz. Cognac
1 Magnum Bollinger or Similar
6 oz. Meths
6 oz. Fernet-Branca
6 oz. Scrumpy Jack
Pour everything into a plain glass
Do not disturb

COITUS says New York hasn't ruled out using the computer-generated abstracts. Can you fucking believe it? This is *after* I'd sent our report to her with a devastating critique of both sets of outsourced abstracts. I even titled the email "Pure shite" so they'd be in no doubt about our assessment. This tells me that my opinion—expert opinion—doesn't count for much.

"If you want low-quality abstracts, Paula, we'd have no trouble providing them for you," I said, probably not the strongest opening argument.

"I'm sure you could, but at what cost?"

"I haven't run the figures, but it strikes me that this is a false economy in the long run. Are you going to release such poor abstracts onto the database and run the risk of losing customers, or are you going to employ more editors to cope with the decline in quality?"

"We're looking into that. We aren't fools. You mustn't make the mistake of thinking we'd jeopardize sales. But at the same time, don't imagine that the market requires perfection. It's a matter of striking a balance, of finding out what the customer is willing to pay for, how much tolerance the customer has before they switch to a competitor. It's all math, really. Equations, formulae, that kind of thing."

"Yeah, yeah, I know what math is." My eyelid ticced. "I'm only saying that I don't believe we've tested the boundaries of what is feasible here. You seem to have shifted the goalposts so that the outsourcers are allowed to operate at a lower level of quality than we are. You haven't considered whether we could meet the modified requirements."

"Because of your cost base. We don't have to pay the rent for the outsourcers' offices."

"Of course you do. It's factored into the price."

"Okay. But the offices aren't in Dublin. They're third world rents. Even in Alabama."

"I'm handling that problem with the subletting."

"It's not enough, Joe. The rates we went in on are very different from those we're getting from the tenants. The simple fact is that your costs are too high. If you could produce abstracts of this quality and drop your costs further, we might be onto something. But as it stands, we have to look at other options."

Twat.

"Would you be able to match the outsourcers' quality with fewer staff?"

"That goes without saying. It isn't like the secret to their low quality is throwing bodies at it."

"And still meet the production targets?"

"Obviously not. Not unless you want to double the number of abstracts for every writer. That'd be ridiculous."

"Well, there you are. They can do it in Manila."

Fucking twat.

"How about I get the editors out of the building? Get the senior staff working from home. That way we could free up some more space for tenants and reduce our overhead still further."

"Do that anyway. Christ, Joe, I don't think you take this job seriously half the time. Why haven't you pursued that option before now?"

"The disruption it would cause. Everything was running so smoothly."

Even at this distance, I could hear her shaking her head in despair at the other end of the line.

"Smoothness is death, Joe. Smoothness is death. Revolutionize the process of production at all times. Change is life, change is progress, disruption is good. The Chinese say 'May you live in interesting times' as a curse. That's why they've never achieved anything except by copying us. We say, 'Embrace interesting times. Interesting times bring opportunities. Opportunities for improvement, for creation, for destruction of the tired old ways.'

Not smoothness. Smoothness is un-American. You don't want to be un-American, do you?"

"Absolutely not."

"Then get with the program. Cut the costs. Cut the wage bill. Double productivity. If being American means living like Filipinos, live like Filipinos. Beat them at their own game. You can do it. You the man."

No, Paula, you the Man. You the Man. Me Cheeta.

I took Sinéad for a night out with Frank, more fool me, partly as a way of helping her to broaden her social circle in Dublin, partly in the hope of ameliorating the intensity of Frank's unsentimental hedonism, and partly, if I'm honest, to form some kind of brains trust, a cross between a think tank and a drunk tank. A thrunk tank. I didn't tell her that Frank was CIA, of course, only that he worked at the embassy as a liaison officer with the Irish government—which is his cover anyway. She seemed happy enough with that.

I suggested that we could make this a regular event, a chance to kick back, mull, provide support for one another, Frank being another blow-in—emotional, intellectual, financial support. It transpired, though, that we have entirely different tastes in food, so I spent the first hour of the afternoon on the phone, negotiating a compromise. Eventually, we agreed to rotate the choice of venue among ourselves, with Sinéad getting the first choice as the woman and the newbie, so that she could select somewhere she knew she'd feel comfortable. She picked Foley's, an unobjectionable tourist bar on the corner of Merrion Row and Baggot Street ("How safe" Frank moaned), followed by Gordon's, a glass-fronted prandial posing palace on Dawson Street.

Between us, we managed to come up with enough change to buy a couple of bottles of Chilean Cabernet in Foley's, so by the time we got to Gordon's I was busting for a piss, but the scene that greeted us as we arrived delayed my relief. We were treated to the spectacle of an old homeless geezer with his trousers round his ankles urinating against the huge front window, behind which sat, forks laden with noodles half way to their mouths, two very demure, fake-blonde Dublin 4 ladies-who-lunch, barricaded by Brown Thomas bags and unable to take their eyes off what is technically known as "yer auld one's mickey."

From the look of disgust on their faces, you'd have thought they'd found smegma in the aioli. Fortunately for them, help was at hand, and their demeanor transformed in mere moments with the arrival of the Gardaí. Indeed, they were orgasming multiply as the good officers' Glocks smashed the old fella's teeth in and rammed them down his throat. Part of me wondered whether we should intervene, intervention in other countries' affairs being our stock in trade, but Frank said no, and besides, nobody else along the street was paying any attention. The Guards went about their job in an almost leisurely fashion, inflicting, for their small audience's delectation, the sort of damage they used to reserve for traveling English soccer thugs. They did it because there were ladies present. To reassure them that the police could be trusted to protect the vulnerable. Never say the Guards don't have a sense of chivalry.

So we stood to one side, beyond the splatter radius, and only when the body was being dragged down toward Nassau Street did I notice that Sinéad was holding my hand.

After a three-minute wait, we were seated toward the back of the restaurant and handed menus by a pinstriped maiden from Mount Anville. Food shortages have forced places like this to be provocatively inventive—meaning like it or lump it—in the creation of dishes, though inventiveness doesn't necessarily imply inspiration, and I didn't see much on the list that I fancied. Frank's body language told me he felt the same way, but rather than hurt Sinéad's feelings, we decided we should indulge her choice of venue. I plumped for the cat's cheese salad, and Frank had the arugula with balsa wood shavings. There was fish on the menu, but it was sole, and Frank won't eat "stupid" fish, stupid being any fish that gets caught by the hundredweight. "How can they be good for your brains? They're thick as fuck." He'll eat dolphins, but only the ones that can do tricks.

Although this was intended to be my inaugural brains trust, Frank spent most of the night moaning about the death of one of his liaisons, a butcher from Dunshaughlin on the government payroll who had been providing him with cash-in-hand information about circus movements, Traveler sightings, and any other activities "affecting American business interests" (his explanation to Sinéad). That, and griping about the incompetents he has to work with in the Irish civil service (read "secret service"). We tend to forget, I think, being citizens of the most powerful country in the world, that other regimes lack the resources and sophistication to take advantage of advances in espionage and military technology. In Frank's case, coordinating activities with his Irish counterparts is complicated by the fact that there isn't really an equivalent to the CIA; no Seamus Bond, no Double-O'Siobhan. What secrets do the Irish have that are worth protecting? How Van Morrison got away with it for so long. That's about it.

In addition, the Irish are still shagging about with outdated crypto, which compromises security and so restricts the level of information it can share with the CIA without risk of leakage. Most European intel that finds its way to Langley is derived from ECHELON, which intercepts all the business calls, e-mails, voice-mails, cell-phone calls, and faxes from European governments and businesses, and PRISM, the NSA's surveillance program. By contrast, encryption over here rarely gets beyond "Cn u gt me sm rd lmnde frm d chppr? Thtd b gr8. Thx." Frank refers to his Irish colleagues as the uninformed services.

"So how did yer man die?" I said once the food had arrived, resigned by that point to the fact that he was going to whine about it all night if we didn't let him get it out of his system.

"Weirdest thing." He took a first mouthful of arugula and pulled a piece of unidentifiable pabulum from between his teeth. "The report I saw said he died from a non-specific attack of gallstones." He made air quotes but only after he'd finished speaking, so they were of no help whatsoever.

"What does 'non-specific attack' mean?"

"Pelted to death with them by medical students." I'd forgotten it was rag week.

"Well, I'm sure you'll miss him, even if they didn't."

"Not a bit of it. Complete asshole. Used to beat his wife regularly."

"I think you mean frequently," said Sinéad, ever the pedant. "Regularly implies that he was following a schedule." Frank briefly drifted off into space—like Laika—before coming back to Earth—like Lockerbie.

"He was. Regularly. Third Tuesday of every month. He'd come home pissed from the pub—after he'd been to his men's assertiveness classes—and take Umbrage™ if his dinner wasn't on the table."

Sinéad winced. "That's awful. You should never mix those designer drugs with alcohol. No wonder he used to go berserk."

I didn't want to hear excuses for wife-beaters, drug crazed or not.

"You can't blame the drugs. Some of them are a right rip-off. They're nowhere near as effective as they're supposed to be, and mixing them with booze is a waste of both."

"Maybe they aren't effective on you, Joe," Sinéad said, putting her fork down carefully, "but that's probably because you've built up a resistance. What's that one you're always taking?"

"Pique Performance™," said Frank, helpfully.

"That's the one." She tapped my forearm twice as she scolded me, touching bare flesh. "If you were a real professional, you wouldn't be doing drugs while you're at work."

"It helps my concentration. Just the right amount of irritation for doing stats sheets and annual reviews." I was trying to stick up for myself but I was distracted by her touch. Had Frank noticed?

"Makes you impotent is what I heard," said Frank, snorting like his brain had burped.

"Hey, I don't have any trouble on that score, I can assure you." Just don't ask me to prove it. "And I take an anti-exasperant to bring me down afterward."

"Besides, Frank," said Sinéad, "You're one to talk. When we stopped at the chemists on the way here, didn't I see you sneak a sachet of Complete Madness™ in with the Nurofen, Golden Bears, and Dioralyte?"

"Fuck off, Sinéad. I like the ads is all."

It was recently reported on *Medical Alert* that Complete Madness™ had been found by the FDA to be constituted largely by slow-release estrogen-mimicking chemicals. Many of the consumers who had bought it in the hope of testosterone-induced fugues found that they were instead developing a number of secondary female sexual characteristics—smooth skin, adipose tissue—and shrunken testes. Many in the CIA think of themselves as big-balled bastards, not big bald bastards.

"Will you be going to the funeral, Frank?"

"S'pose. It's a day off work, isn't it?"

Sinéad recoiled.

"God, Frank. Is that all a funeral is to you, a day off work? That's a terrible thing to say."

"He's pulling your leg, Shin," I said. "It counts as work. He still gets paid. All he means is he'd rather be happy in his toil. Isn't that right?"

"Exactly," Frank said. "Take the ambassador's party, for instance. That's my idea of a working day. Fine wine, fine food, fine women."

"'Fine' is Frank's code-word for 'free'," I explained. "He means 'free wine, free food, free women'."

"The best things in life are fine," said Frank.

"But there's no such thing as a fine lunch," I countered.

"Indeed. Lunch sucks. But since we're talking of fine women, why don't you invite Sinéad here to accompany you to the party? I'm sure she'd enjoy it and there'd be no problem with clearance."

"What's this, Joe?"

"Party at the American ambassador's residence in the Phoenix Park for Veterans Day. At least, ostensibly. In reality, it's nothing but a schmooze-fest. Would you like to come?"

"Do I have to dress up?"

"It is preferred," said Frank. "No pajamas, no slippers."

Sinéad shot me an accusing glare.

"What?" I said innocently, but answer came there none.

"I'd love to go, Frank," she said. "I've never been inside an embassy."

"It isn't an embassy. It's the ambassador's residence. They're two different things. The embassy is that bass-drum building down by Herbert Park."

She paused to picture it.

"Like a spiky biscuit tin," I said.

"That place? Every time I go past, there are loads of people queuing up to get in. I thought it was the social welfare office."

"Those are folk lining up to leave the country. People looking for visas and work permits."

"I wondered why they all looked so happy."

After the main course, I finally managed to steer the conversation round to work. I was looking for suggestions as to how to get head office off my case; Frank can always be called on to think outside the box.

"Have you considered adult diapers?" he said, possibly inspired by my choice of chocolate mousse for dessert.

"Adult diapers?"

"To cut down on toilet breaks. They do it in Japan. Increases productivity. Staff could put them on and take them off in their own time, before and after work. At home if necessary."

"I'm not going to ask my staff to take the bus home wearing soiled nappies, Frank."

He was disappointed by my lack of imagination. "It'd work for telecommuters," he grumbled.

"How about multitasking?" said Sinéad. "Are there any jobs the staff can be doing while they're abstracting and editing? Take phone calls, for instance. You could do away with the Reception. It isn't like there are any visitors to the office."

"Mouth tasks," said Frank, as if it was self-explanatory.

"What?"

"Mouth tasks. Computers have made it possible for people to communicate with one another without having to use their mouths. You're always saying how quiet your office is, Joe. You can find jobs for idle tongues. Licking envelopes and stamps. Taste tests. Grooming. Washing monitors. It'll reduce the need for office cleaners. And if you go the diaper route, you won't need the johns cleaned either."

I was unconvinced.

"I was hoping for something rather more large scale, not piecemeal adjustments like these."

"Pets," said Frank, intent on ignoring me. "Get staff to bring their pets in. Install a generator and treadmills and kill two birds with one stone. The staff won't have to walk their dogs when they get home, and you get cheap electricity."

Sinéad concurred.

"Some rodents are smart enough to man the mail room."

"Are you serious?"

"Make the staff wear nylon socks around the office to generate static." Frank was on a roll now, weaving ideas together. "It could be used to power the coffee machine—make coffee the only available beverage—better still, put socks on the pets too."

"I don't believe any of these ideas will generate the kinds of savings we need."

"Maybe not individually," said Sinéad, "but together, in combination they might." She glanced at Frank for confirmation.

"Sure," he said. "Why not?"

"Otherwise, what are you going to do? New York wants major savings, so you find them or start laying people off. And once you go that route you don't know where it will end. You may find yourself shipping back to the States. You don't want that, do you?"

"Fuck no. I realize I give out about this place from time to time but the truth is that I've come to—what? Love?—really like this place. The filth, the squalor, the absence of any demand for standards of hygiene. The lot."

"Every pock mark and pimple of its streets and its people," said Sinéad.

"Exactly."

"So what will you do? You can't pay them out of your own pocket, can you?"

"I wish."

"So then, we're agreed. It's poo, pets, and static."

"I'll stick with the chocolate mousse, thanks."

In the news this week:

A 1959 Mercedes-Benz 190 D that once belonged to Padre Pio was recently put up for auction at the Auto e Moto d'Epoca show in Padua, Italy. It was a gift to the Capuchin monk from a wealthy family in gratitude for a miraculous recovery from gonorrhea after a visit to Pio's birthplace, Pietrelcina. The car was in good nick, with 50,528 miles on the clock, but did not sell, reportedly because the reserve price of €300,000 was not met, although insiders say the real reason was the constant flow of blood from the door handles.

The *Boston Globe* reports consternation at evangelical think tank the Christian Foundation, who were unamused to find that the message on their order of 5,000 "Spread The Love!" T-shirts had been undermined by the printer's addition of an erroneous letter "m" to the end of the middle word.

No. 68
Oliver's Army

4 oz. Illicit Iranian Vodka
4 oz. Flor de Caña Nicaraguan Rum
Mix with 1 slippery nipple
Drink through a funnel while lying

Well after everyone at the office had finished for the day, and I'd checked with Matt the security guy that the place was empty, I popped back upstairs to lock up and review the latest productivity figures. I'd made a prior arrangement to meet Frank for a few drinks at the Schoolhouse Hotel on Northumberland Road—where all the nerd-birds from the Canal Dock social media businesses tend to hang out—before hitting a couple of late-night places, so I texted him to cancel, saying I wasn't up to it. It wouldn't prevent him from going on his own even though it was a Monday night and there wouldn't be much action on the ground. Or on the carpet. He texted me back to tell me I was a dick-sucking no-mark who was working too hard.

In truth, "reviewing the productivity figures" meant shuffling a few papers around and gazing blankly at the Kandinsky print on my wall while attempting to visualize the faces that matched the names on the reports. Who is Raymond Gash? It says on the page in front of me that he's an assistant editor in the Political and Economic Science department who's recently taken the teleworking option. He's been in the office for four years. Is he the guy who looks like Droopy with a harelip? I don't know. I have no idea whether he's blond, bland, blind, or all three. A blend. What about Stephanie O'Rourke? Apparently she's an editor of Agricultural and Horticultural abstracts but for all I know she could be the rubber plant in the corner of Reception. Simon Chang? Wilfred Larkin? Ailbhe Ni Chonghaile? Norman Haircut? They're all on the payroll but I can't picture any of them. The only face I see is that of Ellie.

I try not to think too much about Ellie, but there it is, the dent in my ego, the chilblain in my flip-flops, the maggot in my porridge, the tapeworm in my gut. It's not only what she did to me, running off with the local Catweazle and blowing dogs behind my back; it's also the fact that it pains me to admit to the likelihood that I would forgive her in an instant if it meant I could get her back. After all the shit she put me through you'd think I'd have had no problem moving on, had nothing to deal with but my rage at the mention of her name, a rage that would subside as the years passed by, to the point where she no longer mattered at all, that I could brush off any thought of her like a September housefly, that she'd join Colm Flynn, Deirdre Cooper, Aisling Power, and Gavin McShit in my gallery of faceless portraits. But that isn't how it works. Even now, I live in fear of my death bed, not because of what it signifies—oblivion—but because of the possibility that, lying there, surrounded by those I love, by my children, my grandchildren, my loving, adoring, mail-order bride, the last name I utter in my moribund delirium will be Ellie. Ellie, I moan. Ellie, my Rosebud. And that, of course, is why I am unable to enjoy a fully committed, satisfying, intimate, caring relationship with a woman. I could not bear putting her through the horror of knowing that her entire marriage was a sham, she a feeble substitute for an absent canine-fellator and adulteress who cast a life-long spell over her husband, their love nothing but a proxy, an overacted performance for want of the original. And also why I am unable to keep a girlfriend. It's nothing to do with me being a misanthropic brothel-haunting boozehound who hangs around with torturers and sniffs bicycle seats. It can't be. Because I was like that with Ellie.

The last time I heard from her, she was back in Dallas, which came as a surprise because she'd always been explicit about wanting to escape the place. We shared that much. One should only return to one's hometown to die.

In the 60s, when I was growing up there, Dallas was barely capable of providing any gainful employment beyond the oil industry, and yet they were halcyon days, before the crisis of the 70s, environmental calamity, the rise of the hybrid, the Bush presidencies. The only ungainful employment—and consequently the kind of work my old man found—related to what I like to call "Kennedy derivatives." To this day, I am convinced that the conclusions of the Warren Commission were part of a vast governmental conspiracy to provide employment opportunities for dingbats. The old man was one of those ingrates who benefited from the far-out wacko kookiness of the American people brought to the surface by the Kennedy assassination. All hail the paranoid style in American politics. The morning after the Warren Report came out, 150 million Americans woke up to find, much to their delight, that they were members of a hithertofore elite and therefore un-American community: skeptics. And the national average IQ leapt a full ¼ point. As a whole new industry was born, my father carved out a niche for himself in the market catering to the various explanations—for both the assassination and the cover-up—that eructed from the cracks in the nation's psyche. At one point, he was selling no fewer than fifteen different versions of the Zapruder film, some with sound, others without, modified using actors and fake footage or re-edited to conform to a particular theory regarding the assassination, each claiming to contain "never before seen" footage. One version showed Kennedy being shot by Governor Connally. In another, you see Kennedy pointing up to Texas Book Repository and hear him saying to Jackie, "Who's left that window open?" A third version showed that the second bullet to hit Kennedy clearly came from the direction of the old courthouse and that its trajectory can be explained by its ricocheting off Jackie's head before entering Jack's. A fourth version confirmed that Jackie was only climbing out of the back of the car to retrieve one of his contact lenses.

One version featured Lee Harvey Oswald. It wasn't the original.

Frank subscribes to the view that Kennedy faked his own death and went off to live behind the Iron Curtain with Marilyn Monroe, Jayne Mansfield, Lenny Bruce, MLK, and the real Paul McCartney. He says he has seen documented evidence that Jack stayed in touch with his brother Bobby via Harold Wilson, the former British prime minister, who used to pop over to East Germany on diplomatic junkets. I try to keep an open mind, and I've never entirely dismissed the possibility of a conspiracy. What was it my old man used to say? "Kennedy? Now *there's* a man who died with a smile on the back of his face."

The world's a bizarre and fucked-up place. How else to explain Glenn Beck or David Bowie? How do we explain Eleanor Finklestein, who awoke a week after the assassination bearing the stigmata of JFK? Whatever happened to her? Was she disappeared by clandestine government forces purely because the hole that appeared in her face was a clear entry wound? And who was Grassy Noel? Shouldn't the Warren Commission have questioned him first? His name alone should have alerted them to his potential value as a snitch. Too late now, sadly. He's gone the way of Umbrella Man, Bridge Man, Black Dog Man, and Mystery Sloth. All dead now. A coincidence? Who can say, 50 years on?

Happily for the Chambers family, the decline of interest in the Kennedy murder coincided with the rise of the Religious Right, and for a few years my father was able to wring a few bucks out of the nut-job home-schooling crowd with his uneducational toys, such as his "Pin the Savior on the Donkey" party pack and Christmas 1982's best-selling boardgame, *Free Will,* with its catchy slogan, "Possibly fun for some of the family." Ironically, those mind-dulling, curiosity-decrying fundamentalist frivolities were the very things that put me through college, gave me the wisdom and knowledge that got me where I am today.

Sitting in a darkened office after hours knocking one out while fantasizing about my treacherous ex-wife.

If I had any sense, it would be Sinéad, wouldn't it? The tremulous undulations of her cleavage when she curses. The rueful look that says, "Screw with me now and you won't screw me later." The magmatic, broiling rage barely beneath the assiduously managed façade of contempt. The dislocated finger, the birthmark on her neck, the drooping eyelid when she's spent too long at the computer. The accent so thick even her writing needs captions. All these glorious virtues should be turn-ons for me, for any man exposed to them on a daily basis, for what is it we desire but that which is just out of reach? Unless it's a cheating whore a third of the way round the planet.

Fuck it, these stats are never going to add up. None of the bright ideas that Sinéad and Frank came up with are going to cut the mustard. COITUS wants big cuts. Maybe she wants the place to look mean and lean so she can sell it, rather than offer it up for asset stripping; most of the assets are already stripped. A takeover wouldn't be so bad if it meant we remained in situ. If we can ride it out in the short term, make it look like we've slashed and burned, until this all blows over, then there may be a chance of coming out the other side relatively intact.

I think I'll give Delia a call.

It's child sexual-abuse awareness week in the U.K., and the papers are doing their usual best to score points against one another: The *Guardian* is featuring a series of articles on underfunding of social welfare services, the *Daily Mail* is running a series on recidivist pedophiles called "Freed to Rape Again," and every day the *Daily Star* has topless photos of models who were abused as children.

Lost one and a half pounds.

No. 66
The 1066

A shot of Archer's, taken in the eye

Lashing rain and reduced visibility can be considered a blessing if you're enduring them on the Northside. I can only imagine that not being able to see the action on the pitch at Dalymount Park is a disability that has been devoutly wished for by many fans, be they connoisseurs of the League of Ireland's particular brand of footility or not. In any case, the purpose of attendance at soccer matches is to express loyalty and solidarity rather than to enjoy the skills on display; every match is more or less identical in terms of its content—only the dramatis personae change. This is why Delia has not missed a single mistimed tackle, sliced volley, red card, or dodgy decision in over ten years. This was also why he brought me on Friday night to watch the Bohemians F.C. soccer team play against the Sligo Rovers in what he informed me was a crucial league match that would go some way to determining which of these teams would remain in the top division of Irish soccer and which would be demoted to a lower one. I could not contain my surprise that there were more than twenty-two men in Ireland willing to engage in this sort of activity on a regular basis—it seemed to involve, for the most part, sliding along wet mud on one's ass—but Delia assured me that soccer is an immensely popular pastime in Ireland and that some people even pay to hire fields of artificial turf one night a week so that they and their friends can frolic in the rain, push each other over, and generally expend whatever energy they have left over from standing in the dole queue or watching porn.

Delia and I experienced the "spectacle" from the relative comfort of the seated portion of the stadium, confusingly referred to as the "stand," in the company of what nouveau riche bourgeoisie the Northside could muster, a minority there as elsewhere but distinguished by its affection for live soccer matches, sheepskin overcoats and jewelry so vulgar it would make a cardinal blush. All the same, their company was not intrusive. Of the several hundred seats, a mere handful were occupied; the majority of the crowd—what I could see of it through the shifting sheet of water that separated us—was congregated in a disconsolate huddle on the terracing to our left, held back from the pitch by razor wire, Plexiglas and several hundred cops with snarling German Shepherds. "Nobody willing to stand for ninety minutes on a concrete step in the freezing rain can be up to any good," Delia explained. "They're troublemakers simply by being there." I wasn't exactly sure why their presence was tolerated at all. It wasn't like their entrance fee—50 cents—contributed significantly to the club's coffers or that they added greatly to the atmosphere with their half-hearted cheers and incomprehensible songs. Perhaps it's a ploy on the part of the police. Sooner the football terraces than the barricades.

Having nobody within earshot, Delia and I were able to conduct our business in a relaxed and cheerful manner, notwithstanding the occasional harangue from Delia directed at the Sligo Rovers striker, who seemed intent on letting every ball passed to him glide effortlessly under his foot and out to touch. One of the generally recognized rituals of the soccer game involves selecting one of the opposing team's players for specific and repeated barracking, the content focusing on the player's perceived deficiencies in some regard, be it his inability to "trap" the ball, his age, his weight, his receding hairline, his past membership of other, especially reviled, opposing clubs, or his appearance in the mass media on account of his extra-marital antics or tax-avoidance difficulties. It is a ritual so central to enjoyment of the sport that Delia was unwilling to surrender it even though he could barely make out the silhouettes of the players through the rain and under the feeble glow cast by Dalymount's floodlights, their strength reduced in accord with the government's "eco-friendly" austerity program.

It was not a night for nuance.

"I need to get in on your coke business, Delia." He turned to face me, I guess to see if I was serious, before turning his attention back to the match. I persisted.

"You did say to me that if I was interested—"

"McAllister! Your legs are laughing at you!" The Sligo Rovers striker looked like a ghost in the mist.

"And you turned me down, Joe. It was too hot for you to handle. I can't have prevarication. What's changed?"

"Circumstances. Circumstances have changed."

A distant, dull thump suggested that the Sligo goaltender had executed a clumsy clearance or had himself been executed by a well-wisher. The appearance of the ball in the vicinity of McAllister would provide confirmation of the former. Delia waited. As the ball arrived, McAllister was challenged by a Bohemians defender, who shoved him in the back with his elbow. McAllister crumpled to the ground like an imploded soufflé. Delia laughed.

"Get up, McAllister, you lazy tart!"

He was still smiling at his bons mots when he returned to our conversation. "How can circumstances have changed so much to cause such a volte-face? I mean, you do understand what we're talking about here, Joe, don't you? This work is very very very very very very very very very very illegal. It isn't a few bottles of duty-free whiskey. It's the sort of thing that can have you sent down—banged up—for years. Decades."

"I realize."

"And that's not to mention the competition. This isn't Hay-on-Wye, Joe, or *Bargain Hunt.* You aren't battling manfully against genteel stamp collectors or experts in art deco table lamps. It's a cut-throat business in every sense."

"Yeah, Delia. I get that."

"McAllister! You've shit yourself!"

He hadn't.

"Is it money, Joe? Do you have debts to pay? Loan sharks?"

"No. It isn't that."

"Because if it is, I can give you a dig-out no probs. Anything. A few grand. Ten. No interest. You can pay me back when you want."

"It's not debts."

"You looking for thrills? Life too quiet? Change of career direction?"

"Anything but. You know me. I'm a man of peace."

"You are in yer hole."

"I am so."

"Piece of work, maybe."

A muted cheer bubbled through the sleet from the terraces. Delia's attention switched to the pitch.

"What was that? What it a goal? Did we score?" We waited in silence for an announcement over the tannoy.

"Goal for Bohemians. In the 29th minute. Scorer: Unknown."

An ironic cheer from the crowd.

"The Unknown Scorer," said Delia. "There should be a memorial for him."

"The flame wouldn't stay lit in this. Besides, they're all unknowns." He disagreed.

"See Levenson there, the number eight? He used to play for Kilmarnock."

I stood corrected.

"So tell me, Joe. What's up?" I wheedled a piece of sleep from the corner of one eye with my little finger and rubbed it into my cheekbone to dissolve it. I was stalling.

"Okay, here's what it is. It's work."

"I knew it."

"But it's not what you think it is. What you think it is, is that I'm bored with work. That's not what it is. What it is, is this. My boss in New York, Miss-management, I like to call her, is on my back to cut costs around the office. They're talking about outsourcing, redundancies—"

"So cut costs. Give 'em what they want. What's the problem?"

"Well, none, if it ends there. But if they're starting to outsource, there's a chance that they'll wind down the whole operation here, bring me back to the States."

McAllister was scythed down by the Bohemians F.C. center-back.

"Ouch."

"Indeed. I don't wanna go back to the States, Del. It's shite. And I like it here, hard though that may be to believe. My hope is that they're trimming things down to sell us on. Maybe then we'll have a chance of staying."

"But you don't know."

"I've no way of knowing. But once jobs are outsourced, we're fucked prettily, so I'm attempting to cut overheads and staff costs to prevent it. And that means paying staff half as much as they're currently being paid and hoping that they'll stay on."

"And you're going to sell coke to top up their wages?"

"That's what I was thinking."

The Bohemians F.C. center-back was shown a red card, meaning dismissal, by the referee.

"That's fucking ridiculous."

"Yeah, he fucking dived, didn't he?"

"Not that. You."

"Oh."

"Seriously. If you want my advice, you consider every other conceivable alternative before you go down this road, before you involve yourself in this. You'd be crazy to be dealing—why?—to give your workers cash in hand at the end of the week. You'd be better off giving them the coke to double their productivity."

"I had considered that, as it happens."

"I was joking. How much do your staff know about this?"

"About the cuts? Not a lot."

"Are they unionized?"

"Are you kidding?"

"Start there, then. Rather than this drastic measure you're thinking of, concealing from head office the fact that you're still paying staff a living wage, why not sign them up as union members and threaten New York with industrial action?"

"Because they'll close the place down without a second thought."

"Not if you play your cards right. Companies are always on the lookout for cheaper sources of labor, cheaper rents, whether there's industrial unrest or not. It's the profit motive. Workers' passivity makes it easier for them in the end to jump ship. But if you can organize and discipline the workforce, you can hold New York to ransom, at least for a time. They'll need the co-operation of your staff if they're going to outsource successfully, to migrate the databases, the platform, whatever they call it. I've seen it dozens of times. It only happens if the staff are compliant."

"And union membership will stop that?"

"It might."

The rain was easing off a little but the wind was still swirling around the stadium. Delia pulled up the collar of his coat.

"As it happens, I'm good mates with the secretary-general of the Printers and Publishers Union. Very nice guy. Works as one of my distributors. Don't look shocked. Needs must. It's a bit of extra cash for him. Union barons are as rare on the ground in Ireland these days as actual barons. What do you say to me arranging for you to have a chat with him so you can discuss the possibility of signing your folk up?"

"Will he go for it? It's rather an odd situation, don't you think? An employer meeting with a union boss to get help organizing his workforce."

"Sure, but look at it like this: Desperate times call for Desperate Housewives."

Some good news for romantics everywhere. According to *Isvestiya,* Yoko Ono and Mark Chapman, the murderer of John Lennon, have announced that they are going to get married. "Some people thought it would be absurd of me to marry someone so patently insane, such a complete psycho, but the more I thought about it, about the gesture of reconciliation that this commitment represented, the more I realized that it was exactly what John would have wanted," an elated Chapman said from his prison cell in Rhode Island.

The *Fermanagh Herald* reports that another couple of pharmers have been suicided, this time outside Blacklion, County Cavan. Their bodies were found swinging from one of the mobile phone antennas, this one prettified by being disguised as a church spire. That's four pharmers in the last three weeks. Someone's keeping busy.

Lost two pounds.

No. 76
The Desert Shield

One bottle of Anima Nera black licorice liqueur
One glass
Fight over it

Frank was out of sorts yet again today—I met him for a drink in the Shelbourne Hotel. He'd spent most of the day tearing hair out, either his own or someone else's, down at the Rehabilitation Hospital. To make matters worse, he'd had to deal with a team of bigwigs from Langley who'd come over to assess his work as part of a performance appraisal program. In their endless wisdom, his bosses have decided to implement a scheme to ensure that not only is the CIA getting value for money but also that its management system is being effectively implemented and in a standardized format at all levels. So Frank has had to put up with assessors sitting in on his interrogations, armed with clipboard and stopwatch, making notes about the number of times he uses open-ended questions, the number of times he elicits a positive answer, whether he refers to torture practices by their right name, whether he clenches his fist correctly when striking a client (it's important that he avoids repetitive strain injuries), and shit like that.

Frank took them into the "special" wing rather than the crimson wing, so as not to scare them too much. The special wing is where they keep the politicos: far left activists, idealistic social workers, smarmy liberals, gullible clergymen, and so on; middle-class dissidents with enough contacts to prevent them from being dispatched without at least some semblance of due process. Daddy might be a lawyer, for instance, or Uncle Mike might be in Opus Dei. Saved, one way or another. The crimson wing is where the less fortunate find themselves assigned, queued up for processing: Travelers, circus freaks, carnies, anarchists, assorted scum. The reason for its name is obvious. The walls are crimson to avoid the need to clean them every day.

Not that anyone in the special wing gets special treatment, you understand. It's special only in that the techniques used there are less crude, designed to elicit co-operation via the disorientation and the isolation of the prisoners, I mean patients. Flashing lights, sometimes strobing day and night, records played nonstop at full blast. It's like the disco at Wesley. I thought the records were to drown out the screams, but that only shows what an amateur I am when it comes to torture.

The music is to scare them. Frank has a penchant for 90s Irish pop—Boyzone, B*Witched, Westlife—and what could be scarier than that? Frank's rationale is that by playing tunes from his victims' childhood or adolescence, it encourages them to reminisce, to become teenagers again, to fill up with nostalgic yearnings for stolen kisses and playing truant down on Sandymount Strand. It renders them more vulnerable, makes them feel more isolated, more distant and separated from those innocent days. Besides, he says, you can't beat a bit of cheery music to help the torturing go by with a laugh and a smile.

My ten favorite records of all time:

10: "Attic Nasty," by the Fabulous Dumps (Quondam Records)
9: "What's Rathmines Is Rathyours," by the Sketchlies (Puma Sick)
8: "Lazarus—Live at the Catacombs EP," by Lazarus (Brillig & Slithe)
7: "Romas Eunt Domus," by Billy & the Racists (Ledge)
6: "I Love Baby Cheeses," by The Cute Horse (Spent Records)
5: "Bring Me the Head of Jerry Garcia," by Do Not Feed the Hippies (Merengue)
4: "Birdshit on My Shoulder, Dogshit on My Shoe," by Plucky Dave (Trenchant)
3: "Betty's Gone Bald (But Her Love Life Goes On)," by Plasma and the Leukocytes (Deaf Music)
2: "I Want It, I Want It, I Want It Now," by L.O.M.A.X. (Petulant)
1: "Put It Back in Yourself," by The Matrons (Vincent Sounds)

This top ten has remained remarkably unchanged over the years, impermeable to the vagaries of fashion, although I did have to remove that old country classic "Soap on Your Ring" from the list a couple of years back. It used to be a sweet little song about a girl who finds out her man is cheating on her when she notices he's been taking his wedding ring off. Last year it was rereleased but sung by a guy, and it wasn't a wedding ring that had soap on it. Ruined the original for me entirely.

"You're a cynical son of a bitch playing them Westlife, Frank," I told him while we freshened up in the Shelbourne's rest room.

"How can you say that?" he protested, purely for the sake of form. "I'm a professional doing a job. The same as you. Do you think I derive personal satisfaction from inflicting pain?"

"I *know* you do, because you're a cynical son of a bitch."

He switched on the drier and flipped the nozzle to dry his face.

"The only personal satisfaction I get is what I'm entitled to. The satisfaction of a professional who does his job well. Job satisfaction."

"That's why you're a cynical son of a bitch." He pouted.

"I didn't ask to be sent here."

"Yes you did, you lying shit." This was a mock argument, meaning I was allowed to be confrontational and offensive, which I never am otherwise.

"Okay, fine. I did, but that's beside the point. I didn't come here specifically to inflict pain."

"No, Frank, not specifically...but it's implicit, given that your brief was to train others in inflicting pain. You've been doing it since you were in Pampers."

"Leave the Pampers out of it. I was wearing them for a bet. This is a profession like any other. How's it any different from being a dentist, say, or a lawyer? Or designing cars. Do you know how many people are killed every year by cars?"

"Cars aren't intended to kill. They're a means of transport." I love it when Frank gets surreal. It keeps me on my toes.

"So is what I do. It gets us from A to B. Death is no more a necessary feature of it than it is of car design. And if I'm good at my job, sometimes people live. Cars are only designed to protect the driver and passengers. Never pedestrians or cyclists."

"But you're good at it because you enjoy it."

"Isn't that the best way to be good at any job? I just show an interest."

He walked over to the urinal, opened his fly, and urinated. In that order.

"It's the same thing," I insisted. "You show an interest because you enjoy it."

He adjusted his jacket with one hand. Urine splashed and spattered around his shoes. I hate ground-level urinals, although bowls aren't much better. You can't beat a good squat for a piss. Even if the squatters object.

"It isn't the same thing at all," he said. "I take an interest because I want to be good at my job. You're putting the cart before the horse. An interrogator who derives too much pleasure from interrogating people is by definition a bad interrogator. He could get carried away and lose valuable information in a moment of self-gratification."

"Let me get this right. What you're saying is that there's an appropriate amount of pleasure to be derived from torture." I am Socrates to Frank's Aristotle.

"I didn't say that. It's getting at the truth that matters. Whether or not you enjoy the process, it's getting results that defines a good interrogator. Results, Joe. Results."

He walked back over to the washbasin, shaking a drop of stubborn piss off his finger.

"I wonder sometimes how you can condone it, Frank. You walk around with Christ dangling from your neck, even when you go down to the cells, and yet you are able to be so objective about human suffering."

"A good Christian has to be objective about suffering. Without suffering, life wouldn't be worth living. Life *should* be painful. It makes death all the sweeter a deliverance. Besides, you forget. I'm not a Christian."

He went over to the basin and washed his hands like Pilate.

"Of course. Have you made any good recordings yet?" He smirked.

"I'm a professional. What do you think?"

He grabbed Christ and turned him on. The washroom echoed with screams and howls of agony. The effect was quite impressive. What a great gift this would make at Lourdes or the Vatican. A model of the crucified Christ that actually screamed in pain. And probably realistic, too. I'm sure Christ *did* scream when he was crucified. Probably pissed and shat himself, too, even if the gospels don't mention it. And why would they? They're biased. Where are the impartial gospels?

The screams faded and I heard Frank's voice—moderated, considered, calculated—issuing from the crucifix. Then silence again. Followed by more screams.

"You've taped your interrogations?"

"All of them. I tape them religiously." He held up Christ and wiggled him before my face, in case I didn't get the joke. "I told you, I'm a professional. Always learning, always perfecting my technique."

"Isn't that a bit barbaric?"

Frank paused to think about it.

"I don't think so."

"Not that. *That.*" I pointed at his trousers, where he'd forgotten to close up his fly. His dick was hanging out, looking for all the world like an enraged dumpling.

"Oh that. Yeah. *That's* barbaric." He started to tuck it away apologetically, wiping his Christ-contaminated hands before doing so. "I was interrogating some fucking circus acrobat a couple of days ago, and somehow the flexible little cunt managed to wriggle free from her cuffs and got hold of the can of pepper spray I had handy, and she sprayed the lot into my crotch. It was fucking agony."

Ow.

"Didn't your pants and boxers protect you at all?" He tried not to meet my gaze.

"I had my dick out."

"In an interrogation?"

He held out his hands imploringly.

"I was fooling around. Shoot me."

From *Which Funeral?* magazine, the answers to last month's quiz, which asked readers to match randomly listed fights with their appropriate funerals.

(a) Child's Funeral – Cabbies with iron bars
(b) Elderly Widower – Elderly widows with handbags
(c) Pop Star – George Michael/Elton John tag team vs. Paparazzi
(d) Jewish Matriarch – Daughters-in-law at wake with expensive glassware
(e) Sportsman – Catfight in heels in rain and mud
(f) Druglord – Gunfight outside cemetery
(g) Millionaire Alcoholic – Sons fist-fighting in car park
(h) Ham Actor/Comedian – Barbed words at *Private Eye* editorial meeting

---

How many CIA operatives does it take to change a light bulb? Three. One to take out the old light bulb, one to put in an acceptable replacement, and one to fabricate the evidence proving that the old light bulb had weapons of mass destruction.

No. 118
The Christopher Hitchens

A Large Famous Grouse
Twenty Rothmans
Frequently drunk in public

Delia had arranged for me to meet Peter O'Flaherty, his union buddy, in a terraced house in Coolock that Delia rents for storage and "administrative" purposes. Delia also supplied a couple of bottles of Valpolicella, carrying them into the living room like a couple of pheasants he'd bagged before depositing them on the coffee table between us and wandering back to the kitchen for mugs.

O'Flaherty's delicate facial features had stuck with him into middle age, undeterred by a deterioration in skin tone and mottling caused by too many Mediterranean cruises. He struck me as nervous, overweight, and moist, not cut out for drug dealing at all but eminently suited to bureaucratic union manipulations, a belief confirmed by the way his chubby, nostril-drilling fingers wrapped around the handle of his briefcase and the oafish thud of his responses when Delia attempted to engage him in lively conversation. From what I gleaned, O'Flaherty had grown used to a lifestyle now beyond his means; twin Mercs for himself and his wife, Winnebago touring vacations in Florida, long weekends in Kinsale. Everything was going great guns for him until the crisis hit, funds plummeted, and those members still in work began to ask what point there was in having a union hierarchy if all it could provide was luncheon vouchers, theater discounts, and hollow promises. At that moment there arose one of those irresistible historical inflections, a straining of tensions that tests the mettle of men, classes, and societies alike: should he defend the interests of his members or his wife's need for Prada? Empires rise and fall on the response.

O'Flaherty was in the happy position of knowing Delia, who had installed the union's servers in its Ely Place offices and designed the software to keep track of members' dues. It was Delia who offered O'Flaherty a way out, a resolution of the dialectic in the form of a distribution job, taking a percentage of new sales, covering the north Dublin suburbs, the Meath/Louth commuter belt and any internal recreational consumption within the union itself. So much for beer and sandwiches in the back room.

"What is the current composition of your workforce?" he asked blandly while extracting a Pitman shorthand notepad from his case and a propelling pencil from the inside pocket of his blazer. "Male, female, under forty, over forty, indigenous, immigrant, graduate, non."

"Erm."

I suppose it's the sort of info I should have had to hand. Sinéad knows it inside out and back to front. She should have come with me.

"About 60–40 female," I hazarded, stereotyping the departments as *science = male* and *humanities = female*. "As far as they self-identify, anyway. Vast majority under 40.

Very few regard it as a long-term career choice simply because of the few opportunities for career advancement, and who wants to be writing abstracts at 63? But also because so few of them have an interest in moving into management. All of them have at least two degrees. Some of them are doctors. Ph.D.'s, I mean. They're either taking a career break or doing a few hours of teaching at the university. You know what academia's like. The definition of a precarious workforce. What value does a doctorate have in the market today? Most of my middle management staff, ironically enough, are the ones either too smart to go into academia or too dumb to be accepted for doctorates. I can't decide which."

"Immigrants and indigenous?"

"Most of them are Irish. Who would want to move here to work? One or two have Irish spouses and so moved here out of love, family commitments. Rob Barton met his Irish wife in Nottingham and moved over here with her after she'd finished her degree in English. One or two others. But ninety-five percent are locals. Is it important?"

He sucked on his upper lip.

"Can be. Very often depends on where they've come from and how worried they are about being sent back there. Or if it's somewhere with a strong trade union tradition, like France or Australia. They might be your first choice for a shop steward. Middle-aged men from the U.K. tend to hate Thatcher, for instance, especially if they're from anywhere north of Oxford. We often find with younger workforces that they tend to take for granted the employment benefits that previous generations have had to fight for and that when they're taken away, they assume it's down to market forces; they don't realize that it can be stopped."

"It's the neoliberal hegemony," Delia interjected.

"Yeah. They think benefits are something granted by businesses out of their need to attract the best labor force, in competition with one another; that market forces will raise workplace conditions on their own. Their naivety would amaze you sometimes."

"The old 'I won't get out of bed for less than a grand' argument."

"Indeed."

"There *are* some immigrants. We've got one Brit, one Yank with a dual passport. Quite a few have lived abroad for a while—Australia, New Zealand, Qatar—but I don't know how much they learned about life from that."

Delia poured out the last drops of the second bottle.

"Does it help that so many are graduates?"

"You'd think so, wouldn't you, but not really. A better education can be a hindrance to class consciousness, if anything. The idea that 'I'm better than everybody else. I've got a plan to get out of here.' It helps that everyone here has a degree, of course, because nobody's special in that respect, and the sense of entitlement that comes with a degree can be used to bolster grievances when demands aren't met, but oftentimes you'll see graduates break ranks because they think they're unique. People who feel they're stuck in a job that offers no way out are more likely to put up a fight because they've got no choice but to stay. Plus, Ireland's always had the emigration option. That's always defused anger. Anyone who can gets out, and realizes how much better things are elsewhere."

"Hah, you're talking to the wrong guy there, Pete," said Delia. "Joe's the only guy I know who actively doesn't *want* to leave."

O'Flaherty eyed me suspiciously.

"We do get a few like that, too. They're particularly dangerous. You never know what they'll do. They're beyond reason."

"Yeah, that's Joe," Delia said. "Mad as a March on Rome."

Selling the idea to Sinéad was as easy as I imagined it would be. "Have you got biscuits for brains, you scuttering geebag? There's not a brasser's chance in Bray you'll be able to pull this one off. Someone's pulling your plonker, Joe, I tell ya."

"Give it a chance, Shin. This guy might be good. A mate of mine swears by him. If he can get the staff signed up before there are any announcements about redundancies or closures, it may be possible to mobilize them to resist it."

"And you don't imagine that people'll think it strange that you've invited a union rep into the office? I mean, talk about tipping folk off to trouble."

"I've thought of that. I'll have a meeting with the senior editors beforehand and explain why I've invited him in. I don't want people jumping for the lifeboats too soon, but if I don't give them advance notice, rumors are going to be flying around the place."

"And what are you going to tell them? That you're letting yer man talk to the staff out of the goodness of your heart? You muppet."

"That the company has decided to adopt a mature and progressive attitude toward employee representation."

"Oh, aye. They'll buy that alright. And what are the fees like, do you know?"

"I don't, but I can find out. Hopefully not too much. I'm going to have to announce pay cuts one way or another pretty soon. If he can get everyone signed up quickly, I can tell New York that there's a problem and to hang fire."

"Janey mack, you're some bucko, so you are. And what are you going to do if nobody signs up?—Stop picking that scab—What if the membership fees are too much? Do you have a Plan B? Or a Plan A and a half?"

I left the scab alone.

"Actually, yes. I kinda do. But I don't know that I should be telling you about it."

"Ah, feck, Joe, you dope. I can't imagine it'll be any more daft than this idea. Have you taken my advice to hire an assassin to take out COITUS? Have you robbed the petty cash to buy some magic beans? Have you blown the lot on lottery tickets?"

"Will you ever feck off, Shin. No. None of those."

"I'm dying to hear. I can't think what other fallback option you might have other than selling us all into slavery. Is that it, Joe? White slave trade?"

"I never considered it, but now that you mention it, I'll write it down. Have you got a pen?"

"Oho, so it's sarcasm now, is it? Sarcasm? You must have a real hum-dinger in that back pocket of yours if you're taking that attitude with me."

"Don't be like that. It's for your own protection. But if you have to know, I'll tell you. You remember how you asked if I knew anyone with access to hard drugs?"

"Jayzus, Mary, and Jonestown. What the feck have you gone and done?"

"Nothing! Nothing yet. But do you remember? I know you were only joking. But as it turns out, *this* guy, this union guy, he has a sideline selling cocaine—"

"Shhhh! Feck me sideways. Don't be calling it that. You have to use a synonym when you're referring to hard drugs. Everybody knows that. Snow. Chalk. Cheese. Choppie. Chub. Nose. Anything but what it is. Walls have ears. Lugs. Wingnuts."

"Oh, right. Sorry. Didn't know. But it turns out that I can get my hands on large quantities of the stuff to sell, and it might—*might*—enable us to keep the office open by topping up staff salaries."

"Topping up staff salaries? By selling Fairy on the streets of Dublin? You must be on the stuff already. That's totally fecking arse."

"Arse? Is that good or bad?"

"Bad! Crackers. Crazy. You're one mad yoke if you think that's a way out."

"It'd only be temporary, Shin. Short term. A stopgap. Once the future of the office is secured, we could wind it down. And then maybe look at unionizing the staff to get their wages back up to current levels."

"And do you think you've got the contacts to be able to sell sherbet on the streets of Dublin without coming to the attention of the Guards or rival gangs?"

"Not yet, no. But I've got friends to show me the ropes, put me in touch with individuals in the know."

"In the know, is it? Friends, is it? Since when have you had friends in the criminal underworld? Since when did a master's degree in Information Management Services equip you to negotiate gangland? You can't use a CMS schematic to find your way around there, you know."

"I realize that. But I trust these guys. They're not gangsters. They're above board. Do a little bit of smuggling. You know? A lot of decent people have had to resort to extra-legal activities to pay the bills. This is nothing different."

"Decent people, me arse. It'll end in tears, I tell you now."

"Let's face that when we have to. It's only a fallback option. We may never have to go down that route."

"I hope not, Joe, for your sake. I know what your map-reading skills are like. You'll end up in a ditch."

This month's *Fora* magazine reports that virtual reality games such as Red Dead Redemption, Death Camp, and Snatch are being superseded among Italian youngsters by new "hyper-real" games combining postmodernity and enigmatics. An example: six months ago, a group of semiotics students from the University of Padua broke into the sarcophagus of Ronald Reagan and stole away with the remains. They proceeded to dismember the body and hide its various parts in specific locations around the world. Members of the global online public were then invited to compete in the retrieval of as many parts as possible. For a mere 200 bucks, contestants received a series of quotations from the works of Schopenhauer, Ibn Khaldun and Kierkegaard, which, taken in conjunction with the cave paintings of Altamira and Lascaux interpreted as a rebus puzzle, directed contestants to the whereabouts of Reagan's remains. The outright winners were Dr. Louise Pearce, an epigenetic engineer from Canberra, and her husband, John. They managed to retrieve Reagan's left ulna, both femurs, most of the pelvis, and a large bag of viscera that had been booked into a room at the Meridien Phuket. Their prize: Forty million dollars. The students for their part got three years' suspended sentences and fellowships at Bologna.

And this just in, closer to home:

Dear Mary-Lou,

Several months ago, I fulfilled a lifetime's dream by indulging in a *ménage à trois* with two 20-year-old nymphets from Tallaght I met on holiday. We had a fabulous night of biting, licking, sucking, penetrative and nonpenetrative sex and… well, you can imagine. They were such cuties and so uninhibited—I'd never heard of an Australian Bead before, let alone been on the receiving end of one. Anyway, to cut a long story short, after that night of unbridled and unprotected lust, would you believe it but they're both pregnant and I'm a prospective father two times over. Don't ask me how. I must have supervirile sperm or something. So, anyway, Mary-Lou, you can see that I'm in a bit of a pickle. Loath as I am as a God-fearing man to recommend that they both do the decent thing and take the boat, the only alternative is to tell the wife. What do you recommend?

Is Mise
Exhausted

(Letter to the "Dear Mary-Lou" problem page, *An Phoblacht*)

No. 119
The Peter Hitchens
A small Grouse

I gathered the senior editors together in the conference room to explain the situation regarding outsourcing and O'Flaherty as best I could. Perplexed is probably the best adjective to describe the response. Explicable, I guess, by the fact that I couldn't give them the whole story. All I could say was that I would do my best to ensure that there were no redundancies or wage cuts. There was no rat to smell, but I think they smelled an imaginary one. The boss coming into a meeting to inform staff that a union organizer would be paying them a visit. It had to be a trick of some sort, hadn't it? All I could do was assure them it wasn't, and they filed out of the meeting with their usual meekness, obedience, and silent confusion.

Another visit to Feargal at the hospital was scheduled for the afternoon. I thought it might be an opportunity to sound him out about the possibility of joining my network of distributors. His position in the pharmacy means he would be ideally placed to give stuff to customers, over or under the counter. I could cut him in on the action in exchange for access to his extensive network of potential clients. I phoned ahead to ask if we could have a chat, and this time I managed to find my way to the pharmacy with little difficulty, but Feargal wasn't at the desk, and because I didn't have the credentials to get any further on my own, I had to give his name so that he could come to collect me. I'd obviously interrupted him in the middle of something. The top button of his shirt was undone and his sleeves were rolled up.

"Joe. Lovely to see you. How's the tapeworm?"

"Not so loud, Ferg."

"You afraid it might hear? Can you feel its ears burning?"

I took the ribbing with good grace. "That might explain the heartburn. I just don't want it to be common knowledge." He pffed.

"Nobody here'll take a blind bit of notice. Your intestines are the least of their worries."

"Still, you never know who you'll bump into."

"Expecting to meet the woman of your dreams *here*? No danger of that, bud. Not among this lot." He nodded in the general direction of the row of patients sat along the far wall. "Can't even guarantee you a one-night stand. Follow me."

He may have been boasting about the efficiency of the Irish health service, but it was unlikely. I took him to mean that they'd all be dead before tomorrow.

He led me past the anterooms of hell, wards and private rooms crammed with kids crying, women rocking themselves and moaning, nurses, some shouting, some prim and professional and applying vindictive calmatives. As we approached his office, I noticed one, very insistent voice getting louder. Frantic. Screeching. As we turned the last corner, the source became apparent: a tiny old woman. Very old. Very tiny. Teeny tiny. A gray toddler. Presumably, that was why she had been put in a crib and wrapped in what looked like swaddling. She knelt, her face scrunched up like a brown paper bag, and rattled the crib's wooden bars as she harangued a male nurse attending her.

"Give me back my teeth! Give me back my teeth!"

I'm not sure who was more embarrassed, me or Feargal. Mentally, I crossed her off my list of potential mates.

"I want my teeth! You're all cruel, you are. Cruel."

"What's the deal here?" asked Feargal, edging up to the nurse so as not to look like he wielded any authority.

"Gah, nothing, Ferg. She's a bit loopy. Bit of the Alzheimer's I'd say. Doesn't know what's going on."

"That makes two of us," I interjected, failing to introduce a bit of levity to the situation.

"Ninety-two I am. Ninety-two and they won't let me have my teeth."

"She's been like this all morning," the nurse continued. "She was pulled in at six after a raid in Phibsboro. Still in a state of shock, maybe. She's attached to one of those EU monitoring agencies. Kraut, I reckon. Fecking meddlers."

I could tell Feargal had already lost interest but for appearance's sake felt obliged to demonstrate concern.

"What's she doing here? Shouldn't she be over in the special wing?"

The nurse shrugged.

"Full up over there. Bit of a backlog. Logjam. Backlogjam. We're keeping them sedated over here before transfer."

"Sedated? She doesn't seem very sedated."

He turned to the crone with a benign smile glued unnaturally to his mush. The old woman was still rattling her bars.

"Calm down, dear, calm down. We'll soon have you sorted out. You can't have your teeth because you're going to the theater."

Well, of course, that confused her even more. Her face lit up.

"The theater? The theater? Who's on? Is it a good show?"

"Not as good as this one," I thought.

"The operating theater, love," Feargal explained considerately. "They're going to make you better." He didn't say better than what, but she didn't believe him anyway.

"I want my teeth! Give me my teeth, you stinking pig."

And with that, she let fly the oldest, greenest lump of spittle I've ever seen. She was obviously out of practice, or perhaps age had reduced her accuracy, because the gob landed on the breast pocket of Feargal's shirt, on the cap of his biro, instead of in his face, which is where I assume she was aiming. The nurse and I took a deep breath and waited for Feargal's smile to crack, but he held firm, pulled a handkerchief from his trouser pocket—there was some blood on it, I noticed—and wiped the thick mucus off his shirt. It came off in one go; hospital staff are supplied with easy-clean shirts because of all the bodily fluids they deal with.

Conscious that he was being watched and that all was suddenly quiet, Feargal turned to the nurse and raised his voice so all could hear.

"Give her back her teeth. I'll see that she gets looked after."

The nurse wisely chose not to protest.

"And give her something to eat. Whatever she wants."

"But that'll mean she can't go to theater."

"Doesn't matter," Feargal said. "Just do it."

I was surprised by the respect with which Feargal's orders were being received. I'd imagined him to be a mere subordinate here in the hospital. I knew he had qualifications coming out of every orifice, but the nurse's deference and the change in attire suggested that perhaps he had greater authority than I'd imagined. All to the good.

He ushered me into a quiet and compact office. A small, uncomfortable-looking sofa and an uneasy chair competed for space on one side of the room while being stared down by an animated coffeemaker gurgling on the laminated office table opposite.

"I'll get your package for you on the way out, Joe. I'm sorry there isn't somewhere else more luxurious for us to meet."

"No worries, Ferg. It's not a problem. I've been in a lot worse kips than this."

Which wasn't particularly true. I was once in an illegal shebeen in De Kalb where a girl onstage shot ping-pong balls out of her asshole into the audience's cocktails. But at least it served cocktails.

"What was it you wanted to have a chat to me about?"

"It's a job opportunity. Of sorts. Now, look, this has to be entirely between us, Ferg, okay? And if you want to say no, I understand entirely. I'm approaching you because I know you're someone I can trust completely and you've done me so many good turns over the years. I thought I might try to return the favor."

"What are friends for?"

"Exactly. My feelings too."

"Do you want a coffee?"

"No, I'm good. You go ahead, if you want."

"Thanks. Tell me more."

I sat down in the uneasy chair while he mucked about with the coffeemaker.

"Okay. Well, I'm about to come into possession of a sizeable amount of non-prescription medication that is generally unavailable in high-street stores and I'm looking for someone who can help me to get it to market in a manner that is unobtrusive, low profile, but at the same time accessible to all those who might be interested in its purchase."

He stirred the coffee pensively, head bowed and face hidden.

"This non-prescription medication. Is it highly sought after?"

"Yes, and for many different reasons, but it has a very enthusiastic customer base."

"Is it very moreish?"

"Not really. It usually comes from South America."

He turned and laughed.

"No, I didn't mean Moorish, as in North African. But that's okay. You've told me, now. What sort of quantities are we talking?"

"Nothing huge to begin with, Ferg. A few grand a month, say. And I'd be willing to pay on commission or you could take it off my hands at a wholesale rate and keep whatever cash you manage to get for it."

Raised eyebrows and pursed lips meant either bitter coffee or an interesting proposition.

"It's very tempting, I must say, and thanks a million for coming to me first. Of course, I don't know anything about the quality of the stuff, and I should tell you that I already have a thriving business going here, you know?" He winked. "Cash in hand, off the books."

"You mean stuff from the pharmacy?"

"Are you shocked?"

"It never occurred to me."

"I'm flattered by your estimation of my incorruptibility, though it makes me wonder why you would think of me for your own scheme."

"I thought I'd be doing you a favor." He took a sip of coffee.

"And I'm very grateful, believe me. But people can't afford to hang around waiting for opportunities to fall into their lap these days. Look at me, Joe. I'm perfectly placed to deal in black market drugs. Are you genuinely saying that that didn't enter your mind?"

"I didn't think you were the sort of guy who'd—"

"What, be corrupted until you came along to corrupt me? Maybe you don't know me as well as you thought." He tittered.

"Maybe not. Perhaps I should think twice about dealing with such a dodgy customer."

"Perhaps you should. Look, it isn't like I don't appreciate the offer, Joe, but I do already have a good thing going here, and I'd be a fool to jeopardize it by getting caught up in a web I know very little about. I mean, where are you getting this stuff? Who else knows you're dealing? What are the dangers I'm likely to face if I come in with you."

"I can't tell you any of that, Ferg. You know that."

"I do. And that's precisely why I have to say thanks but no thanks."

"Sure."

"Do you know the people you're dealing with? I hope your judgment of character is better than you showed today."

"Ha ha. Yeah, I must be a fool to think you're a great guy. I really should get my head examined."

"Not your head, bud. Your eyes."

He was right. I was out at the front of the hospital and half way to the taxi rank before I realized the old lady had gone.

The Reality Channel

9.00 a.m. *Chef Island*
Top New York and London chefs left on a desert island without utensils or balsamic vinegar are expected to survive on tree bark for six weeks.

9.30 a.m. *Are You Older Than a 10-year-old?*
An hour and a half with the innumerate.

11.00 a.m. *Drunken Mutts Wedding*
Arranged marriages between the family pets of violent East End alcoholics.

12.00 p.m. The weather. (Fiction)

12.05 p.m. *Funeral Swap*
This week, a devout Christian family from Huntingdon see their father burned on top of a traditional Hindu funeral pyre, and a Muslim family from Leeds watch as their mother's remains are blasted into space.

1.00 p.m. *Property Ladder*
DIY experts vie for supremacy by battering each other with stepladders on a bouncy castle. In the dark.

1.30 p.m. *Animal Hospital*

This week the beloved drummer from the Muppets carries out open-heart surgery.

2.00 p.m. *Fat Race*
A documentary about Texans. Part of the American Idle season.

3.00 p.m. *The Liver Birds*
Two women in need of a transplant take part in a series of challenges as they compete for a dead man's liver. We also catch up with Mark Halstram, winner of last year's show, *The Kidney Kids,* and find out what happened to all the losing contestants.

4.00 p.m. *Talent to Burn*
This week the teenage arsonists are let loose in a caravan park.

4.30 p.m. *Airport: Celebrity Hijack*
Terry Christian and Linda Lusardi are stuck on the tarmac at Luton as the bodies pile up around them.

5.00 p.m. *Big Bother*
Secret video footage of people looking bored or sleeping. Or both.

6.00 p.m. *Whose Child Is It Anyway?*

Parents compete to see how much neglect and abuse of their children they can get away with before they are taken into care.

7.00 p.m. *Your Money or Your Life*
Noel Edmonds kidnaps bank managers.

7.30 *Sex Tourist: Banged Up a Broad*
A coachload of single men from Guildford compare their STDs.

8.00 p.m. *Flog Him!*
Slave auctions from Liverpool, with David Dickinson and Michael Barrymore.

8.45 p.m. *Dancing with Wolves*
More ballroom shenanigans from Molineux with Kenny and the lads.

9.30 p.m. *It Shouldn't Happen to a Bulimic*
Dieting competition, plus a report on the latest radical weight-loss craze from the USA: amputation.

10.00 p.m. *Before the Beak*
True-life small claims court cases presided over by a trained Pelican.

10.45 p.m. *Fuck Yourself, Skinny*

Gordon Ramsay insults a roomful of supermodels nonstop for 45 minutes.

11.30 p.m. *How Long Will You Live?*
Special episode on the recent massive rise in the number of people dying in their sleep for no apparent reason whatsoever.

12.30 a.m. *A Bedtime Prayer*

12.35 a.m. Close.

Who needs reality anyway?

No. 91
The Costa Concordia

6 oz. Limoncello
Lots of Water
Serve on the rocks

The English-language edition of the Spanish magazine *Spyhole* (it isn't a magazine we index at work; I have my own, private subscription) has a quiz in it this month entitled "Do You Have What It Takes to Be a Spook?" I thought I'd give it a go.

The correct answers were as follows: 1) 15 minutes; 2) super; 3) biliverdin; 4) Zanzibar; 5) Tracey Emin; 6) Aubergines; 7) SMERSH; 8) Neither of them; 9) October Surprise; 10) Bill Clinton.

My answers were 1) The Bosnian Quarter of Shanghai; 2) Three missing deadly sins; 3) Tony Blair; 4) Zeugma (½ mark for being close); 5) Tracey Emin; 6) Sputnik; 7) A morose wardrobe; 8) Both of them; 9) Ram's Bladder Cup; 10) Chocolate Fingers.

Tests like these don't prove anything anyway.

Another Traveler met her maker in Antrim today. Wow. There, are enough murders in this country to keep the economy going on formaldehyde production alone, though they'll need super strength thread as well if they hope to patch up this one. Someone really went to town on the poor woman. Slashed her perineum right open so that her rectum and vagina made one big gaping hole. Bayonet wounds to the neck, nipples torn off, blinded. Like someone wanted to make it look like sexual assault but didn't know how to; to me, this suggests a death squad composed entirely of priests.

Because of the loss of foreign tourist bucks and a tightening of security, the Hilton Hotel isn't what it used to be. The doormen's uniforms are still the same, although somewhat incongruous—braiding and pistols don't go well together—and they still try to be polite and welcoming, opening the door for you with one hand as they finger their holster with the other. The seats are all gone from the hotel lobby, and the walls are adorned with prints instead of originals, which all makes sense. You can't loiter here anymore to admire the paintings, and the prospects of a bomb taking out Old Masters would send insurance costs through the roof. Both the lobby and the bar have a claustrophobic, depressed feel to them, thanks to the poor lighting. Three years ago, a suicide bomber strolled into the Westin and detonated a homemade device in the lobby, killing two coachloads of Italians who, for reasons best known to themselves, were about to depart for Avoca. Most of those who died were killed not by the blast but by fragments from the lobby's glass roof. Shards rained down on the already injured, impaling them, slicing through arteries, followed by a needle rain of the finest slivers, piercing and puncturing tanned and bloody Italian flesh, working their way under skin, death by several thousand cuts. The delicacy of the surgery required was generally beyond the butchers who fill Ireland's hospitals—several of the victims died on the operating table—and the ensuing humiliation was enough to prompt the government to require the removal of all plate glass from hotel lobbies in Dublin.

The Hilton used to depend heavily on natural light, but now the place is lit entirely by fiber optics, millions of points of light drawn down through the ceiling and the walls. The fibers are flexible rather than friable, so there is less danger of them taking your eye out than glass might, but much of the light is dissipated and the cost of installation so great that most hotels elected to go with a gloomy, turn-of-the-century Havana-style brownout ambience rather than to pay top whack. Besides, the infrared security cameras can still pick out suspicious packages and persons in the half-light.

I was dressed for the party in a white tux with matching pants. I borrowed Frank's iron to do my suit. "It's not my iron. It belongs to the Company," Frank told me, rather ominously. I made a point of checking it for dried blood.

I'd taken a stool at the bar facing the door, so I could spot Sinéad the moment she came in. My only company was an elderly couple in the corner away from the bar sucking glasses of fizzy orange, and a middle-aged guy with a face straight out of *Scanners*—pink, blue, and purple patches on his cheeks and a homely, bulbous, vermilion nose like a cozy fireside—shirt open at the collar, no tie, of course, and an ancient charcoal gray suit, heavily creased and stained from the requisite number of wakes to make a stereotypical maudlin Irish drunk. I was impressed that he had managed to sustain the stereotype even in an era when booze was hard to come by. That sort of style requires either bottomless pockets or total devotion to the cause.

I was twiddling a swizzle stick and sipping a Bloody Mary when she arrived. I'd also treated myself to a Glenmorangie before leaving the apartment, possibly not such a good idea on an empty stomach, but I tried to look as blasé as possible when I got up to greet her and fell off the stool.

She, goddamn her, she glided across the maple floor in high heels and a low boatneck velvet dress, Balenciaga or some such, I imagine, mauve but translucent so the sun shining through the foyer behind her revealed her shapely legs. She carried a black silk purse on her wrist and wore her hair loose and slightly tousled. She kissed my right cheek and I inhaled Agua Fresca de Rosas.

"Howya Mr. C. Ready to show a bad girl a good time?"

Fuck me.

I swallowed air and said, "Sure. How about some fancy liquor?"

"I'll have a drink first, if that's alright with you."

Beautiful *and* filthy. What more could a man want? I helped her up onto the seat next to mine. Gentlemanly, I thought.

"Of course, Shin. What's it to be?" She never took her eyes off me but raised her head a little and opened her mouth slightly so that I could see her tongue press against her teeth. Lo-lee-ta.

"Lager top. Pint."

"A wha—?"

She giggled—since when does she giggle?

"I'm fucking with you. They don't serve it." She placed a hand carefully on my thigh and leaned forward. "I'll have a quinine."

The barman came over. I remained admirably composed despite the thought of Sinéad fucking with me.

"Quinine for the lady…another BM for me." Sinéad squeezed my thigh.

"BM, Joe? Are those genetically modified tomatoes?"

"At these prices? I do hope so."

The barguy wandered off and left us to make awkward conversation. I tried to think of some of Delia's jokes to break the ice. Quick as a flash.

"Did you hear the one about the dead epileptic who wouldn't fit in his coffin?" She was polite enough to feign amusement.

"Very good, Joe. I haven't heard that one, which is surprising, because my mother's epileptic."

"Shit. Is she? Not shit, I mean. Fuck. I mean, oh, I'm so sorry, Sinéad. That was insensitive of me."

She waved away my apology. "Forget it Joe, you weren't to know. Besides, even if my mother *hadn't* been epileptic, it would still have been insensitive of you."

The drinks arrived before I could dig myself a bigger hole.

"Let's put it down to you hanging around too much with Frank."

Yes. Let's. It's better that she believes that Frank's responsible for my thuggishness than the truth, that I can manage it perfectly well on my own. I told her it was very perceptive of her and allowed that he can be a bit extreme at times.

The sun was setting by the time we left for the ambassador's residence, nicely sozzled, for the party. To be honest, I rarely enjoy parties: as a guest, one has no control over who else might be there, and people are such a pain. The last party I attended in Dublin was over a year ago. I say party, but actually it was a reception at the French embassy on Ailesbury Road after a particularly filthy rugby international in which both sides lost and two players from either side were dismissed for fighting, which is how rugby players bond. You can imagine what the reception was like, trying to make conversation with people whose idea of sophistication is raising their pinkie as they drink a pint of the scrum-half's piss. I spent the entire night talking to guys whose breath smelled of telephone kiosks.

In a moment of the most outlandish optimism, I managed to convince myself that this evening's affair was going to be different and I was comforted by the knowledge that it was taking place on home turf, at the ambassador's residence, a building I think I know my way around fairly well. The hotspots are easy to avoid because the usual debauchery one finds at parties attended by the rich and obnoxious is corralled into rooms on the upper floor, where the sane and less well-heeled fear to intrude.

We walked through the Phoenix Park, it being so balmy and gentle. The evening was already mopping up the long shadows like a resentful janitor, but we still had plenty of time to chat. I found myself relaxing in Sinéad's company, always difficult with smart, sharp, witty women who are not intimidated by bank balance or possession of a penis. About halfway across the park we encountered an assortment of English ex-pats, West Brits, and Jackeens playing cricket, all dressed in whites. I was bemused and distracted by this bizarre and ostentatious display of anti-social activity when Sinéad said,

"Smile, Joe. You're on *Candid Camera*."

I failed to get the reference at first, but she directed my attention away from the cricketers toward where they had parked their cars, along the opposite kerb. The third car in the row was in gear, its engine running, and sat in the driver's seat was none other than Seymour Stiveley, amateurishly snapping away on a zoom-lensed digicam pointed straight at us. The moment he realized I had recognized him, he dropped the camera onto his lap and grabbed the steering wheel. He pulled out without checking his mirror—irresponsible and ill advised—and stuck his foot to the floor. I briefly considered giving chase, and as he was passing, I leapt in his general direction. The smirk on his face vanished in an instant at the thought that I might catch and humiliate him, a response sufficient in its pathos to satisfy the sadist in me. There was no need to run too far: I wanted Sinéad to see that I was fit and virile, but I didn't want her to see me knackered.

Stiveley accelerated away in first gear and I returned to a more pleasant pursuit.

"Who the hell was that?" she asked as I returned to her side, making a show of how out of puff I wasn't.

"That, Sinéad, was Seymour Stiveley of British Intelligence. Which tells you everything you need to know about British Intelligence."

"Stiveley? What kind of name is that?"

"Ridiculous, isn't it? I understand it's an old Saxon name, meaning 'symptom-free bearer of syphilis'."

"Ah. That would explain the odd behavior. But why is someone from British Intelligence taking photos of you?"

"That is a very good question indeed. I wish I had an answer for you. I think it's industrial sabotage."

"They're hoping to pick up some tips from the way you're running Whetstone?"

"Ha ha. Very funny. I think you mean 'a cutting-edge information-gathering resource for the 21st century'."

"British Intelligence is trying to entrap you, is that it? Following you around to find a way to blackmail you to pass on all your top secrets."

"Who can say? I only know that Frank tipped me off through a friend at the embassy that I was being targeted. Maybe it's for my looks."

"Now who's being funny?"

"Not funny. Self-deprecating. You're supposed to find it attractive."

"Keep supposing."

"All I know is that there have been a couple of break-ins to my apartment, a few anonymous letters, that kind of thing. I've just ignored them."

"Are you serious? Why haven't you alerted the Guards or the papers?"

"What's the point? It would only attract more attention to me, and I don't want that. Besides, you've seen him. He's totally useless. The very fact that you *have* seen him is proof enough. He's the least clandestine clandestine operative ever. I mean, normally the English are great at blending into the background, with all their apologies for existing and what have you. But not Stiveley. He's not even good at being English."

A sigh of resignation and forgiveness escaped the clutches of her better judgment.

"I do hope you're right, Joe. You've enough on your plate as it is."

"And we haven't even got to the buffet yet."

"Now who's *not* being funny?"

Crassness itself would be ashamed of the new security measures surrounding the ambassador's compound. The guards displayed their weapons like mounted fish for all to see, the searchlights on the two new watchtowers either side of the main gate were blindingly obvious, forgive the pun, and a new strip of razor wire had been strung along the top of the 12-foot brick wall that encircles the residence. Presumably there had been problems with break-ins by people to whom 20,000 volts is just provocation.

We flashed our ID to the guards. No smile, but Sinéad took my hand and led me toward the entrance hall. On the soft evening air, I could already hear chamber music, laughter, sparkling conversation, and the braying accents of the wealthy and influential. I stiffened my resolve not to be unjustifiably prejudiced against the arrogant, parasitical, motherfucking scumsuckers.

Glasses of Bollinger presented themselves to us as we stepped into the entrance hall, and I was relieved to find that I recognized no one. I'm not much good at mingling, and nonmingling suggested itself as a perfectly reasonable alternative, so we opted for the latter, happy enough to find a corner where we could chat and I could keep an eye on Sinéad's flesh.

The American ambassador's residence wasn't built to impress so much as depress: a low-slung two-story Georgian edifice taken over from the Brits when they cleared out and left the Irish to fuck the country up for a change. Wellington lived here, and so did Churchill, for a while, but the only spirits here are 40% proof. The decor, I suppose, could best be described as postmodern eclectic, the consequence of each ambassador's spouse adding something of her own middlebrow taste to the interior—oriental rugs, crystal chandeliers, Arizona tat. Fortunately, the present ambassador's wife lacks any sense of taste, middlebrow or otherwise, with the consequence that the residence has been rehung with paintings by contemporary Irish artists: John Kingerlee, Pauline Bewick, Louis le Brocquy, others I didn't recognize. This decision was partly one of necessity, since the U.S. government ended the Art in the Embassy Program a few years back, requiring each ambassador to make ad hoc arrangements. Whoever decided it would be a good idea to commission local artists to produce portraits of past ambassadors either had a great sense of humor or had never seen Irish art in action.

"Joe, will we go and explore some of the other rooms?" I quickly realized that Sinéad's low boredom threshold could threaten the chances of an uneventful, conversation-free evening. I stalled.

"In a while, if you like. I did say to Frank that he could find us here."

She drained her glass.

"Well, it's eight now. What time did he say he'd meet you?"

"Eight."

She caught a waiter's attention and signaled for another drink. "Okay, but I'd like some one-on-one time with you, Joe...later, maybe...upstairs."

With a flick of her head she indicated the staircase. I nodded noncommittally. Had she come along with an agenda?

I'd noticed on our way in that one or two guests were strolling around with pints of stout and soon deduced that they were coming up from the staircase that led down to the underground rooms, usually reserved for private communications, secret meetings, and the shredder. Free stout was too good a gift to pass up.

"Sinéad, I've got to go for a slash. Can you stay here and look out for Frank?"

She looked disappointed, but she's a grown woman for pity's sake.

"I won't be long. It was the champagne."

I took her silence for consent and headed off.

My instincts were right. The ambassador had turned the conference rooms into a miniature frat party, with barrels on tap and Green Day's MOR anarchy whining over the sound system, obviously the artiste à la mode when the ambassador was at Yale. The barman was most helpful—I told him I was getting a pint for a friend as well—so it was with some cheerfulness and self-congratulation that I returned upstairs, only to find Sinéad engaged in an animated discussion with Frank and a slight, well-groomed woman I'd never seen before. The moment they saw me, their conversation ended and Frank made a dive for my extra pint.

Now I like Frank, but I realize he's not to everyone's taste. Many's the time he's happily offended friend and stranger alike after we've exploded out of some dump onto the Dublin streets at three in the morning with a bottle of fucking Jack Daniel's in either hand. He's a wonderful dypsomaniac when his children can afford to go without. But there's a time and a place for such cheerful antagonizing, a rule of etiquette that either went unmentioned in CIA training or which Frank chose unstudiously to ignore. He wouldn't be your go-to guy for the furthering of international diplomacy, and at a party like this he's as conducive to affability as a bulimic puking in the punch.

I could see he was already unsteady on his feet, so decided not to wind him up excessively, fun though it might have been and despite him robbing my extra pint.

"Frank, how's it going, stranger?"

"No stranger than normal, Joe." Ah, wit. So, not totally out of control, and he showed enough dexterity to stroke the ass of the young woman with him, although a swift raking of her left arm brushed it away.

"Joe, can I introduce—what's yer name, love?—Yasmina, that's it. Yasmina, this is Joe. He's a good friend of mine. And an utter gentleman." Yasmina offered her hand. "Turkish, Joe. From Turkey. What do you think about that?"

Sinéad interjected before I could reply. "Yasmina works for the UN Commission on Human Rights. She's monitoring possible abuses committed against Travelers by the military."

Talk about keeping your friends close and your enemies even closer.

"A pleasure, Yasmina. I think there's only a small Turkish community in Ireland. How are you finding it?"

"With a microscope."

"?"

"Do you get it, Joe?" said Sinéad. "How are you finding the small Turkish community? With a microscope."

"Ah yes. Very good."

"You'll have to forgive Joe, Yasmina," Sinéad continued. "He's American. I'm sure you're already familiar with American men." She shot a glance at Frank.

"I find their company…soothing." Is that meant to be a compliment? "And they provide me with entertainment, of course."

Not shy in expressing her opinions, as you might expect from a fucking liberal human rights do-gooder. And her small, oval face had something characterless about it, an absence, a blandness. Like she had opinions but no personality. Almost the exact opposite of Frank's ideal type.

"You hear that, Joe? We're the fucking entertainment." Frank wrapped his arm playfully but clumsily around Yasmina's waist. "You don't want to know the kinds of ideas I entertain, Yasmina."

She shared a resigned pout with Sinéad and snared Frank's hand to stop it wandering.

"Great, this, isn't it, Joe?" Frank waved around the room with his free hand. "Have you ever seen so much quality pussy in one place? No offense, Yasmina. I'm including you, obviously. It's fantastic. An extrava…an extrava…an extravagina."

I almost felt sorry for Yasmina. Almost.

"Not that there's anything wrong with the tired and trusted, like Sinéad, I mean."

"Frank!"

"Sorry. Tried and crusted." Yasmina facepalmed.

"Where's Margot?" I asked out of badness. "Was she not able to come?" Frank did a quick recon of the room without focusing.

"Not here…Busy."

"That's a shame. I'm sure she'd have liked to have attended."

"Yasmina, I hope you'll excuse us for a moment," Sinéad said, taking my elbow to lead me away. "I need to have a word with Joe. It's lovely to meet you."

I do like a decisive woman.

"What's the story, Shin?"

"Nothing. But Frank bores me, and I wanted to get you on your own. Listen. You pop upstairs and find an empty room. I'm going to use my feminine charms to get us something more substantial than these piddling glasses they're giving us."

An Advent calendar for deviants is the best way I can describe my search upstairs for an empty room. Each door I opened revealed a scene of some depravity or other: couples coupling on floors stark naked or mates mating up against the fireplace. Some rooms gave me pause to think I'd encountered an entirely separate, fancy-dress party that nobody had been told about. Highwaymen in split-crotch panties, pirates with massive dildos strapped to their foreheads, bishops and whores spinning on shagpiles in a perpetual cycle of mutual masturbation.

The bishops weren't in fancy dress, mind. I just recognized them from the papers.

As I approached the—I really don't know—the 13th room, say, I chanced to glance down the adjoining corridor to my right, where another row of rooms, as numerous as the first, appeared before me. Activities of a similar bent were presumably being perpetrated behind their doors.

I let myself into room 13. Empty. But no key in the lock, so anyone could walk in on us.

Tough.

It was a reception room, a mahogany-paneled disaster decorated with some of the portraits of former U.S. ambassadors, the windows offering a disconcertingly clear view of the cross erected to commemorate the visit of Pope John-Paul II to Ireland. Four well-upholstered brown leather armchairs formed a semi-circle around a dead hearth. Otherwise, the room was sparsely furnished, an empty Cavan Crystal fruit bowl being the melancholic centerpiece on an otherwise uncluttered circular maple table.

I had barely oriented myself when Sinéad showed up. To be honest, I wasn't feeling all that great by this point. My stomach was starting to hurt and I was a bit dizzy. No food. Lots of booze. Confusion regarding Sinéad's intentions.

"Found you," she said playfully, brushing past me, the eager grin on her face further confounding me. She flaunted a champagne bottle before my face as she passed, at the last moment handing it over. "Didn't take me long to get this, did it? I've still got my pulling power."

I took the bottle, imagining it would be safer in my hands. She spun away from me, waltzing, laughing, trying to hum, her inability to do so making her laugh even more. I stuck the bottle on the mantelpiece, where Sinéad could easily reach it, and hiccupped before drawing the curtains and bidding farewell to the cross. My head was beginning to swim, and I've never been a great swimmer. I'd have to get something to eat or else throw up in the hearth.

Sinéad was oblivious to all this and flung herself into one of the armchairs, apparently worn out by her efforts at what she must have thought was dancing.

"That was fun. What'll we do now?" Her tongue rolled in a way that was almost *too* obscene, like an ecstatic death throe.

"Sit down."

"I'm already sitting down."

"Me…I need to sit down." The room was beginning to spin and swirl. Seriously. This was going to be a major hurl. I just about made it to the seat next to Sinéad's and flopped down. Big mistake. The moment I sat down, she was up from her seat and into my lap.

"Joe…What is it? Are you okay?"

At that moment, it seemed, things began to feel a little better. Not because she was sitting in my lap but because a wave of incredible tiredness swept over me, and the nausea was carried away to the horizon of my consciousness. Now, if only she'd let me sleep.

I felt Sinéad sliding off my lap and undoing my trousers. There was nothing I could do to resist. My strength was failing rapidly. Besides, why would I want to resist? I haven't been sucked off in years.

I don't recall if I said it out loud, but the last thing I remember thinking was, "I can't believe I'm going to miss thi-"

No. 43
The Cold War Breeze
Two large Powers on ice

I opened my eyes tentatively, getting used to the glare. Panoramic windows revealed ragged, scummy gray clouds wandering aimlessly and forlornly across the sky like semen in dirty bathwater, here and there clinging to the Dublin Mountains in the distance. I was home.

The last thing I expected was to wake up alone. And in my own bed. I checked my cock for lipstick and was reassured. Then I checked the mirror to make sure I wasn't wearing lipstick. Some things hadn't been imagined then. But I had no recollection of getting home, of any of the rest of the party, or of leaving the ambassador's residence. Did I get a cab? Was I on my own? Did I fuck Sinéad? Did I lick her kebab? I had no way of knowing, short of asking her, and what gentleman wants to admit he can't remember something like that?

My clothes were strewn around the floor of the bedroom like I had flung them off rather than having been undressed, but it's not something difficult to fake. But faked by whom? Stiveley?

Always revert to the most prosaic explanation. I was feeling sick before Sinéad even laid a finger on me and had passed out even as she went to work. No doubt, she eventually gave up and let me sleep until I recovered and was able to get home under my own steam. It'll all start to come back to me after a couple of coffees and an anti-inflammatory. And another nap. Another nap.

—

Sunday was a complete washout. I slept right through until my alarm and the Monday morning fog. Maybe the fog was in my head: I managed to get into work on autopilot. No sign of Sinéad; she had rung in before I arrived at the office and left a message on the answering machine to say she'd come down with a bout of food poisoning and wouldn't be in but she'd go to the doctor tomorrow if she wasn't any better. She was hoping it was a 24-hour thing that'd clear up once she'd "evacuated" her "holding bays." It wouldn't be done for me to phone her from the office to check on her during work hours. I'd have to give her a ring in the evening from my mobile or home phone to check she was okay.

As consolation and compensation for Sinéad's absence, I had Peter O'Flaherty's company in the afternoon. He wanted to fill me in on his meeting with the senior editors and update me on the progress of his efforts to unionize my workforce.

"It's pretty much as I anticipated, Joe," he said through croissant-flecked teeth—we were meeting in a patisserie (*the* patisserie) in Irishtown—"I have made no progress in my efforts to unionize your workforce." Or words to that effect.

"None at all?"

A dismissive flick of the hand.

"One or two of them expressed an interest and were what I'd describe as reasonably pro-union. They'd got parents who'd worked in social welfare. Most of them were put off once I told them how much membership was. Said they didn't think it was worth it."

"Wow." I knew there was a lot of apathy among the young for political activity, especially among those in work, who, practically by definition, were middle class and had obtained employment by virtue of a private education or contacts, but I'd have expected at least some of them to bite.

"Are they not worried about the changes afoot in the company? The expansion of the teleworking scheme. The rumors of wage cuts." Rumors we'd been careful to circulate non-attributably.

"It's sauve qui peut, Joe. You get this among graduates. Like I said to you: Everyone has their own escape plan. It isn't fertile ground for solidarity."

Escape plan? What's mine?

"This is why I took on the extra work with Delia," he said, wiping the corner of his mouth with an index-finger-backed napkin. "Jobs that last a lifetime, jobs offering career pathways, career development, they're disappearing fast. There used to be plenty, especially in the civil service, because the government wanted a stable workforce, a workforce it could rely on to be professional, permanent, to run the state. That made the civil service an ideal place to organize. You had a long-term commitment to a career. People were in deep. Not now. Cops and prisons are the only arms of the state where the workforce isn't being eroded. And some of the hospitals, of course. The rest has gone to buggery."

"I blame the parents."

"Me too."

"They brought their kids up in blissful ignorance."

"No, Joe. If anything, they educated their kids too well. They taught them to fall in line with the prevailing ethos: Identify those in power and suck up to them; everything's done through the priest, the GAA, and the local TD—if you want anything done, see them. And most of all: Never give a sucker an even break. I tell you, Joe, Irish kids are suckled on cynicism. They have the attitude long before they have the experience necessary to justify it. It shapes everything they do. It's the rotten heart of Catholicism: Nobody is perfect but Our Lady. Don't expect anything good from humans because they're tainted from the start."

"That's a very noble speech."

"Hah. I don't exempt myself, Joe. I'm as cynical as the next teenager. But I do have the experience to support it. It becomes a self-fulfilling prophecy. If you think people are unreliable, you come not to rely on them. And you forgive yourself for being unreliable, you allow yourself to be no better than the rest. It's the only way to survive."

"So the parents are looking out for their kids by teaching them what they need to get by."

"When you put it like that, I suppose you're right. Everyone and no one is to blame. What can you do?"

"You do what you need to do."

"Indeed you do. Has Delia given you any of his product yet to sell?"

"No. God, no. Did he tell you that he was going to?"

"He said you'd expressed an interest. Didn't say what or why. I wasn't sure how far things had gone."

"Right. It was something I was hoping to avoid."

"Sure. It isn't a business you want to get into if you don't have to. How much do you know about it?"

"Almost nothing."

"Have you ever taken any?"

"Not a whisper."

"Christ. You need to know what you're getting yourself into, Joe." He dug into his briefcase and pulled out a wee baggie.

"This is a quarter of a gram. Okay? It's about twenty euros. I know. It's nothing. Take it home. Give it a go. This is the stuff that Delia hands out. It's good quality, but you can cut it and double your money without too much difficulty. I'll explain to you how to do that if you decide to take him up on it."

I reached for my wallet. He stopped me. "No need. It's a favor. I owe you at least that for not being able to get your people to go with the union."

"Thanks, Peter. Appreciate it. How many of these do you sell a week?"

"These? These are samples. I never sell baggies this small. I sell a gram at 80, two grams at 150. That's a pretty good night out. Probably twenty grams a week—without having to push myself—but double that if I focus."

"What's that work out at? Sixteen hundred on an easy week, three grand plus if you really work it."

"Yeah. Not bad, eh? Of course, you're minus the initial outlay you give to Delia, which is maybe half. It depends on how greedy you are, how much you cut the product, how much of a monopoly you have over your customer base. And remember, this is nothing like what it used to be. That kind of money might sound good to you as a top-up to your salary, but it's not so great for someone trying to earn a living from this."

"I hadn't thought of it like that."

"You've got to keep an eye on the competition, Joe. Everyone wants a monopoly. And they don't plan on achieving it by letting the market decide. Markets are for greengrocers and fools, not cabbages and kingpins."

"I'll bear that in mind, thanks. And won't ask which one am I."

—

ALR: This is a remarkable claim.

McGilovitch: But the evidence is more than circumstantial. The Memory Palace mnemonic technique has been around for thousands of years. According to Cicero, it was invented by Simonides of Ceos, but the most famous version is the memory palace devised by Matteo Ricci, a late-16th-century Jesuit missionary to China. The Jesuits taught this technique widely in their schools.

ALR: Is it as complicated as it appears in the novel?

McGilovitch: Not at all. The term "palace" is elastic. All you need is a location that you know intimately. It can be your home, your workplace, your school, or, as in this case, a city. You determine a route through that location, and along the way, you pick out landmarks that you then associate with the items you need to remember. It's really very simple once you've mastered it. And invaluable for exams. I must confess my surprise that no one has spotted this before. Even the title of the book is a mnemonic: The consonant sounds—l, s, s—stand for the numbers 500. Route maps show that the old 500 tram followed exactly the route described in the book, in effect, the path through the memory palace.

ALR: So the references to Greek mythology are an attempt to disguise the novel's real purpose.

McGilovitch: Purpose? No. My suspicion is that the book was the result of a bet. We know how excited Jean-Paul Sartre was by the possibility of philosophizing about a glass of beer. I think someone simply bet Joyce that he couldn't write a book based on his weekly shopping list.

ALR: Extraordinary.

McGilovitch: And yet it's all there, hidden in plain sight: kidneys, lemon soap, burgundy, Gorgonzola.

From an interview with Marshall McGilovitch, Eustace Professor of Irish Literature at New Amsterdam College, in the fall issue of the *Albany Literary Review.*

No. 13
The Rainbow Warrior
3 oz. Orange Juice
3 oz. Lemonade
3 oz. Cranberry Juice
3 oz. Blueberry Juice
1 oz. Blue Curaçao
1 oz. Grenadine
1 oz. Crème de Menthe
Serve with an Armagnac depth charge in a New Zealand Port

New words to learn today: floughrous – spinning out of control; froadate – to nullify, to cancel; bhent – a downward spiral; gimnal – a joined work, the parts of which move within each other; swivet – a state of extreme agitation; grutch – to begrudge; darry – to weep spontaneously or for no apparent reason; yawp – to make a raucous noise, to complain; strill – covered passageway for gases; pules – gangrenous limbs; probang – a thin rod with a sponge on the end for removing objects from the esophagus; birrey – a paper cut; imbroglio – a state of great confusion or entanglement; barricize – transform a suburban area into slumland.

Sinéad took an entire week off work with food poisoning. I suspect she was trying to do us both a favor. When she came back in on the Monday, we were careful to avoid bumping into each other in the kitchen or the elevator, but there was a personnel review appointment scheduled for four in my office that we both knew could not be put off. I had a carefully prepared monologue that I thought would defuse the tension, but she decided to go straight for the jugular the moment she came through the door.

"Have you been avoiding me, Joe?"

"Avoiding you? Of course not. You're the one who's been off work for five days. Why would I be avoiding you?"

"Avoiding me out of embarrassment."

"Embarrassment? For what?"

"For the way you behaved at the party. I figured you must be ashamed of what you did."

"Why should I be ashamed? I've got nothing to be ashamed of."

She licked her lower lip in contemplation. Somewhere upon high, a coin of small denomination acted in accord with the laws of gravity.

"You don't remember, do you? I *knew* it. I said to Frank, 'He'll have forgotten all this by tomorrow, you know.' I was right."

"Bullshit. I remember everything."

"Go on then." She settled herself down into her chair. "Tell me what you did." A bit of canny guesswork required.

"Well, I remember the Guinness. The champagne."

"Go on."

"The cigars." I was already at my limit.

"What else?"

"The sex."

"Kah! You're already making it up."

Dammit. I didn't fuck her.

"Not with you. Obviously. Someone else."

She rested her elbow on the desk and her chin on her fist.

"Highly unlikely given your inability to stand up, let alone get it up, but I'll give you the benefit of the doubt. Who did you shag on Saturday night?"

"Nobody you'd know. You wouldn't have seen her. I met her later on. After the party." She sat back, her eyes shining with merriment and contempt.

"You are so full of shit. You don't remember Frank calling you every name under the sun because we made him take you home in a taxi and he had to leave the party when he thought he had a good chance of screwing that Yasmina from the UN? Do you not remember that? You kept telling Frank that he was the best friend you'd ever had and then the next minute that he was a treacherous cunt because he was trying to steal Yasmina off you. You were convinced she had the hots for you even though she barely said a word to you all night. Do you remember getting hold of the microphone and telling the band to play 'Ever Fallen in Love with Someone You Shouldn't Fall in Love With' and then when they wouldn't, singing it anyway while starting to strip, until you were led off the stage by the Garda commissioner, who happened to be a guest but also related by marriage to the ambassador's niece? That was a highlight. I'm surprised you don't remember that. Maybe you were disoriented by all the camera bulbs flashing. Have you checked Facebook yet?"

"You're winding me up, Shin. I'd have remembered stuff like that."

"Apparently not. What's the last thing you *do* remember?"

"Honestly? Promise you won't get mad?"

"Of course not."

"It was going upstairs with you and swigging champagne and then you unzipping my fly."

"Unzipping your what now?"

"My fly. My trouser zip."

"I know what it is, but I assure you *that* did not happen."

"Now I *know* you're winding me up. I remember it clearly."

"Some yoke you are. What kind of a woman do you take me for? Do you think that I, a good Catholic girl from Kerry, would go down on you, my boss, at a party at the American ambassador's residence? Is that what you're saying? That I'm so, so, so awestruck by opulence and power that the only thing on my mind could be to get my lips around your puny limp cock out of some kind of—what—phallocentric worship of the patriarchy? Is that it?"

"No! No! Not at all. I just meant *you* were a bit tipsy and happy, and *I* was a bit tipsy and happy, and—"

"And that translates into a blow job, does it?"

"I'm only saying that's the last thing I remember. You promised you wouldn't get mad."

"No I didn't. I said I didn't promise not to get mad. Read back."

"So you're saying that your recollection of what happened upstairs is better than mine, is that it? That I imagined you kneeling on the floor in front of me."

"You've got that right." She'd had enough of this conversation. She was making to get out of the chair. "I won't deny that we were having a bit of fun, Joe, but when I came over to sit on your knee, you practically pushed me to the floor before puking up on the carpet and passing out. It was a miracle how you managed to avoid getting any on your suit. It all went onto the rug. But you were only passed out for ten minutes or so. Seemed to get your second wind. Poured the rest of the champagne on the puke, smuggled us out of the room before anybody noticed, then dragged me back downstairs to mingle with the other guests again and grab something to eat. You ate like a horse. All those vol-au-vents. That quiche."

Christ, no. None of it. Maybe I should make light of this. Try to change the tone. Be a good sport.

"I ate like a horse because I'm hung like a horse."

I managed a feeble grin, concealing regret and bile. She nearly laughed, but I don't know if it was at my wit or at the discrepancy between a horse's penis and my own.

"You're a dark horse, Joe, that's for sure. A dark horse in a black sheep's clothing."

"May as well be hung like a sheep as a lamb."

Whatever that means. Suddenly, she leaned across the desk and squinted.

"Hold still."

She was close enough to me that I could smell her perfume. I inhaled deeply. To distraction. To such distraction that I failed to realize what she was doing. When she pulled away from me again, she'd picked a booger from my nose. Gross.

She wiped her fingers on a tissue and turned to go.

"Okay. We're good."

"Good. I'm glad we're good. It's good."

Sprezzatura

560 Pine Valley Boulevard

There is no better champion of regional Italian cooking than this swank and semiformal Midtown restaurant rooted in the traditions of the Adriatic coast. Some of the recipes come directly from the owners' family, and the kitchen cultivates an authenticity that will delight you. Chef Jose Relago, originally from Corsica, has a police record for violent assault, a foul temper, and an even fouler-looking daughter whom he worships. References to paper bags and doing her with the lights off should soon escalate into hand-to-hand combat, but if you have enough money to cover the bill when the pigs arrive, Jose will be sweet and refuse to press charges. Make sure you try the spaghetti with fresh clams and cured guanciale before you kick things off. The Pecorino and pear salad tossed with local honey is an elegant starter and can be used to heal cuts.

Bread and Roses

24 East Ponce de Leon Avenue

There is nothing flashy about the way young chef Billy Allin and his wife, Kristin, offend guests in their endearing restaurant in the downtown area. New arrivals are offered the choice of sarcasm or knives by the maître d' and choose according to how best they think they can match their wits against former standup Kristin and three-time state knife-throwing champ Billy. It's a testament to the panache of Kristin's material and the accuracy of Billy's throwing that diners keep coming back, regardless of the humiliation or number of stitches they endured previously. Lots of local produce and wine by the liter mean that the couple are usually hammered well before the first diners arrive at 6.00 p.m. but this never seems to impair Kristin's repartee, although Billy is more inclined to get the machetes out of an evening just to make sure he doesn't miss.

Bisquite

2040 Naughton Place

There is a huge discrepancy between the formal decor and the casual dress of the wait staff at this one-of-a-kind dessert bar, the place to come for a proper, mob-handed ruck with, say, a stag party or a rugby club outing. You'll generally want to tool up in advance of visiting Bisquite Bar because only staff members have access to cutlery and glassware. Something with a long reach, such as a baseball bat, is always useful; it keeps the waiters at arms' length and reduces them to throwing bottles at you, which you should be able to fend off, for the most part. Pastry chef Aaron Roberts is particularly proud of his petit fours and delicate geranium-scented biscuits; try referring to them as "lumps of shit" and clicking your fingers at the owner's wife if things are a bit quiet. The cheese plate is particularly aerodynamic.

M&W Seafood and Oyster Bar

31 Chubb Hill

"Suave" is the first word that comes to mind when trying to describe the way head chef Jon Schrempp stamps on fingers. A wound-up man in Doc Martens, Schrempp always wanted to work as a full-time ballroom dancer but ended up in haute cuisine when he discovered how much violence he could inflict on staff and customers alike. Whether diners hop onto a stool at the lively oyster bar or relax in a dining room designed like an intimate, comfortable brasserie, they never know when Schrempp is going to leap out like an Argentinean and slice off an earlobe. The tension is only increased by the disconcerting presence of Schrempp's club-footed mute son Colin, who means no harm but is clumsy around hot fat. Strip lighting is intended to make things easier for staff to locate diners and land punches better, but it also has the effect of improving the visibility of the food, rendering most of it inedible. Come for the music, stay for the swearing.

The Electric Diner

427 Edgewood Lane

The synchronicity between the environment and the food—both elegantly minimalist and good for the planet—soothes the soul even as you blacken the waitress's eye in chef/owner Martin Sweeney's mostly vegetarian hovel. The sensibility in TED, as it is affectionately known to regulars, is as close to Broadmoor as it gets in a laidback, spontaneous format, and since the menu changes almost every day, diners can always expect novel forms of abuse in the form of subtly poisoned dishes served at farm tables that encourage mutual distrust. Avoid the mushroom soup.

Restaurant reviews from the *Hostile Planet Guide to New Hampshire.*

No. 8
The Edward Snowden
A Bitter in Cider

You won't believe the fucking trouble I had today trying to find someone who'll sell the coke I'm going to get off Delia I can see that I'll probably end up taking it all myself well you can't flush it down the toilet the way people used to when the cops turned up because ounce for ounce the cost of fucking water is more than cocaine isn't it, not that the cops would find it in my apartment of course I'm not that stupid they could turn the place upside down looking for it but they won't find it no they won't because I'll have stashed it somewhere smart in a lock-up in Grangegorman or in the trunk of a hire car like Delia or maybe two hire cars one of them a decoy what do you think of that? And then the rest of it I'll keep it in the office in the ceiling space they'll never think of looking for it there even if they bring in sniffer dogs you know Sinéad said to me the other day *Why do they call them sniffer dogs and not sniffing dogs, surely it would make sense to call them sniffing dogs seeing how they have seeking helicopters* I felt like saying *Sinéad, you dumb bitch, it isn't seeking helicopters it's Sea King helicopters, that's the name of the model, they're built by Sikorsky, Sikorsky Sea King helicopters, not seeking, it isn't seeking and sniffing, it's sniffer and Sea King,* but of course I didn't did I, I kept schtum and shared a knowing glance with Frank who rolled his eyes without Sinéad seeing and then said *Yeah Sinéad, you're right it doesn't make sense does it, some fucker ought to sort that out you know, why don't you write to the papers or get in touch with RTE?* and she said *You know, I think I will* and all the time there's me thinking Frank, you bastard you'd let her as well wouldn't you, and he's smirking while she's thinking so highly of him for backing her up and telling her what an astute and perceptive chick she is, which is typical of Frank, isn't it, just typical so anyway I paid a visit to Jane Bondage out in Glenageary without Frank knowing, this is, you know, without telling him, so she was a bit surprised to see me because you normally have to make an appointment but I wanted to present her with the great business opportunity of helping me to shift my coke it was a deal too good for her to pass up and I was doing it not because she would be a phenomenally good outlet but also because she's a good friend and I knew I could trust her I was almost thrusting it on her, the coke that is fnur fnur but she was saying she already has enough problems there and hadn't she already warned me that Estímulo doesn't allow customers to bring drink and drugs onto the premises it could result in police raids and lord only knows what trouble that might cause you wouldn't know who's going to be in the building when the Guards arrive although I'm not that naive I know they would always tip Estímulo off so that there wouldn't be anyone in the building who he didn't want to be there but I didn't take no for an answer straightaway, I thought she was being coy and angling for a better percentage *You don't have to be an escort, you can be a consort, a snortscort, you would be really well placed to make a fortune out of this* but when I pulled the little baggie out I got from O'Flaherty she almost had an eppy *Get that stuff the fuck outta here, Joe, I already told you once you'll get us feckin killed so you will, times are bad enough as it is* but I ignored her and cut some lines out for us both so she could sample the product and after a bit of cajoling well she didn't say no did she, she did it all under protest and by the end of it she was laughing her leggings off and I said do you think I'm sexy and she said seriously Joe you must be high already that's really amazing stuff and I said you're darn tooting I am and that one made her laugh as well because we were both darn tooting we laughed a lot really a lot but she still didn't want to run the risk of dealing out of Knockmerry so I changed the subject we can always come back to it I figured so I asked about the new girl and what had been happening to her but now I can't remember what Jane told me or even if she did tell me anything I couldn't pay attention and in any case I had this brilliant idea I thought maybe if instead of asking Jane to sell the coke for me what if I got her list of clients off her and approached them myself then that would get her off the hook and she wouldn't have to do any work or compromise herself in any way just tell me who her customers are, not even tell me, really, drop hints maybe draw a picture of them maybe do a Pictionary sketch and let me guess it shouldn't be that hard after all most of them are easily identifiable and you'd see them on the telly all the time, judges barristers chat show hosts radio pundits deejays business tycoons so all she'd need to do really is a caricature of their most prominent feature like say a shiny bald head which is really just a curved line isn't it or else say a squiggle representing the outline of a particular county so I'd be able to identify the TD being referred to or even if she just shat in her hand I'd know the shit she'd be referring to I think we all would but Jane wasn't having anything of it *I'm not going to play feckin pantomimes with you Joe, especially not in the state you're in, if you had any sense you'd go straight home now and get some sleep, you look like you haven't slept for days, Sure I have* I said *Once I slept for three days that time I fell off the terrace at the Merrion, That wasn't sleep, you were in a coma* she said *It doesn't count* so I said *Well if you're going to be like that I'm going to go now* but of course I wasn't going at all because I'd got it into my head that it would be a good idea to have a look around the building, see who else was there of a Friday afternoon that I might recognize, not out of any malevolent intent you understand not for blackmail or anything but to see if there might be anyone interested in purchasing my wares but somebody I don't know who must have tipped off security or else they have security cameras watching for this sort of thing or maybe I said out very loudly *I'm going now but first I'm going to look in all the rooms of the house* whichever it was I'd got no further than the door of her boudoir when these two big burly cunts burst in and grabbed me by each arm and dragged me out the room and pulled me down the stairs and round the back of the Reception, avoiding the waiting room so nobody could see me being ejected, down through past the kitchen, round by the dungeon/bondage cellar, straight past Manuel Estímulo's office/panic room/armory, onto the back patio, making sure to rabbit punch my kidneys and bang my head on the wall as we go and along a secluded bush-lined alleyway that eventually spewed out into the fields backing onto the local junior school where I was unceremoniously kicked in the nads and told not to be showing my feculent fizzog anywhere within half a mile of Miss Whipcream's establishment again if I didn't want it summarily sliced off at the jaw, peeled away using the ears as winding handles and the space where my eyeballs used to be crammed with dog turds, well that was me fucking told wasn't it isn't it it's remarkable that I had the good sense to come straight home and write this down as evidence so that when I take the bastards to court for assault and battery I'll have a complete account of everything that happened and all in the exact order and they won't be able to wriggle out of it because I've got Jane Bondage as a witness and anyway I bet I can subpoena the tapes from all the video cameras and that will show how wrongly done by I was and maltreated and manhandled, I'm pretty sure Jane will stick up for me anyway, she understands that I'm trying to look out for her and me and Delia and that you've got to look after your mates.

This is funny.

A baker's dozen of little-known facts about the philosopher and mathematician Bertrand Russell:

1: He was the nephew of Isaac Poundland and inherited his chain of family shops from him on his death.
2: On Sunday mornings, he used to make prank phone calls to Malcolm Muggeridge pretending to be the voice of God.
3: In the introduction to his *Principia Mathematica,* Russell unknowingly outlined the format for the future TV smash hit *Countdown.*
4: Although a pacifist, he was often seen cycling round London wearing nothing but a Comanche headdress and carrying a tomahawk.
5: While Russell was in prison in the 1960s for his involvement in anti-nuclear protests, fellow inmates the Kray twins arranged for a 12 oz. tin of rough-cut ready rub shag tobacco to be smuggled into the prison up the rectum of Frank "Mad Axeman" Mitchell and delivered to Russell as a mark of respect.
6: The sight of children's shoes drove him into fits of uncontrollable rage but he was never able to explain why.
7: He burned down the Reichstag.
8: His first break in maths came with his discovery of the formula for sexual congress, which is $f(x) = x + 1$ where I'm the unknown quantity and you're the one, honey. It got him laid at parties.

9: Having discovered that friend and rival Ludwig Wittgenstein had served in the German trenches during World War I in a search for authenticity, Russell attended the launch of Wittgenstein's *Tractatus Logico-Philosophicus* talking in a high-pitched voice and wearing a Prussian helmet with a baby impaled on the spike.

10: As an avid Gooner, he would ring A. J. Ayer before every North London derby to arrange a pre-match scrap.

11: In 1966, Russell played the Joker for Richmond in the first ever episode of *It's a Knockout.*

12: For his Ph.D. thesis in 1904, he presented an irrefutable argument that demonstrated his own non-existence. He was consequently denied his doctorate by the board of examiners at Cambridge.

13: During a séance in 1973, he assaulted medium Doris Stokes from beyond the grave.

No. 30
The Berlusconi
1 Bottle of Prosecco
1 Viagra
Shake vigorously, surrounded by naked women
Pop cork
Deny everything

Holy fucking shit there was a bomb. I'm watching it now on CNN, although it seems to be footage from last night. Bodies being dragged from smoking wreckage. It's Connolly Station. Connolly fucking Station. In Dublin.

Ow, my fucking head.

There's the ticket office. What's left of it, anyway. I recognize the façade. Turn up the volume.

"Most of the victims were innocent commuters buying tickets, waiting for their trains or queuing up at the Complaints desk. Even though it was well past rush hour when the explosion occurred, the station was busy because of the usual delays: leaves on the line, a suicide in Raheny, commuters from Sligo sabotaging their train so they wouldn't have to go home to Sligo for the weekend. There was no warning and no expectation that something so monstrous might occur, even though it was Dublin on a Friday night."

He thinks that's monstrous? He should see the food in the embassy canteen.

"As yet, no one has claimed responsibility for the blast. Antiterrorist experts say it has all the hallmarks of a dissident group, which narrows the suspects down to two and half million people. Police are presently using social media to round up all self-identifying anarchists, circus performers, tattooists, anyone with piercings, rail users—"

I turned the volume down. The usual lack of reliable info from the MSM. I clambered off the bed and searched for my pants. Usually they're conveniently at hand, on the floor next to the bed. I pulled them on and picked up the phone, as if whoever I phoned would know I had no pants on.

I tried Frank's number at the embassy first. It was outrageously optimistic to hope Frank would be in the office on a Saturday morning and I got the answering machine. I tried his home number and had more success. Janet, his wife, answered.

"Janet. Thank God. Is Frank there?"

"No, Joe, of course not. He often stays out on Friday nights. You heard about the bomb, right? I imagine he's in work. Or on his way. What about you? Where are you?"

"I'm at home. I thought he might cast some light on it. He isn't in the office."

"Try the hospital. He might be checking on casualties. Maybe Connolly itself but I doubt it. He tries to avoid crime scenes in case there are photographers. Last thing he needs is to be seen at the site of a bombing. Did you phone his mobile?"

"Good thought. Thanks Janet." What an idiot. Me, I mean. I was still half-asleep. But Frank had his mobile turned off, the stupid bastard, which meant if I wanted to find out what was happening I'd have to go over to the hospital myself. Well, it was a Saturday and I had nothing better to do. Not that I imagined for one minute that Frank had anything to do with it or that the explosion was part of some kind of broader military-industrial strategy to protect American interests in the region. That *never* happens.

But first, a wash. And some proper clothes and non-prescription drugs. If I went the way I was, I'd be mistaken for one of the casualties.

The walk from Herbert Place to the bus stop would give me time to piece together what I knew. Or what I thought I knew. Atrocities like this intrigue me, bring out my inner parapolitical investigator. The first question you always have to ask when these things happen is *cui bono?* Who benefits? Who benefits from blowing up Connolly Station? Where do the cards fall when the dust has settled?

Where do you want to start? The construction industry. Car manufacturers. Bicycle shops. Bus Éireann. Architects. Northside Dubs. Ambulance crews. Journalists. Talking heads. About the only people not likely to benefit from this explosion were the winos and bums who sleep in Connolly every night amidst the piss and shit and rubble and noise. The ones least likely to notice the place has been blown up. And the ones most likely to be rounded up and shot.

I trotted down the steps at the front of the apartment, still adjusting my tie—something suitably muted—and was about to open the front gate when I was accosted by a gabardine-clad weirdo with hunched shoulders and a képi trying his best to look inconspicuous but failing conspicuously as a result of the sartorial mismanagement that had matched a gabardine and a képi. He also had what I took to be a false beard, but I didn't try pulling it because it looked so ridiculous it could only be genuine.

"Joe."

Bugger me extra-terrestrially. It was Delia.

"Let me guess. Fidel Castro. No. Milošević on the run."

"What?"

"Your fancy-dress costume. A hipster flasher, is it?"

He spat his salmiak out onto the sidewalk. I was right.

"Will you ever feck off, Joe. This is serious. Haven't you seen the news?"

"Of course I have. I'm on the way to the hospital now."

An army chopper flew overhead. Delia glanced skyward, furtively, and paused before replying, like he didn't want to shout his reply.

"You'd do well to keep your head down, Joe. This…the bomb…it's a set-up. An excuse. Next thing is the clamp-down. The backlash. You know. The roundups."

Jesus, a conspiracy nut. And entirely correct, of course.

"What's that to you, Del? You're not in trouble, are you?"

His look said he thought I was an utter moron. Again, entirely correct.

"Come on, Joe. Think! This provides them with a chance to tighten their grip, to squeeze out the last drops. You don't imagine all this—" he waved his arms around generally but I think he meant the helicopter, "is out of fear of what Travelers can do, do you? Jesus. It's about *control,* man. *Control.* They reserve the right to have a finger in every pie. And they're running out of pies. There's nothing left to cannibalize."

"But why the disguise? It's a bit Inspector Clouseau isn't it?"

"Joe, they'll be doing door-to-door within 24 hours. Don't you listen to the radio? There're already roadblocks on every route out of the city center. You won't believe the trouble I had getting here to find you."

"Find me? What for?"

"Because I don't trust the phone network. Not mobiles, not landlines. I had to warn you to get hid. They'll want to know about me and the coke. They'll want to know if you know me. And I don't want you to have to go through interrogation."

Bless him.

"Genuinely, Del. That's not going to happen."

"...because I know you'd snap like a Twiglet and spill the beans, you fecker."

"Don't be daft, Del. You're being melodramatic. I'm sure you could have phoned."

"You're kidding. Every phone call is monitored. Not just mine. Everyone's. They'd've picked us both up straight away using GPS."

He was hopping from foot to foot like Rafa Nadal. The only thing they have in common. He needed to calm down.

‘"Look, Del. Relax. It isn't going to be a problem...I have other contacts besides yourself, you know. I can make all of this go away."

He scanned the street impatiently.

"What? All of it?"

"Well, no, not all of it. I mean anything to do with us. A couple of phone calls. Honest. The American ambassador. People like that. With pull."

He eyed me skeptically. That same army chopper returned, back from the direction of the Hilton. Delia took it as a bad omen. It was time for him to head off.

"Might do for you, Joe. But don't be surprised if the American ambassador isn't in on it."

"Now you're being daft. The American ambassador never knows anything."

"I hope so, Joe, for your sake. But keep an eye out all the same. Make sure you aren't being followed. I'll see you again when this has all blown over."

"Where're you going?" He tapped his nose.

"Going underground…like Paul Weller."

"Paul Weller died? When?"

"Style Council. Maybe late Jam. But that's irrelevant now. I'm off. Can't tell you where. You're a Twiglet. Spare the rod and spoil the broth."

The chopper began to circle. I shielded my eyes from the afternoon rain to check it out.

By the time I turned back, Delia was at Baggot Street Bridge.

Frank's office in the hospital is much sparser than the one in the embassy. Few luxuries on offer but piped music through the speaker system: Gregorian chants while I was there. One luxury he did have, though, was a drinks cabinet, from which he obligingly drew a Club Orange for me, simultaneously mocking my refusal of an alcoholic beverage. He took a Rémy for himself and sat down behind his desk in his black leather swivel chair.

"What's the latest on the bombing? Any clues as to who's behind it?"

"Fucking Travelers behind it, Joe. Dissidents. The Sinister Fringe. Who d'you think?"

I gave him my I-Can't-Believe-It's-Not-Bullshit look, but there was no point contesting it. Because they're behind everything, aren't they? Bombings, theft, arson, embezzlement, tax evasion, gay marriage.

"Is there much evidence? Has anyone confessed?"

"I've got dozens of confessions, but it hasn't been decided which ones to use yet."

"Well let me rephrase my question. *Besides* confessions, do you know if the Irish security services have got any evidence?"

"I'm sure they have, Joe." He took a slurp of Rémy. "That's nothing to do with me, though. That's forensics. I just handle the interrogation side of things."

Indeed. Hence the confessions.

"What about the choice of target? Any suggestion the bomb was aimed at someone in particular?"

"Couldn't tell you, Joe. Train stations, though. A classic target. Atocha, Bologna, Mumbai. London Underground. Tokyo Underground. They're an easy target, for one thing. Lots of people milling round. And nobody of any consequence uses public transport, so low security. Plenty of escape routes."

"Not a suicide bomber, then?"

"Haven't ruled it out, but who wants to die in a train station?"

We don't have that many suicide bombers in Ireland, thanks to Catholic guilt, except for the infamous Sylvia Plath Battalion, a crack unit of circus performers formed five years ago and dedicated to suicide missions against top-ranking military and government officials. On one occasion, several members were dispatched into the countryside to contract rabies and were then infiltrated into Dublin, where they attempted to bite the president himself and three of his aides at the parade celebrating the death of Gay Byrne, when everyone gets a day off work in lieu of pay. Fifty-three people were shot dead in the ensuing mêlée on that day, including the minister for education.

The president survived, even though he was bitten by several people. It turned out that none of them were rebels, just ordinary citizens taking advantage of the opportunity.

Frank finished off his Rémy.

"Enough of this persiflage, Joe. I'm going to be liaising closely over the next couple of weeks with Irish intelligence, see if we can't close this one up quick. I'll have Washington on my back like a randy mastiff if I can't generate a plausible explanation toot sweet. Have to pull in all my agents and see what the word is. Step up interrogations, increase roundups. I'll have to get something."

"Sure." I got up to go.

"Oh. I forgot to ask. What the hell happened with you and Sinéad the other night? You disappeared upstairs and then she comes running down telling me you've upchucked over the carpet and passed out on the sofa."

"Yeah. Not one of my most stellar moments."

"Then, by the time I got up there, you were back on your feet and dancing to Abba."

"Doesn't sound like me."

"Dancing Queen."

"Maybe, so."

"You didn't get a chance to do her, anyway."

"Nope."

"I knew it. You could barely raise an eyebrow."

He pulled open his drawer and tossed a bottle of pills over.

"Have these on me. You never know when you might need a bit of help."

"Ha fucking ha." I placed the bottle back on his desk. "Your need's greater than mine, Frank."

"They're not mine, you dick. They're currency. Some of my guys insist on being paid in Viagra. The stress of the job. Takes its toll."

"I'm sure."

"Not that Sinéad's that kind of girl, anyway, as I'm sure you've realized by now."

I nodded, inwardly dejected at the news.

"Her idea of a good night out is midnight mass. You'd be much better off trying some extramural activities, if you get my drift." He picked up the bottle of pills and fiddled with it, thoughtfully. "Have you heard anything from Ellie recently?"

Strange question.

"Not a thing. We don't have much to do with each other since…well, since…"

"Sure, of course…I understand. I only meant that it's better not to confuse business and pleasure. Know what I mean?"

"Sure. And how did you get on with that...what was it...the Turkish human rights woman?"

"What? Yasmina? You mean *your* bird? Oh, excellent, Joe. Excellent. I've always liked Stiff Little Fingers. Just never had them up my ass before."

The latest edition of *Brewer's Dictionary of Phrase and Fable* features several new additions to its Collective Nouns section:

- An absence of epileptics
- A congress of rabbits
- A coterie of painters
- A dearth of Irish ecologists
- A shortage of midgets
- A crewe of trainspotters
- A battery of chip shops
- A bevy of barmaids
- A division of spectacle wearers
- A shitload of nappies
- A mass of Latin Lovers
- A meeting of butchers
- A drove of joyriders
- A Quorum of tribute bands
- A gunch of ventriloquists
- An armery of amputees

- A murder of lorry drivers
- A minion of shallots
- A gaggle of masochists
- A wrap of black film directors
- A livery of pubs

and

- A knot of pessimists

Lost half a pound.

No. 10
The Georgi Markov

8 oz. Bulgarian Vodka or whatever's your poison
Serve with an umbrella

Steve the tapeworm is being a stubborn little bastard right now. I took my third capsule last night, but there's been no response. He's probably digging his hooks in deeper, dodging the Niclosamide as it shoots down my intestine.

"I don't like the look of that," he's saying. "There's no way I'm touching those things. I know what that fecker's up to."

No doubt like every other malignant entity in this country, he's developed some resistance to society's efforts at self-defense: the antibiotics, the anthelmintics, the antivirals. We shall have to box clever and find new ways to get rid of these enemies of the people. In my case, I'm trying to get Steve drunk as possible so that he loses the ability to hang on.

It turns out Delia was right about the clampdown. And with a vengeance, too. Not so much a clampdown on freedom of expression or freedom to criticize the government; the papers can be trusted to censor themselves, focusing on nothing but the bombing at the train station—speculation about the perps, made ever more speculative thanks to police tip-offs—prurient details about the casualties, atrocity-porn photos, all that stuff. But closer to home, under the radar, on the ground, I hear tell of a carnival of reaction.

Reports of wholesale slaughter in Clonmel, pogroms in Antrim, police riots in Ennis. As though the bomb was a starter pistol writ large. On your marks, get set, kill.

This is what states do when they have lost all legitimacy. They let loose the dogs of fascism, the gangster class, the criminal underworld; they give ordinary punters a taste of something worse. "You need us to keep these dogs in check," they say, as though these dogs are not the state's own beasts, its bastard offspring, its *ultima ratio,* its id. "Only we know how to tame them, only we have the tools to protect you from them. Quick, let's pass these emergency laws before it's too late. Before everything descends into anarchy. We'll worry about the fine print later. Give us your trust and your DNA and everything will be fine. We need it to eliminate you. As a suspect, we mean. Obviously."

Around Grand Canal Dock, you wouldn't notice much change. A couple of extra armed Gardaí at the traffic junction and reduced foot traffic because the DART only goes as far north as Tara Street now; those Northsiders who have jobs on the South side have had to drive in or get the bus. Nobody is particularly garrulous. Maybe folk are watching what they say and who they say it to. Maybe they're just anti-social bastards.

Other than myself and Sinéad, foot traffic into Whetstone is non-existent. Today was the first day in the office without the senior editorial staff, who are now all unconditionally on the teleworking scheme. The office is no quieter than it was, given that Sinéad was always the noisiest, but it's eerie to wander between the empty cubicles and to try to identify the people who only last week were sitting there. Maybe one of them was Gavin McShit. Who knows?

COITUS was on the phone to us first thing, of course, wanting to know if we'd managed to find someone to lease out the office space.

"I have a couple of potential clients coming to have a look later this week, but from the responses I've received so far, few of them are interested in renting out half a floor."

A stapler whizzed by my left ear. Sinéad was the only suspect. Her grinding teeth lent conviction to my suspicion.

"You'll need to look at that, then, Joe. Who's left in the office now besides you and Human Resources?"

Gah. Feck.

"Nobody. That's what we were aiming for. But of course we still have the servers in here, and Tom who looks after them has to come in whenever there are electrical faults or hardware upgrades required."

"Yes, well, servers can be anywhere, can't they? It was only for the sake of convenience and consolidation that we put them and the abstracting offices in the same location. Reduced the rental costs. I mean, in principle, we could have the servers over here, couldn't we?"

That sound is Sinéad pummeling the partition wall with both fists.

"In principle, you could, but you'd have to consider the extra costs involved. One of the advantages of teleworking is that the staff pay for their own electricity and Internet connections, remember."

"Are you suggesting that Tom has the servers in his own home?"

Sinéad's arm waving gave no indication of pattern or message. It was random, demented.

"I was merely offering some blue-sky thinking. Thinking out aloud. Trying to find ways to attract new tenants while lowering our costs even further."

Silence.

"Good for you, Joe. Glad to see you finally get on board. God knows it's taken you long enough. But it doesn't have to be Tom, does it? If he doesn't want to have the servers in his home I'm sure we can find some loophole to put them somewhere else. You can always let Tom go and find someone more amenable if he kicks up a stink, right? Do some research. See if there are server farms that can do this on the cheap. You've got the databases there, after all. Use them."

"Will do."

"Good man. Enjoy your afternoon."

I phewed. Sinéad? Feud.

"You are determined to see us on that slow fucking boat to China, aren't you? Not content with getting all the staff out of the office and not stamping down on the outsourcing option when it first cropped up, you're now shipping out all the hardware from this place so that there's no reason I can think of for any of us to be in Ireland at all. Unless, that is, you're planning to go round all the floors on the last day of the month to collect the rent money from the tenants personally."

"Don't be daft. You heard her. I was giving her some chum."

"Like a shark, is it? Placating a shark? Well, don't you be surprised, boy, if she doesn't hack off a limb the next time she swims round this way and you haven't got anything to feed her with."

"I'll throw her you."

"Oh, will you now?"

"I'm winding you up."

"I know you are. Because right now the one thing you *do* need to have is a Human Resources officer, someone who's familiar with Irish tax and employment law, because until such time as those writers and editors are made redundant—and neither of us knows how long that will be—the only person who can keep track of their holidays, their sick pay, their legal entitlements, their rights under Irish law—is yours truly. Your job, on the other hand, any big eejit can do."

"Thanks a million, Shin."

"Can I take it you had no luck with yer union fella?"

"O'Flaherty? Not really. He says there's no interest among the staff. What can you do? They've no experience of union activity. They only encounter it when they can't get into the office because of a rail strike or when they can't go on their holidays because of a work-to-rule at the passport office. They see union activity as something of an inconvenience for themselves as consumers, not as a means of exercising their rights as workers."

"He says that," she sneered, "But that's the fecking union hierarchy for you. Too much effort for him. Doesn't want to know. I swear to God most of them hate the people they're supposed to be representing. They have more in common with management in terms of lifestyle."

"Maybe you're right. Seems a bit harsh. I thought the guy was genuine. And he did give me advice on how to go about selling the…erm…sugar."

"The what?"

"The sugar. You know. The salt. The sherbet. The shampoo."

"The cocaine?"

"Sshh. Yes."

"You aren't still on about that are you?"

"I don't see that I have any alternative now, Shin. We're cut right to the bone. The only way we're going to compete is by wage reductions and keeping people happy with cash in hand."

"It's fecking ridiculous. You haven't got a clue."

"My mates will help me. I'm going to meet them again as soon as I can and get things moving."

"At a time like this, Joe? You'd be a fool."

"Yeah. That's what they said."

—

Meeting Delia wasn't going to be as easy as I anticipated. He wasn't answering his mobile—it was registering as an unrecognized number—and his landline went straight to voicemail. I guess he was serious about me lying low and him going underground. This was going to complicate matters. I really needed to get going if I wanted to have enough cash to cover the wage cuts COITUS was talking about, but if I couldn't get hold of Delia, then I was stumped. I tried to get hold of O'Flaherty to see if he knew where Delia was holed up, but he was incommunicado too. No sign of either of them. I shall have to get Frank to track them down for me.

—

Here are *Billboard*'s top ten shows currently in pre-production or casting that it recently tipped as Broadway or West End smash hits in the next 12 months:

10: *G.I.'s and Blow-Up Dolls*
A historical musical on efforts to prevent the transmission of venereal disease among U.S. troops during the Vietnam War.

9: *Seven Child Brides for Seven Mormon Brothers*
An arranged marriage musical set in rural Utah. A guaranteed laughfest.

8: *The Pirates of Penang*

A cheery light opera about life on the Malaysian seas among nonstate entrepreneurs engaged in attacks on corporate shipping.

7: *Oi! Cal Cutter!*
Love is the answer to knife crime and East End gang violence according to this all-singing, all-dancing, all-nude production.

6: *Catscan*
An Andrew Lloyd-Webber–inspired history of computed tomography, from its early days in the work of Italian radiologist Alessandro Vallebona, through to Hounsfield and Cormack's Nobel Award acceptance speeches, all told through the medium of showgirls in revealing hospital gowns.

5: *Osama bin Laden's Hair!: The Afghan Tribal Love-Rock Musical*
Faithful to the original Rado/Ragni/MacDermot show, expect this updated version's profanity, depiction of the use of illegal drugs, treatment of sexuality, irreverence for the American flag, and naked death scene to cause much comment and controversy.

4: *Oklahoma Bomb!*
White supremacists take no prisoners in this revisiting of the classic Rodgers and Hammerstein show.

3: *Rentboy*
Life among the New York subcultures and underground is sympathetically dealt with via the touching and heartfelt story of a teenage street drummer who discovers how much more money he can make by selling his ass to strangers; with hilarious consequences.

2: *Take That Come to Town*
A light-hearted romp set in the world of sperm banks and in vitro fertilization.

1: *Columbine High School Musical*
Misfit American teenagers find the answers to their alienation in the form of pop music and automatic weapons.

No. 7
The Cristiano Ronaldo
A Tumbler and Some Wines

Who was it said, "You know who your friends are?" Julius Caesar, I think. He was the first one to realize you can live alongside someone, day in, day out, habituate yourself to their foibles, even find those foibles endearing, then suddenly the day arrives when you realize that you never knew them at all. That they were stringing you along without any concern that you might value their friendship, their company.

I'll tell you what I mean.

I left work at 4.30 today and got back to Herbert Place by 5.15, intending to change into my tracksuit to pop over to the church hall on Haddington Road for Weight Watchers, but I got to my front door and fumbled for the keys in my pocket only to realize that I'd left not just my keys but also my Nicorettes, my mobile, and my wallet, with my ID card inside, back at work. Seeing as how I had to make it to the church by 6.30, I figured I'd give it a miss this week and headed back to the office to get my stuff.

It was a fresh evening and quicker to walk than drive, so that's what I did. When I arrived back at Whetstone House, I swapped the usual expletives with Matt the security guy, who was manning the newly installed metal detector, and used the stairs up to my office because the elevator was locked out.

I made it up the two flights only to find the floor in pitch darkness. Shut down. Or so I thought. As I groped for the walls, my eyes slowly adjusted to the darkness, and gradually I was able to make out a narrow slit of light beckoning to me from beneath my own door at the end of the corridor. I assumed that it meant the cleaners were doing their rounds, although they normally don't show until about 9, but it provided me with a horizon, a way of keeping my balance and locating my destination. The darkness had come as a bit of a surprise, but then I figured that because the cleaners are all blind—we use the same company as the embassy—they don't need the lights turned on. More of a surprise were the moans and murmurs I began to hear as I got closer to my office. Not the moans and murmurs of conversation, you understand. More like the moans and murmurs that blind people make when they're knocking one out. I imagine. I don't know. I'm speculating. Anyway, these faintly repellent, oddly sirenic sounds persuaded me that I should continue my approach more stealthily, imagining, well, imagining I don't know what. What do *you* picture when you think of blind people masturbating?

Closer still and my attitude changed. These were noises made by more than one person. I had been bemused. Now I was fucking annoyed. Two blind people fucking in my office. I was really going to give them a piece of my mind.

Although part of me thought it might be worth watching for a while, since they wouldn't know I was there.

So when I threw open the door of my office, I thought there'd be little left to surprise me. I was wrong. It wasn't the office cleaners at all. It was Frank. Frank Prendergast. Frank Prendergast down on all fours, stark bollock naked and eating Cointreau and cream out of the anus of an equally undressed Sinéad. Not equally undressed. Forgive me. Sinéad was wearing a mask. A tight, close-fitting mask, of my fucking face.

Needless to say, I was horrified. Cointreau at room temperature. Disgusting. He should at least have had ice in his mouth.

I suppose I must have stood there for two minutes watching, Frank tonguing and probing away, Sinéad throwing her head this way and that in rapture. It's possible, I suppose, that her muffled cries were efforts to call Frank's attention to the fact that they were not alone, but they could just as easily have been growls of ecstasy, and Frank certainly took them for that, because he seemed only encouraged by her wriggling and ejaculations.

And I credit my fervent heterosexuality for the fact that I'd been there for two minutes before I noticed that Frank was pulling himself off. And it was only when he came—shooting his diseased yellow jism all over my fucking carpet, mind you—that I managed to say, "Well, honestly!" and he realized that something was up.

You know, I don't think I've ever seen a dick shrink so fast. Not that his starting point was so magnificent, you understand, but it was funny nonetheless. Frank sprang to his feet—cock boinging—picked Sinéad up and crouched behind her, so that all I could see was a naked, masked Sinéad—okay, that wasn't so bad—but with Frank's limp dick peeking through from behind, hanging between her legs.

"Joe! Joe! What the fuck are you doing here?"

I gestured toward his spunk on my carpet.

"You could at least have worn a condom, you filthy bastard."

Sinéad ripped off the mask, her chest still heaving, either from shock or orgasm.

"Why aren't you at Weight Watchers?" she asked.

"Forgot my keys. How the hell did you get in here?"

"I have your keys. Spare set."

"How many times have you been up here to fuck, you fuckers?"

"It's only the second time ever, Joe, I swear," she said, and I considered believing her. Frank was pulling her over to my chair, where they'd piled up their clothes. I was trying not to laugh now that I had them on the hook.

"You could have fucking asked."

"You know how it is, Joe." Frank was pulling on his boxers inside out. That wasn't accidental, by the way; he reckons he can get two days' use out of underwear by wearing them inside out as well as inside in. "Didn't like to ask. Didn't want to embarrass you. Adds an extra frisson for Sinéad to do it on the sly. Boss's office and all that."

"And the mask?"

Sinéad turned it over in her hand, but Frank was grinning like an idiot.

"Nothing to do with me, Joe. That's all Sinéad. Gets her off big style. She likes to watch us in the mirror"—He indicated my full-length mirror in the corner of the room—"I think the idea of watching you have sex turns her on."

I corrected him.

"The idea of us having sex, Frank. Me and you. That's what she sees. She doesn't like the idea of you fucking her, so she gets off on the idea of you fucking me."

This was an idea that didn't sit well with him. I could see him checking Sinéad's expression for confirmation. She gave nothing away.

"Let's agree to disagree," he said.

"Yes, let's. And who else knows about your shenanigans?"

"Nobody," she said, but then she would say that, wouldn't she? I looked to Frank for the honest answer—more fool me—but he simply shrugged as if to say, "What she said."

"Right. I'm going to walk around the office for a couple of minutes to see if I can figure out why everything's turned off, and hopefully by the time I get back, you'll be fully clothed."

"Got yer," he said.

I couldn't figure it out, as it happens. It wasn't a fuse that had blown. The whole place must have been shut down and turned off after I left, even though the servers need to be kept running all weekend so that the teleworkers can upload and download their files. Even given that there was a bank holiday weekend coming up, it doesn't stop the teleworkers from plowing straight through so that they can take off the Tuesday and Wednesday instead.

Frank and Sinéad were ready to tiptoe past me by the time I returned to the office, Sinéad carrying her high heels. Frank was putting the mask into a plastic shopping bag and absent-mindedly massaging his semen into my carpet with the sole of his shoe.

"Jesus, Frank. Don't try to make amends. Do one, will yer?"

"Aye aye, Cap'n."

He made to leave, trying his best to look shamefaced, but that's difficult for Frank.

"Just one thing, Frank, before you go."

"Yes, boss." He stopped in his tracks, willing, I suspect, to do anything.

"Where'd you get the Cointreau?"

The *Anglo-Celt* reports that the body of a 70-year-old bloke was found yesterday on Clones Golf Course with the old Salvadorean necktie: throat cut from ear to ear and tongue pulled through to drape down the neck. The middle finger of his right hand had been cut off and pushed up his nose. I'm not sure of the significance of this, but the necktie, I think, is a sign that the guy was an informer.

The June issue of the South Korean gentleman's magazine *Haengun Palgi* (literal translation: *Lucky You Erection*) offers advice to its readers on "How to be a Cool Dad."

- Do not throw full ashtrays at the family pet.
- Remember that your children look up to you, so learn how to lie proficiently.
- If food falls on the floor and there are children in the room, make a point of explaining all about bacteria and blow on it before putting it in your mouth.
- Children like to know that they live in a happy home, so always kiss your wife hello and goodbye. Unless she has been on the floor, in which case you must blow on her first.
- A cool dad buys his kids interesting pets. Swearing mynah birds are totally out of date. Kids today want hamsters that stutter, a paranoid dachshund, or a gibbon in a beret.
- A cool dad will let his children drive the car home from school.
- Put a lock on your drinks cabinet. Drunken children are neither funny nor clever, even if they think they are.
- Your children do not want you to be their friend. They want to hold you in esteem.

If you let them give you a nickname, make sure it is respectful, such as Big Chief, Sage, or The Fathernator, not contemptuous, like Running Sore, El Tedio, or The Stenchmaster.

- Learn how to fart the theme tune to *Bang Gui Dae Jang*.
- Avoid playing sports with anyone younger and/or better than you. Do not play sports with women. Retain dignity at all times. A cool dad knows that it is better to referee football matches or women's wrestling than to take part.
- Kids love foreign cultures, so speaking in another language will impress them. Learn a few English phrases, such as "Get me a beer" and "You're no son of mine" to throw into conversation whenever the kids have friends round.
- A cool dad does not hit his children. He sets traps for them so that they associate bad deeds with violent retribution from God.
- A cool dad never eats fruit.

Lost half a pound.

No. 113
The WTF?!

6 oz. Whiskey
6 oz. Tequila
18 oz. Fanta
Serve repeatedly until comatose

I met up with Sinéad and Frank by the statue of Bill Clinton this evening. It wasn't originally a statue of Clinton, it was Molly Malone, but as a tribute to Clinton's role in the peace process they'd stuck his head on it rather than cast a whole new statue.

I decided to forgive and forget what happened at the office last night, mainly so I'd have someone to go out and drink with. The atmosphere at first was strange and strained—they were still embarrassed—but since Frank doesn't take anyone's feelings seriously for long, he soon got over any hurt he might have caused me or any feelings of guilt. In his defense, he's been distracted since the bomb at Connolly, which has forced him to ratchet up the intensity of his interrogations—always a source of pleasure, but also stress, to him. A further source of pleasure was the fact that it was Frank's turn to choose our dining venue this week, and he was keen for us to try out a couple of new places: the wine bar we went to first, de Boer's, and the new Jap restaurant at the Pembroke Hotel, Zetsubō.

De Boer's, on Nassau Street, takes the concept of bad taste and runs with it down-market. The theme is apartheid-era South Africa: photos of Selous Scouts on the wall, tires hanging from the rafters as a humorous reminder of the necklaces that Winnie Mandela wanted to use to free the country, sjamboks hanging behind the bars over the mirrors and, to complete the effect, segregation, with the white wine served upstairs in a plush lounge, while non-whites are served in spartan surroundings in the basement, the real apartheid, of course, being the sign on the front door of the bar that says "No Travelers Allowed." Frank gave in to his love of the picaresque, taking us downstairs; we clubbed together to buy a bottle of Tokay and settled on a bench well away from the restroom doors and close to the jukebox. We could squeeze two glasses each out of the bottle, so it worked out at a mere 18 euros a glass.

Returning from the bar with the bottle, I gradually picked up Frank's voice and recognized the spiel he was giving Sinéad: he was reciting the list of interrogation options he makes his trainees memorize in case they find themselves short of ideas. Rub chili powder in the subject's eyes; stick his head into a polythene bag of dogshit or petrol; play a tape of screaming in the next room and tell him it's his wife and kids; put electric wires into his mouth, especially on his teeth, or better yet, to his teeth and his ears at the same time, a technique known as the telephone; put electric needles under his nails; burn him with cigarettes; slowly squeeze his testicles; and sleep deprivation, disorientation. I've known Frank to come into an interrogation room and kiss his victim passionately on the lips, so pleased is he to have them there as a guest.

I don't enjoy our nights out that much when we talk shop, but this was Frank trying to impress Sinéad—not exactly chat her up, because he didn't need to do that now—with the odd witty anecdote about torture. He's clearly dropped any pretense about his job at the embassy; who knows, maybe that's how he got Sinéad to fuck him in the first place. Anyway, in his charge today was a member of the "sinister fringe" who he'd been pursuing for ages, hence his cheerfulness.

"Tell me what you did to him then," said Sinéad, showing what I thought was an indecent degree of interest. Not quite salivating, but certainly with no consideration for *my* feelings.

"Ahh…not much…give us a peanut…we just wire-brushed his helmet."

I winced. "He wasn't English, was he? I understand they love that sort of thing." Frank briefly reflected on the possibility.

"Could've been. He got a boner anyway. Spewed all over the cell, the dirty fucker. And we'd only had it cleaned the day before." He split a peanut between his front teeth. "Didn't tell us much either. There's a real dearth of info out there at the moment. People are disappearing right, left, and center…mostly left." He snorted at his own joke. Or possibly the peanut.

"Not that that's anything to do with you, Frank."

"Joe, disappearances are not my style, you know that. They're terribly amateurish."

"Quite...quite. And I know how you hate helicopters."

We laughed and took simultaneous swigs. Sinéad checked out the barman's profile. Eugenically superior stock.

We left de Boer's in a light-hearted mood and headed for Zetsubō via Grafton Street, even though there are still enough buskers, balloon manipulators, poetry reciters and statue impersonators in this country for a stroll down Grafton Street to make the case for Pol Pot. In the 60s, all these kids would have been educated for emigration, trained to head off for decent jobs in the U.K. and the States so they could send cash back to their indigent relatives. With the demise of higher education, or rather, of careers requiring a higher education, anyone who didn't fancy selling their body parts was faced with either joining the Gardaí or learning to juggle. Their omnipresence today proves there are still some things a self-respecting Dub won't do.

And which also means there's a natural enmity between the Gardaí and the street entertainers. The latter are tolerated and nothing more. When the tourists disappear, around about October, these guys very wisely start exploring the transplant option, because when the tourists go, the witnesses go, so not only is there no one to throw a euro in your cap, there's also no one around to see your head being caved in. Spring and summer return, and these fuckers seem to sprout like kudzu, congregating near waste ground or derelict sites in the Grafton Street vicinity to make a rapid retreat when circumstances demand.

It was while we were walking up past Davy Byrne's that Frank broke the shocking news.

"Joe, you remember that Turkish bird, Yasmina. The one working for the human rights group? The one you fancied fucking."

"The one who had her fingers up your ass?"

"Yeah, that one. Did you see she was killed in the bomb blast at Connolly?"

"You're shitting me."

He sniffed the air abruptly and looked back at Davy Byrne's.

"You really didn't see? Her photo was in the *Mail* this morning. Do you smell fire?"

I paused to verify his sense-data.

"I get cabbage soup. Licorice. Maybe the Guinness brewery's ablaze." He smiled at the thought, like he found it comforting.

"In the *Independent,* too. Not the kind of shit they'd both make up."

"True, but maybe they had the same source. The Guards. They'd both reproduce it without question."

"Sounds like you don't want it to be true."

Maybe I don't.

"What was she doing at Connolly?"

He shrugged then scratched his neck, just under his ear. "Same as everybody else, probably. Wondering where her life had gone, wondering where the Maynooth train is, wondering what's in that package over there. Are you sure you don't smell fire?"

"Yeah, I'm sure. Maybe you're having a seizure."

"Maybe what I can smell is the flame you're carrying for Yasmina. Fat lot of use it is now."

A lanky young woman with a moustache and an apron held a bucket out at us and asked if we'd like to make a donation to leukemia research. Frank told her, "Only if I can watch," and she skulked off.

I'm rather more partial to Indian and Chinese food than Japanese, but it was Frank's choice of restaurant and there aren't any Chinese restaurants left in Dublin, not since they all buggered off home to open fish and chip shops when the "free market" kicked in. Anyhow, Frank told me that this was Japanese "with a difference," so I strapped on my adventurous face to impress Sinéad and decided to give it a go.

It *was* different. The decor you normally expect from sushi bars is minimalist and hyper-real, whereas this place was 18th-century Victorian, with green marble floors and ornate friezes, a bit like the restaurant at the Hotel Adolphus back home. The food was different too.

There are two things that I thought I knew about lobsters, and it turns out only one of them is right. The first thing I knew, from reading *Scientific American* at work, was that no matter how fast lobsters walk, their heart rate never exceeds 80 to 90 beats per minute, and their ventilation rate peaks at 175 to 180 and refuses to go higher, irrespective of any increase in speed—I don't know how this was discovered; lobsters on treadmills is my guess.

The other thing I thought I knew was that before being eaten, lobsters are boiled alive, and although they're an orangey pink when they reach your table, they are a dark, greenish black in their natural state. The orangey pink is their scream.

They are indeed a dark, greenish black in their natural state, though with a hint of midnight blue, but they aren't necessarily boiled alive before you eat them. At least, not at Zetsubō, which, it transpires, is a sushi bar that specializes in *ikezukuri*, a form of sushi preparation in which the meat is cut away from the selected animal while the still-functioning internal organs are left intact.

So the first time I threw up was when the chef plucked Frank's red snapper out of the tank next to our table and expertly flensed two slivers of meat from along either side of its body and presented them on a plate to Frank before gently placing the snapper back in the water so that we could watch the confused and panic-stricken creature swim around in search of its nether regions.

The second time I puked, my lobster was making a game attempt to escape, crawling off my plate with one claw, three-quarters of its body, and one eye. What actually made me hurl, though, was Frank offering me an octopus arm—"Try this, Joe, it feels really weird"—the disembodied arm still curling and uncurling between his chopsticks like a snake, and when I put it in my mouth, rather bravely, I thought, the tentacles started sucking on my tongue and on my soft palate, and then the arm unwound and reached down my gullet and triggered my gag reflex. Everything came up. Tokay, bits of lobster, Tayto cheese and onion. I whacked back my entire saketini, which stung my eyes, and at this point I realized that the octopus arm was hanging on, having withstood the onslaught of vomit, clamping itself to the inside of my cheek and swinging out of my mouth like a drunk around a lamppost, unfurling like a banner and enabling me to pleasure all the women in the room at the same time without having to leave my seat.

Frank did his best to console me by pointing in my direction and laughing loudly, but eventually boredom kicked in and he decided instead to pat me on the back and, using a napkinned hand, pull the octopus arm free and dab my chin sympathetically.

"Must've been something you ate," he said.

I gasped for air while Frank ordered more drinks and Sinéad looked a little nauseous at the sight of me. Frank picked his moment.

"Joe, before I forget…sorry, Sinéad, this is a little indelicate…Joe, you didn't happen to come across my crucifix anywhere in your office, did you?"

Despite the sad state I was in, I shook my head with some concealed delight, schadenfreude, no less, since it was obvious that he would be in deep shit if he failed to return it to R&D.

"I'll have a better look round, tomorrow, Frank," I said, weakly. "I'm going to pop into work."

"Great. If you would, mate. I'm pretty sure that's where it'll be. I think I misplaced it there when..." His voice trailed off before he could say, "I was eating out Sinéad's ass." I considered completing the sentence for him, but I could see Sinéad's complexion reddening.

"Don't worry," I reassured him.

"I'll be at the hospital if you want to get in touch."

"I'll do my best, Frank." He frowned in confirmation.

"I know you will, mate. You always do. You're very good to me. Listen, dessert's on me. What'll you have?"

"Sleep."

According to the *Alabama Star,* a 15-year-old schoolboy went berserk yesterday at his campus in Luttrell, Tennessee. Piloting a stolen U.S. Navy F/A-18E/F, the young student bombed the gymnasium, library and science labs before strafing the playground as his terrified classmates ran for cover. Since state laws were changed in 2009 allowing pupils to wear concealed weapons for self-defense in the event of a school shooting, the students were able to return fire, but their efforts were largely futile; their schoolmate was determined to go out with a bang, crashing the fighter into the main building of the school without ejecting. At least 230 students and staff are reported missing, and so far ninety-seven bodies have been found. A spokesperson for the NRA said, 'This goes to prove our point that it isn't guns that kill people, it's people who kill people. If only those kids had been allowed to arm themselves with surface-to-air rocket launchers, their assailant would have thought twice about blowing them to smithereens.'

Local Christian fundamentalists were briefly mobilized for the Rapture by their Chapter heads when a TV station announced that, "Authorities believe a number of the dead will rise," but this was an editorial error. The announcement should have read, "Authorities believe *the* number of the dead will rise."

No. 49
The Afghan Hound

Bottle of Tennessee Whiskey
Bottle of Absinthe
Egg whites
Bottle of Russian Standard Vodka
Mix whiskey, absinthe, and egg white to make as many sidewinders as you need
Chuck out the Russian Standard

I checked the papers after Frank's revelation and confirmed that Yasmina Yıldırım had been one of the seventy-three victims of the explosion at Connolly Station. Police are working on the assumption that the bomb was either detonated remotely or using a timer, which narrows things down a bit, doesn't it? While everyone else in the vicinity might have been suicidal, apparently the bomber was not.

Frank's crucifix turned up. It was on the floor of my office behind the desk. Sinéad must have torn it off him in wild abandon. I hold it in my hand, toy with it, think of her clutching it, of it digging into her palm, of her using that pain to delay and intensify the moment of release, the firework display in her brain. And I find I can't restrain myself. The saddest wank I ever had.

Still no power in Whetstone House except for my office. I can't figure it out. Admittedly, we only need power now for me, Sinéad, and the servers, so it makes sense to turn off everything else, but Tom wouldn't have turned off the servers, would he? And I'm sure COITUS can't do it from New York.

The Irish Medical Board has produced a report showing that a preparation made largely from the marrow of dogs will prolong human life by at least 20 years. The Taoiseach has greeted the report with delight as a vindication of the government's policy on shooting stray dogs, but this isn't the first time that dubious claims have been made about the beneficial effects of canine supplements. Only two years ago, a team of gynecologists from Queen's University claimed that the salivary glands of puppies could be used in the treatment of a range of genito-urinary disorders. Unfortunately, the publicity campaign that followed was uninspired, and potential consumers turned their back on the products. Who, after all, is going to be seduced by the slogan "Help lick genital warts"? It was biggest marketing gaffe since Mattel was boycotted into bankruptcy after bringing out a children's vibrator.

I've nearly run out of Glenmorangie. Only a couple of bottles left. I've been mawkishly trawling through Scotch whisky websites as a means of distraction. Here's some fascinating information from the Strathmullen home page:

Scotland has been part of the United Kingdom for more than three hundred years, but it is unlike anywhere else in Britain. Here are some important things you should know about the country:

1. Many phenomena traditionally regarded as Scottish were actually invented in England, such as the kilt, the haggis, alcoholism, and domestic violence.
2. The Scots did, however, invent the television, the telephone, and penicillin, thereby making Babestation a possibility.
3. They also invented tarmac, tires, and hollow pipe drainage, thereby making *Top Gear* a possibility.
4. The Clyde is the country's longest river. It is celebrated in the national anthem, "Flower of Scotland."
5. Famous Scottish thinkers include Adam Smith, David Hume, Alasdair MacIntyre, and John Loch.
6. Built before the perfection of the arch, the longest Roman viaduct in the world links the Irish and North seas. Later Roman architects sarcastically referred to it as Hadrian's Wall, and the name stuck.
7. Saltire is the result of a poor Scots diet.
8. The sporran is named after the Scottish martyr Saint Sporran, who was hung by the goolies.
9. The title of the head of the Salvation Army in Scotland is the Right Reverend Captain Kirk.
10. Edinburgh was the first British city to have its own fire brigade. And Boys Brigade. Glasgow was the first to have a Red Brigade.
11. The correct way to serve haggis is with neaps and tatties. "Neaps" and "Tatties" are old Scots dialect words for breasts.

12. People elope to Gretna Green to get married because of a loophole in the Act of Union.
13. Temazepam is a savory substance used to improve Scottish fruitcakes.
14. The Scots are stereotypically depicted as mean, as exemplified by the tale of Greyfriars Bobby, a border collie who starved to death guarding his stash of bones.
15. During the 19th century, Scottish Shortbread was confusingly sold in England as "Ginger Biscuits."
16. A Shetland pony is £20.
17. It is a testament to the importance of literature and poetry in Scottish life that the majority of hospitals in the country have a Burns unit, named after Robert Burns. Many also have a Urology unit, named after Joan Ure and some even have a Trauma unit, named after Thomas the Rhymer.
18. Many people mistakenly believe that the singer Ruby Murray is Scottish. In fact, she's an Indian.

No. 77
The Dubya

Sake and Sour Grapes in an empty vessel

"You fucker. When did you do it?" Frank's first response was a watery smile. His second was more assured.

"You've come here straight away, I'm sure. You must have only found it this morning."

The pleasure in contradicting him was slight.

"Night before last, actually. But I had to listen to the recording several times to check I wasn't hallucinating."

He was indifferent to the revelation of his own fallibility. He motioned casually down the corridor.

"Walk with me."

I'd found the fecker at the hospital, exactly where he said he'd be, although he put off meeting me once I got there; I had to wait until he came out of the interrogation room. Part of me wanted to storm right in there, create a scene, maybe kick a few chairs, punch the suspect myself a couple of times to demonstrate how crazy and unhinged he'd made me. Sadly, I am nothing if not professional. Instead, I sat there until he'd finished putting Band-Aids on his knuckles. Now he was leading me outside so he could have a smoke and prevent his minions from seeing me give out.

Exiting the rear door of the hospital was like stepping into a furnace. That dry heat again, the aridity of a

Dublin spring morning catching in my throat, pounding my temples.

We both coughed. The corridor through the hospital had taken us past interrogation rooms, a part of the crimson wing where I had rarely ventured, rooms in which suspects are "debriefed," often literally, before being dragged out here, round the back of the building, for the final stage of their processing. Over to the left, maybe 30 yards away from the back door, skirted by stoical berms of earth, lay a patch of scrubland where they are knelt down to be shot in the head or the heart, as appropriate, depending on the surgeon's requirements.

Further on along the hospital wall, not even out of sight of the execution grounds, was the entrance to the surgery, where the bodies enter for dismemberment and evisceration, and beside that entrance a large metal grille atop a raised platform indicated the disembarkation point for the pharmers' lorries, where the other patients arrive. The lorries come down a winding, secluded drive that meets an otherwise little-used back road out toward Dun Laoghaire.

Frank lit up a fag and offered me one before attempting an explanation. As he was about to start, there was a rumbling like thunder that made him hesitate, but it was only a lorry making its way down the drive.

"Joe. Mate. I'd've liked to have told you sooner, honestly. But we had to be sure of our case before proceeding."

I laughed awkwardly. It wasn't a day for laughing.

"Sure of your case? Since when has that ever mattered?"

"Come on. You can see that this is different. This is a breach of security."

Not very convincing, but he was keeping a straight face, trying it on for size to see if I'd buy it. But I was all spent up.

"I can't fucking believe this, Frank. Are you suggesting that Delia had befriended me in order to spy on you? On the Company? For what? For who?"

"For *them,* who d'you think?" Quick drag. "And I think you'll find that it's 'for whom,' not 'for who.'"

I wheeled away.

"Ahhh, fer Christ's sake, that's ridiculous. Delia's solid. What possible motive could he have had?"

"He's Irish. He could have had all manner of motives. You've been here long enough to know what they're like. Even you don't fall for that *céad míle fáilte* stuff. They'll do all sorts behind your back if you're not careful. The *only* motives they have are ulterior ones."

"Jesus, Frank," I said, assuming he was referring to Delia's black market activities, "He was trying to keep his shit together, trying to make a living. How do you expect them *not* to resent us? We come over here with our money and our jobs and we expect them to love us for it, then we fuck off with our money and our jobs and imagine we've left behind fond memories."

He waved away my protests.

"Doesn't matter." He heaved up a gobbet of phlegm and aimed it at the trees. "We're not here to defend rights and wrongs. We're here to look after U.S. interests. That's where the morality ends."

How can life be so easy for someone so twisted? Maybe life *is* easy if you're twisted, and it's complicated if you're sane. Is that why people go crazy? To keep things simple. Retain their sanity.

"And *do* you have any evidence against him?"

He nodded, eyeing the lorry as it approached.

"Enough." An exhalation of smoke. "He had the contacts."

"He was trying to make a living. Which of us isn't compromised?"

I didn't like the look he gave me. Menacing.

"It's a capital offense. I did him a favor."

"You're a piece of shit, Frank. You know that, don't you?"

"Fuck off, Joe. You don't want to make an enemy of me."

I couldn't believe this. He was threatening me. Frank fucking Prendergast. My oldest buddy.

"When did you pick him up? No, wait. Let me guess. It was last Friday, wasn't it?"

No answer.

"It was either then or the morning after, because that was the last time I saw him, the last time I met him."

Frank stubbed out his fag.

"You're lucky you're still alive. We've got photos of you meeting him, you know—"

"—Photos?! Fucking Stiveley."

Revenge is a dish best served by someone else.

"What?"

"Never mind. Look, Frank, Delia supplied me with knocked-off goods, yes. We played tennis together. He was a mate."

"You have no idea what kind of risks you were running. You could have wound up in the canal with a bullet through your brains. His contacts…for all you know… they might be killers."

My forehead was hurting as it was. It was the sun. It was stress. It was rubbing my hand back and forth across my brow with a lit cigarette in it.

The lorry we'd heard had worked its way down the drive and was reversing so that its back door broached the raised platform. I'd expected to smell pig, but then I saw the symbol on the driver's door. It was the peace sign. The sign used by PACS, that charity outfit I donated my clothes to.

"In the long run, Joe, you'll thank me."

Frank was walking vaguely in the direction of the lorry, for no good reason that I could tell. His tone was still friendly but reproving. I tried to maneuver so as to square up to him, but he kept turning and I didn't want to look silly.

"Thank you? You'll be a long time waiting."

"We'll see. We'll see."

"Meaning what, exactly?"

He opened his arms to me, generously, like the pope, as if to embrace me, a prodigal son, a lamb to the slaughter.

"Ours is not to reason why."

"You shit."

He grinned, almost as if he enjoyed being insulted. Well, he does. He placed what he must have thought was a comforting hand on my shoulder, but I swiped it off, stifling a laugh of disbelief. The metal grille on the platform was raised now, and I could see more clearly what was going on.

Trying to be paternal, he said, "You know the best thing to do, don't you?"

I blanked him.

"Just get on a plane and leave. Go somewhere nice. Maybe try calling Ellie. I know it's a long shot, but she *might* want to listen."

I wasn't paying too much attention. Fucking Stiveley. He'd got me.

The back of the lorry had been opened by a hospital porter who was now throwing piles of clothes out of the hospital and onto the platform, and from there into the lorry. The driver of the truck climbed down from the cabin, glanced in my direction as he saw me approach, and smiled a little inquisitively.

He had no idea what I was going to do. Neither did I. At that point, the red mist had already descended; my head was an alarming shade of scarlet and had swollen to twice its usual size. I was on an impromptu walkabout that any nonpartisan onlooker might have taken for the dance of a berserker, but which was nevertheless intentional, motivated. Motivated by the fact that I'd recognized my red leather Pierre Balmain jacket on the driver of the lorry. *My* fucking Pierre Balmain jacket, which I'd given in good faith, expecting it to be passed on to some unsuspecting wino to puke over and urinate in. It only struck me then. PACS doesn't pass on all the clothes it receives to the homeless. It only gives them the clothes being thrown into the back of the lorry, the clothes of the already dead. It recycles the clothes of the homeless. Fuck it, they probably use the clothes as a way to identify the next batch to be rounded up. I bet they have trackers stitched into them.

So I threw a right hook that connected with the driver's jaw at such an oblique angle that he actually fell toward me, already unconscious, and I had to step out of the way so that his teeth could hit the concrete. It was a satisfying punch—how rarely one gets it right—but I couldn't stay to enjoy it because, if you recall, I was crazed and maniacal. I wanted to get out of that place as quickly as possible. I was in such a state of delirium, though, that it was all I could do to follow the wall of the hospital round in the hope that it would bring me to the front gate.

I didn't look back, but I think I heard Frank clapping.

I managed to make my way to the entrance in time to see the army making another delivery. A canvas-covered truck screeched up to the door, nearly knocking me to the gravel, and four troops jumped out, dragging a number of detainees in handcuffs down behind them. When I saw the first of them, pulled out by his feet and dragged up the steps—his big red nose, his comic white face—I thought, "Christ, they're rounding up the kiddies' entertainers now," but on closer inspection I realized that it was someone I knew. It was O'Flaherty. They'd obviously stormed in on him while he was shaving and given him a bloody nose when he put up his puny resistance.

You won't get puny resistance from me. I legged it.

Libération reports that six people were killed and over forty were injured in Chantilly, France, when heavy fog descended onto the racetrack and five horses plowed into the stands. This was the first accident of its kind to occur in France. Many still remember the chaos following the Munich equestrian disaster two years ago when the stands collapsed during the dressage event and over two hundred spectators died in their sleep.

The Top Ten Boys' Names in Norway for last year were as follows (previous year's position in brackets):

1. Henrik (1)
2. Olaf (3)
3. Wolf (2)
4. Satan (17)
5. Rebel (4)
6. Prince (6)
7. Snarl (5)
8. Ignog (35)
9. Agbonlahor (10)
10. Ghostface Killah (7)

No. 27
The Pinochet Slammer

4 oz. Pisco
Take the Pisco through a straw
Drink until Alzheimer's appears to set in

Stiveley was lucky enough to get a house to himself, even though he's single. The British embassy owns a place on Ailesbury Gardens, a walk away from the embassy itself but a bus ride away from the hospital, so you might have expected that I'd have calmed down by the time I got there, especially seeing how the bus was stopped four times on the way at army checkpoints. But no. When I buzzed the intercom to his suburban pad, I was still seething.

"Who is it?" Stiveley has a deep voice but a camp delivery. Prick.

"Joe Chambers. Open up."

"Joe, old boy. A second, please."

I was intentionally fidgety, trying to sustain my anger. I could hear him coming down the stairs and unlocking the door. He opened it fully and offered me the kind of enthusiastic, accommodating welcome anacondas offer goats.

"Come on in, old chap," he said, but I didn't wait for the invitation. I barged past him into the hallway. He feigned offense.

"Well, Joe, I must say. I hope you aren't expecting a drink."

I wasn't listening.

"Where is it, Stiveley? Where is it?"

He appeared confused by my agitated state.

"Where's what, dear boy?"

"Your fucking camera, Stiveley. Where is it?"

"My cam—?"

I was at his throat all of a sudden and a look of terror flashed into his eyes. My grip was loose but I could see tears forming in his eyes.

"Your fucking camera. You know."

He managed to croak out "upstairs" and I let go. I rushed up the stairs with him close behind. "In the front room," he added, helpfully. Feebly.

The front room was sparsely furnished but in very good taste—I don't know if that's a gay thing or an MI6 thing. There was a large Chinese cabinet in the corner beside the window, accompanied by an oversize white leather couch, Roche Bobois. In the middle of the room stood an ochre Antonio Citterio table, on top of which lay a couple of recent issues of *Elle Decoration* and Stiveley's camera. I picked it up before realizing I didn't know what to do with it. In the old movies, you always saw the goon open up the back of the camera and expose the film, but this was one was digital. How do you fuck up a digital camera?

Stiveley followed me in. I waved the camera at him.

"I hope you're satisfied now, Seymour."

"Satisfied, Joe? Hardly. The closest we've ever been was moments ago when you tried to strangle me."

I was still raging.

"Do you have any idea how much trouble your photos have caused? Do you realize they've quite possibly led to the death...certainly the torture...of one of my best friends?"

He took a step away from me, toward the door.

"But Joe. No one else has ever seen them. I swear. I would *never* let anybody else see them."

"You expect me to believe that, you fuckwit? After all that harassment, after all the break-ins, you expect me to believe you wouldn't drop me in the shit? Squeal to the Guards. Rat on me."

The tears were welling up again, but he was trying to collect himself, to keep in mind that he was an Englishman and a respectable one to boot. He was probably thinking of the Queen Mother.

He pulled himself up to his full height.

"Joe Chambers, you insult me. I have no idea what you think me capable of, but at least give me some credit for the way I play the game. When I lose a round, I take it on the chin in good faith and carry on. I concede unconditionally that you got me—good and proper, too—in Athens, and I say well done, sir, well done. But to suggest that I would stoop to dobbing you in to the authorities, I must say, that indicates more about your lack of faith in human nature than it does about me."

"Yeah, yeah, very noble, Seymour. Now tell me. What's on the film?"

Matter-of-factly, he said, "Photos of you, Joe. What else would you expect?"

"Show me."

And he fucking did.

He sat me down in front of the Chinese cabinet and opened the doors. Inside, there was a state-of-the-art 30-inch flexiscreen with a sliver port for his memory card. More impressively, the interior doors of the cabinet, the walls of the cabinet and the internal cupboards of the cabinet were all plastered with posters and pictures of me. Pictures taken in Athens. Pictures taken of me strolling along Herbert Place. Pictures of me leaving the embassy. Stiveley had erected a fucking shrine to me in his front room.

Not just a shrine, of course. It took a moment for me to realize, but you've probably sussed it too. This is where Stiveley jerks off. Looking at pictures of me.

Hmm. Suddenly, I felt distinctly vulnerable, a vulnerability I attempted to deflect with aggression.

"What the fuck is all this, Stiveley?"

"Are you going to tell me you hadn't figured it out, Joe?"

There was an element of bemusement, perhaps disappointment, in his query. Never meet your idols, isn't that what they say? He inserted the memory card from the camera into the slot and flicked on the screen.

"Let's see what we've got here."

What *had* we got here? Some gay guy fixated on me? Fuck. I know I'm a total cock-hardening pussy-wetting stud-muffin, but I never thought I'd get myself a stalker.

They were the photos Stiveley had taken in Phoenix Park, and nicely taken shots they were too, although Stiveley had clearly had plenty of practice, and the zoom lens was obviously powerful. These photos were professionally framed, with attention paid to lighting, chiaroscuro, contrast, angle, mood. Lovingly crafted. I probably admired them for too long, because it took a while for a common feature to strike me. A common lack of feature, I should say.

"Where's Sinéad?"

"Excuse me?"

"Where's Sinéad? I was walking through the park with Sinéad when you took these photos."

"Oh, *her*. What would I want with pictures of her? She'd spoil the shot, wouldn't she? Ruin the...the atmosphere."

He was right, of course. She would have been intrusive. And a quick scan of all the photos in the cabinet told me the same thing. Occasions when I'd been with Frank, with Delia, with Sinéad: all cropped. Just me. Me in glorious isolation.

"Did you somehow imagine that I bore you a grudge, Joe? You, of all people? The very man responsible for my presence here. The man I followed here."

This conversation was taking on a decidedly unsavory cast. I rose from the chair.

"When you say you followed me here, Seymour, I take it you mean purely in a chronological sense."

He chortled and moved to put a hand on me. I recoiled and he thought better of it.

"Don't be absurd, dear boy. Once I found out where you'd been sent, I had to put in a request for a transfer. I was in Sitges, in Spain. Do you know it? Frightful place. The Dublin transfer couldn't have come at a better time. I was going mad. I thought you would be long dead before I got here."

Thanks for the vote of confidence.

"Why the break-ins, then, if you weren't seeking revenge?" He drew back and refocused to see whether I might be joking.

"Are you serious? You didn't realize what I was up to?" He cast his gaze to the heavens as my innocence and stupidity became apparent. I was trying to keep the rage going, but embarrassment was winning out.

"After you told me—and everyone else, incidentally—how you got me booted out of Athens, you made me realize how unprofessional I'd been. How lax my security was, how trusting I had been. When I began photographing you, I discovered that you were meeting up with some little dark-skinned chap who was providing you with illicit alcohol—don't deny it, Joe, I saw you. And before you make any accusations, you've seen the photos. There are none of the little chap in any of them. If the Guards have photos of you with him, they didn't come from me. Trust me."

Trust him? The guy was a nut. Who just happened to have good taste in men.

"It didn't take me long, Joe, to realize that you were in great danger of getting into trouble, so I thought I might tip you off, get you to appreciate the dire risks you were running. I broke into your apartment so you'd realize how poor your security was, like mine was in Athens. Okay, so, yes, I admit I used the opportunity to take one or two items of underwear and some other…delicate personal possessions, but I figured you wouldn't notice that if I focused on your…alcohol intake."

"Yeah, thanks, Stiveley. You just reminded me of another reason to throttle you."

He clenched his teeth and stamped in a hissy fit.

"Don't you understand, Joe? Your drinking could have killed you in any number of ways. I was trying to warn you. What did you think the cards were for? The instruction to give up the drink. The Al Anon card with the threat to send off your address to them: "I know where you live." I was telling you to stop your boozing. I was worried about you. It was going to get you into trouble. And now it looks like it has."

Fuck me. I hate being lectured at the best of times, and the last person I wanted to look an idiot in front of was Stiveley. After all, here was a guy who was mad about me, who thought I was cute, sexy, and now I'd let him down through my utter obliviousness. Feet of clay.

I eased myself out of the house. I couldn't bring myself to apologize because I still felt entitled to anger of some sort, but about what? The fact that he stalked me or that he was so obtuse in his warnings?

Part of me was blaming myself—I used to be a spy, goddammit. How could I not have read the signs? Simultaneously, though, another, more defensive part of me, the cowardly part, was excusing me: after all, I'm out of that game now. I'm a respectable office drone. I'm not fucking Sherlock Holmes. Why did Stiveley have to assume that because I was handsome I was brilliant, too?

Yes, it was Stiveley's fault. Blame him.

—

Nothing from Sinéad. The office is still deserted. Spotted this in the *Irish Times*:

According to the British government's Border and Immigration Agency, based in the Home Office, the following circus acts are banned from performing in the United Kingdom for the foreseeable future:

Sultan Bryan Reynolds and His Obedient Harem of Goats (animal gymnastics from New Zealand)
Dirty Little Stevie (underage regurgitation act from New Mexico)
The Swinging Majors (prosthetic trapeze act from Namibia)
Willie the Electrician (vicious clown, origins unknown)
El Depresso (Spanish raconteur and self-harmer)
The Toecap Zoo (flying animals from Belgium)
The Daring Buds of May (topless juggling from Sweden)
The Indifferents (contortionist family from Idaho wanted in 12 states)

Scott Macrae and Kitchenware (eunuch self-degradation act from ex-pat based in Hamburg)
Mr. Rainbow (lurid weather impersonator from Holland)

and

Magnificent Madge and Her Discriminating Dobermans (anti-semitic dog act from Pretoria)

No. 112
American Spy: My Secret History in the CIA, Watergate, and Beyond, by E. Howard Hunt
Cognac

What price should we put on betrayal? Should it be a higher price if you are betrayed by someone you love, or, because it's someone you love and therefore someone you're more willing to forgive, should the price be lower? Does betrayal modify the nature of that love simply by virtue of its subversion, its falsification of the love you thought you had, the object of that love revealing itself after all to be something other than you imagined? Or do you factor in the likelihood of disappointment before making the decision to commit to loving someone in the first place? And how many roads must a man walk down before he gets a taxi in this fucking country?

I've got a lot of stupid ideas galloping around my head tonight. Galloping? Gamboling. Anne Boleyn. Could be confusion. Could be that I haven't been drinking. Could be that men just can't help acting on impulse. I'm frothing at the mouth with rage and shame and existential angst and a million other emotions that Kierkegaard never even dreamed of in his philosophies, Horatio.

Should I up and leave like Frank says, the one thing I've been trying to avoid all along? Forget about everything that's happened, make a fresh start, and put everything behind me. Who could blame me, after all? And what obligations do I have to anyone here who's still alive?

A part of me, though, a big part, is seething. Endless, pointless seething that won't stay still long enough for me to sit down and analyze it. I want to believe that it's rage at injustice, an unbridled desire to avenge, a noble urge that forms my core, my real self, my underlying self-respect. But my real self actually fears that it's nothing like that at all, that it's actually anger at myself, at the humiliation I've allowed myself to undergo, a burning shame at having been made to look an idiot, not in the eyes of others but in my own eyes, the ones that count. I'm a fucking fool. An impotent, incompetent fucking fool.

After I left Stiveley, I came home and sat in silence, the rear window open, looking over onto next door's roof garden, hoping to catch a glimpse of Mrs. Sharpey at Number 42 sunbathing so I could have a wank and distract myself. I listened to the police and ambulance sirens on the warm wind. Now and again voices would carry across from the other side of the Pepper Canister and I would try to make out what they were saying.

Mostly, though, I just stared at the walls—or the ceiling, for variety—and listened to Frank's crucifix, trying to decode the meaning of the various shufflings and slaps and screams and snorts, every so often picking up Frank's sneering interrogation, sometimes hearing a shaky response, on occasion defiant but more usually honest and fearful. There were a number of interviews recorded, so

I had the benefit of Frank's entire repertoire. "Please feel free to die now," I hear him say at one point to a sobbing guest. Typical showboating. I expect he was trying to impress the trainees in there with him. Or entertaining himself while inducting them into the ranks of torturers, which is, after all, one of the principal purposes of torture: to compromise those with clean records. It isn't to get at the truth, no matter how many State Department lackeys tell you it is. The victims will tell you whatever they think you want to hear. No, the purpose of torture is to create a bond between the torturers, or between the torturers and the witnesses, at the same time as degrading and dehumanizing the enemy. I exclude the victim here, of course, who simply facilitates the bonding and is most likely going to die anyway.

The more obscene it is, the more compromised those involved. If it happens to be the case that some interrogators derive pleasure from torture, if they ejaculate over writhing bodies, well, there's no harm done, so long as there are silent onlookers present to witness the atrocity, to be initiated into sin. Because torture without witnesses is just sadism.

Frank's voice on these recordings has its own identity, an assuredness, a definite and distinct owner. Not because he is closest to the crucifix but because it has confidence and logic on its side. To anyone who understands his strategies, his questions make perfect sense. It's almost possible for you to hear his mind at work, to predict his next move, the next question, almost touch his mind. I advise you to wear gloves. Not so the voice of his victims, who generally have no idea how to respond correctly. Very few of them have been tortured before. Their answers are ambiguous, hedging their bets, non-committal, pathetic. Their burbling, reticent voices have a hard time escaping their mouths. And you can only tell them apart by their screams.

Except one.

I have played the tape several times this afternoon, much as I did the past few nights, in an effort to re-create the brain-numbing horror I felt the first time I listened to it. The time I heard a nearly familiar voice, close to laughing, say,

"Actions speak louder than mimes"

before a loud, bestial, slurping and gurgling noise wiped away any semblance of humor, of humanity, a sound that I still cannot bring myself to imagine the meaning of.

In front of me I have a passport photograph that I took today in the kiosk in the Powerscourt Center, and although it looks nothing like me, which is probably a good thing, I gaze at it like it's a mirror and wonder whether the asshole looking back at me is as bigger fool as I am.

Yeah. A lot of stupid ideas in my head.

The *Armagh Bandit* reports sightings of caravans of camels and elephants traipsing cross-country around Tandragee. These movements are widely assumed to be the resistance on maneuvers, their numbers bolstered by reinforcements from the fairgrounds of Bundoran and Portrush now that the holiday season is coming to an end. This means the rebels will be a much tougher proposition on the battlefield, freshly armed with air rifles, darts, and ping-pong balls.

From the February issue of *Advertising Age.*

Many much-loved household brand names have their origins in the strangest of places. Here are a few of those we have uncovered, and we'd love to hear from you if you know of any others:

Marmite: The delightful, beefy flavored yeast extract gets its name from the French word for a casserole dish.

Scotch Tape: So named because, in the First World War, members of the Grenadier Guards used it to tape bottles of Scotch to their legs so that they wouldn't lose them in battle.

Lego: A Latin word, meaning "I choke."

Kracka Wheat: A corruption of the phrase "Krakow Wheat," a kind of tasteless, unleavened bread eaten in the ghetto of that city during the Second World War.

Andrex: Named after the ancient Persian king famous for amputating the left hand of anyone who incurred his displeasure.

Snickers: A disease of the hands, caused by fungal growth, common among peanut harvesters in Latin America.

Bovril is the German word for bolt gun.

Ryvita: So called because the surface of the biscuit resembles the skin disease *Ryvita nervosa*.

Hobnobs: The original recipe was based on the scrapings found around the dials of gas cookers.

Xerox: Named for a court fool and impersonator who features in Plutarch's account of his visit to Assyria.

Ritz: The original name of the notorious army cracker game, short for "one off the wrist."

IKEA is the Swedish word for "terror."

No. 111
The Rimington Fizz

A Pint of Stella
Sprinkle liberally with bugs

This is the saddest day of my life. Never did I think that I would find myself drinking the last two bottles of my stash of Glenmorangie. I'd always promised myself that I'd save them for the day my divorce papers came through. Or the birth of my first grandchild. Or the death of Kathleen Turner (it's a long story). Whichever came first.

I usually find that getting down a bottle of Scotch gets easier the more I drink, but this time around I found there was an inherent tension. I had no way of replacing the booze once it was gone. Thus, much as I might normally delight recklessly in the hot golden glow of a wanton gulp, every atom in my body, every nerve, every tendril, was tweaked to high alert, straining to savor each drop, extract the essence from it, attentive even to the ghostly vapors emanating from the glass, trying to absorb them into my being, make them mine, make them me. And I think I absorbed pretty well all of them. From the first bottle, anyway, which took me a good hour and forty minutes to finish. After that, things started to get a bit silly. I put the plug into the bathroom sink, emptied my very last bottle into it and immersed my head. There's nothing like a whisky facial. I held my breath for as long as I could manage and then, with all the self-control I could muster, drew a snort up each nostril to let the liquid really suffuse my sinuses.

There was some screaming.

I performed an ill-advised pirouette in the bathroom, smacked my head on the shower door, and searched frantically for a towel to clear the whisky from my eyes. The first bottle had dulled my senses, but not so much that I was inured to agony, only common sense. I managed to make my way to the kitchen, where I dug out my favorite Longhorns mug (Go Longhorns!) and started to bail out the sink, scooping the Glenmorangie into a tureen that I occasionally use to toss salads. When I was done, I carried the tureen into the living room and placed it on the coffee table for ease of access. Then began the process of bailing out the tureen, using the same Longhorns mug, and scooping the whisky into me. In deference to the significance of the occasion, I sat upright, keeping a straight back and a stalwart demeanor, knowing that while I was bound to get maudlin drunk, it was better than the alternative: maudlin sober.

So, after two mugs, it now being 6.30 p.m. and beginning to hit dusk, I'm sitting there in my living room in a Verner Panton chair, sweating, half naked but still wearing my shoes, with a fishing hat on, listening to *The Clash's Greatest Hits* over and over on the CD player, staring at the ceiling and recalling how Europe put all its rejects, misfits, and psychos on the *Mayflower*. And grinning, the drool falling triumphantly from both corners of my mouth onto my unbuttoned shirt. Around this time, I got my second wind, and some instinct for self-preservation manifested itself because I decided to restrict myself to shots. Not that this would mean drinking any less. Just slower. And with more effort. Assuming I'd be able to find the shot glass with the bottle, and then find my mouth with the glass.

At 7.50, it was well dark and the bottles were finished. I could still stand and pull up my pants, but now I was shouting the lyrics to "Rock the Casbah" even though the CD player was turned off. I picked up the empty bottles to take over to Percy Place, where there was a dumpster by the rear exit of the old Bank of Ireland offices. I had it on good authority that the security camera attached to the wall and targeted on the back door didn't work, so there'd be no recording of me getting rid of the bottles, the good authority being the little old lady at Number 34, who I'd caught leaving cardboard boxes in the same bin one Sunday evening. That was good enough for me.

Carrying the bottles in both hands meant using my elbows to steer me down the stairs, using my arms as leverage off the walls, then the banister, then back off the walls, stepping gingerly but with the persistence built into every drunk's DNA that allows him to overcome trams, traffic cones, trouser zips, and tremors. At the bottom of the stairs, I took off the fishing hat and left it on the table in the hallway. I had to put down the bottles on the table first to take off the hat, but when I picked them up again and found myself confronted with the front door, I realized that I'd left my keys in the door to my apartment. I turned to head back upstairs and got to the bottom of the stairs before the redundancy of taking the bottles back upstairs dawned on me. I put the bottles back on the table and went back up the stairs, less gingerly this time, since I only had myself to damage, and retrieved the keys. To save time, I fell down the stairs to the hallway. I managed to get the front door open and scrambled down the front steps, through the gate, and across to Huband Bridge. Then I realized I didn't have the bottles with me. I scrambled back up the steps, spent eight minutes trying to get the key in the front door, retrieved the bottles, and then fell down the front steps, determinedly protecting the bottles as I fell because I was on a mission to put them in the bin.

When I came back, I found that all the exercise up and down the stairs had loosened my guts and I had to run for the john. With my pants barely down, my innards dropped out with a SPLOOSH! that soaked my ass. I felt like I'd shat a placenta.

I studied the bulbous mass of shit but held myself back from prodding it to see if it moved—it isn't like I'm German. At first, I thought it was my stomach, then, joy of joys, from underneath the dense stew, a little white lump bobbed to the surface and clung to the side of the turd like a shipwreck survivor. It was what I'd been hoping to see for months: Steve the parasite's head. Finally, the poor bastard had bought the farm.

I considered fishing it out so that I could mount it, his departure striking me as both timely and symbolic, and by the look of the pile in the pan he'd taken another couple of pounds off my weight, which compounded my joy. No more Weight Watchers for me. From now on, I'll be putting on weight.

I haven't been this happy in years.

No. 31
The Juan Carlos

4 oz. Bourbon
An ivory swizzle stick
Serve in a foiled coupe

After breakfast, I got a phone call from Frank to meet up. I took four paracetamols and a pint of water and slipped into something long and uncomfortable—the 11.15 DART from Lansdowne Road to Greystones—and Frank met me at Killiney Station instead of Dalkey, his local station. He didn't want his neighbors seeing him consort with people of my ilk.

We exited the station and took the underpass down to a deserted and windswept Killiney beach, never my favorite spot—too stony, desolate. I'd had the sense to wrap up, had put a scarf on, although I'd forgotten gloves, and my Hush Puppies had seen better days. The tide was right in, roaring and slamming against the groynes, thrashing the shingle so that our small talk was accompanied by a background hiss, like a Greek chorus inserted into a pantomime.

"You've really screwed up the whole show with your lack of professionalism, Joe," he began. We were walking side by side in the direction of Killiney Hill, which meant he was shielding me from the sea—very thoughtful—but also that I could hear him clearly, understand his meaning unambiguously.

"Don't lecture me on professionalism, Frank," I protested. "You and your buddies are running around like a bull in a China shop breaking a butterfly on a wheel."

He grimaced.

"What kind of fucked-up metaphor is that?"

"I'm sorry. It's the stress."

He nodded understandingly.

"You don't have to tell me. There's all hell let loose beyond the Pale. A breakout at the detention camp in Mosney. Half the refugees have managed to escape. If they organize, we could be screwed right royally."

A hundred yards ahead of us, a black Labrador appeared out of nowhere, tearing toward the waves in delight. It gave Frank cause to stop in his tracks. We'd have to head back before anyone saw us.

"And not only do I have to deal with that, but you, *you,* have put me in this position where I have to…to *improvise.* Like I don't have enough to worry about."

I grabbed his arm and stopped him in his tracks.

"Excuse me? Don't try to stick anything on me, Frank. You're the one who has put yourself in this position. You were the one who picked up Delia. You were the one whose voice I heard on the recording. You're the one who's out of control. When you could have come to me. Could have talked to me. Like old times."

"Like old times? You moron. Why do you think I was sent here? Old times, my ass."

"You came here because you wanted to. Left to your own devices, isn't that what you said? How many times have I kept my mouth shut because you're a buddy?"

His face gave no sign of comprehension.

"Buddy? You dick. I was sent here to clean up the mess. After your fuck-up in Athens and your risible attempt to hold the Company to ransom. Do you really think they'd give in to blackmail? They put you here for a purpose, you idiot. And sent me because I knew you. Because you'd trust me."

I pulled a packet of stale Cohiba Minis from my inside pocket and offered him one, but at that very same moment he pulled out—from where exactly I'm not sure—a beige A4 envelope, which he held out insistently. Our eyes met and I realized from his glare that his offer had precedence. I took it from him and he set off walking again, a little ahead of me, while I put away the Minis and examined the envelope's contents.

They were photographs of me, not taken by Stiveley—too clinical—showing me engaged in various forms of activity with Yasmina. They didn't look Photoshopped. They looked genuine. Me fucking her up the ass from behind, me going down on her, she sucking me off. All posed. It looked like the ambassador's residence, but I couldn't be sure. The background wasn't really the issue. *These* were the photos Frank had been referring to the other day. Not Stiveley's.

So maybe I did get laid that night after all. It does count if both our drinks were spiked, right?

Frank had wandered off down the beach. I ran to catch up with him.

"Are these meant to buy my silence?"

He shrugged.

"Your call. I had to ask you the other day if you knew she'd died at Connolly in case you'd already heard and suspected something. But since you haven't figured it out, I'll tell you how it plays. Even as we speak, Yasmina Yıldırım of the United Nations Commission on Human Rights is being exposed in the Irish media as the suicide bomber responsible for the explosion at Connolly Station, working in cahoots with a sophisticated anarchist underground of dissident republican elements, asylum seekers, illegal immigrants, the Travelers' resistance, and the Irish Circus Army, a dangerous new organization that has infiltrated the legitimate street entertainment and public performance community. She was only able to carry out this act of barbarism as a result of her network of collaborators with links to the criminal underworld—smugglers of cigarettes, duty-free booze, and so on—and the use of her feminine wiles, which she used to beguile a former CIA operative into betraying his country by providing her with the local knowledge he acquired through his work as the boss of an international information-gathering business. The whereabouts of this traitor, this low-life, are unknown. It is possible that he died in the bomb blast with his lover, blown to smithereens, and no trace of him remains, or that he knew in advance that the bombing was about to happen and so made himself scarce. There are rumors that he has been spotted in Venezuela. Someone saw him in Ecuador with Julian Assange and Freddie Mercury. The evidence is inconclusive."

I waved the photos in front of his face.

"There's no way anyone will fall for this."

"You're kidding. They'll lap it up. People love conspiracy shit like this. You should know. Ask your dad. They think it empowers them."

"What about Sinéad? Have you killed her, too? You fuck her, then you kill her, is that it? You'll have to, now. She knows the truth too."

"Joe," he said, like he was about to lose his temper, "Don't be a schmuck all your fucking life. Sinéad was at the ambassador's residence. She was sent over by New York to keep an eye on you. To keep you distracted. Supervise the winding down of the office while conning you she wanted it kept open. Who do you think turned out the lights?"

My self-esteem shrank to the size of a small ball of mucus and bounced around my belly.

"Winding down?" I knew exactly what he meant, but I wanted him to spell it out. He inhaled deeply.

"If you're fucking friend Delia hadn't got in the way, everything might have gone smoothly. We'd have wound down the office, pinned the explosion on you, and I'd have got a medal and a few decent fucks from Sinéad." He smiled to himself. "You know, Joe. I actually think we might have a future together."

"I'm fucking delighted for you. What do you mean 'Delia got in the way'?"

"The guy was finding ways to keep your office open. O'Flaherty the union guy. Selling cocaine to top up wages. I mean, it's useful now as a tie-in to smear Yasmina, but at the time we figured he was compromising the operation. Had to be taken out."

"'Taken out' being today's euphemism for 'tortured and murdered.'" He waved my pedantry away.

"I can't be standing around here all day debating niceties with you when there are Travelers to be rounded up and asylum seekers to be interrogated. The decision's yours to make. I'm doing you a favor, out of the kindness of my heart. You can do a runner, disappear, wherever you like—I'll give you a day's start—or you can do the decent thing—bottle of pills, slit your wrists in the woods, on the beach," he motioned toward the water, "or wait for them to come for you. But remember, they're not going to give you a chance to talk. Believe me."

He started to walk up the beach and took a few steps past me. I grabbed his arm.

"I can't let you go, Frank. Not until you've told me to my face that you killed Delia. That you tortured him. To my face."

His shoulders sagged with impatience.

"Fuck off, Joe. Don't be so melodramatic. Will it make things any easier for you if I say yes? In that case, yes. Will it make things more difficult? In that case, no."

"It's not so much the truth I want, Frank. It's whether you're prepared to look me in the eye when you tell me."

He retraced his few steps and stood toe-to-toe with me, glaring.

"Here. Is this close enough for you? I'm looking you in the eye, do you see? And I'm telling you. Yes, I tortured Delia Brennan, Joe, yes. Yes, I killed him, yes, I slit his throat, and yes, it gave me pleasure. Yes, I said. Yes. He was a fucking fly in the ointment. He got in my fucking way. Is that what you need to hear, good buddy? He was like a fly to me. As we are to the gods."

He stepped back, his lips tight and unsmiling, and still he glared. I don't know what kind of response he was expecting. I elected to speak in measured tones.

"That's all I wanted to know, Frank. That you could look me in the eye. Because I tell you what. I was hoping you couldn't. I was hoping you'd feel some shame. Some guilt. Now I know that you have no remorse. It will make things so much easier."

I reached inside my overcoat and pulled out Frank's crucifix. He gave no hint of recognition, betrayed no surprise. I flicked the stop switch on Christ's wrist and pressed playback so that Frank could hear his own confession over the growl of the waves.

"Give me that fucking thing, Joe. It's not going to do you any good."

"So why do you need it?"

I started to back away.

"It isn't mine to lose, Joe. I'm beta-testing it, remember?"

"Of course. How silly of me. Well how about this?" I detached the crucifix from the chain and popped it in my mouth.

You've probably never tried to swallow a crucifix, so let me tell you, it isn't as easy as you'd imagine. I had the necessary saliva, or so I thought, but the peristaltic wave that forms around the bolus of food normally sent down one's gullet doesn't cope so easily with something cross-shaped. Like a cross. It scrapes. It stabs. It tries to come back up again. And *that* really fucking hurts.

I was doubled over coughing and retching when Frank grabbed my arm, pulled me down to the sand, and kicked my stomach. Perhaps he was trying to be helpful, figuring that the rapid expulsion of air would contribute to forced exit of the crucifix. Like the Heimlich maneuver but with more bruising. It didn't work, anyway, which was probably why he attempted to crush my Adam's apple instead. My immediate thought was, "That's not actually helping at all," although the pain served as a palliative in that it took my mind off any internal bleeding I might have had.

I tried to break Frank's stranglehold, but he was even more tenacious than Steve. And when I looked up at him kneeling over me, it became clear that I meant nothing to him, that even now, he was just doing his job.

He said to me once, "You know, Joe, if you were to dehydrate the human body entirely, the chemicals that you're left with can be bought over the counter in a pharmacy for 13 euros; some people's lives are worth much less." Well, that may be true, but add water to those chemicals and, when arranged in a particular way, they're surprisingly unwilling to surrender that human life. I never knew my body wanted to live so much.

Frank was squeezing my throat with such vigor that despite the cloudiness of my vision, I could make out that purple vein on his temple, pulsating. "If he's not careful he'll kill himself," I thought.

Frank altered his grip to get a better purchase, and by moving down my throat, he forced the crucifix up. It popped out of my mouth like a jack-rabbit, and we both followed its trajectory, Frank easing off momentarily, out of surprise and indecision. With my right hand, I reached out for it among the pebbles, only a couple of feet away from my head, and as I turned my head, Frank's grip became less secure. He wasn't sure whether to beat me to the disc or strangle me first. I took advantage of his indecision and grabbed a stone, baseball size but egg-shaped, so that it protruded from the palm of my hand, and when I aimed it at his head, I aimed it so that the pointy end made contact with that throbbing purple vein at his temple.

It was a roundhouse blow but a clean shot, making contact perfectly. Clean, but bloody, dislodging Frank and knocking him to the ground next to me, semi-conscious, groaning. I was coughing and sore, but at least I could breathe, so I pressed home my advantage. As Frank came round, he attempted to pull himself up to a kneeling position. I rushed him and swung again, catching him more or less in the same spot, opening up a gash along the side of his head, round to the socket of his right eye. He went down face first but still wasn't out.

I pulled him over onto his back and hit him again, full in the face, on the bridge of his nose. That's where you aim to drive the bone up into the brain, although my intention was only disfigurement. I hit him again on his right cheekbone and felt it give way under the solidity of the stone, saw the bone through the grazing, saw the blood pour into his eye.

In retrospect, it's difficult to decide whether I was killing Frank because he'd killed Delia or because he'd betrayed me. Maybe Delia *had* been a member of the underground. Maybe he *had* been using me without my knowledge. But so what? It had felt like a proper friendship, and he was all I had.

Well, him and Frank, but it turns out I didn't have a friendship with Frank.

Another couple of minutes battering Frank's face and neck was enough to convince me he was dead. At that point, I felt I should check whether there had been any witnesses, so I gingerly looked up from my work and surveyed the scene. The black Labrador had gone. Not a soul around.

I returned my gaze to what remained of Frank's face. Urgh. Poor Frank.

I dragged him over to the nearest groyne, only a matter of yards away, and propped him up against it at the edge of the water.

I looked for the crucifix among the pebbles and pocketed it.

I'd sat Frank up so I could search him for identification. I started on his outside pockets and found some tissues, then reached inside his coat for his wallet only to discover that he'd been packing. Under his left armpit was a small holster containing a Saturday night special, fully loaded. Why the fuck hadn't he thought to use it?

I threw it down, cast it away from me. Then I slapped Frank about the face. Severely. "You fucking, fucking idiot, Frank. You fucking, fucking idiot." He could have used the gun on me, could have whipped it out and shot me dead, yet he chose to try to choke me, to scare me into handing over the crucifix, to force it back up my gullet.

I wept. I put my head on his shoulder and wept.

I hugged him until I felt the tide lapping at my left trouser leg. A sudden burst of hailstones began to rattle the pebbles like applause. Time to go. I picked up the gun, put it into Frank's right hand, aimed it into his mouth and pulled the trigger.

I'm not proud of it. It just made sense.

I left the gun next to his body and turned him onto his stomach, face down on the pebbles. The sea began its work.

According to *Business Week*, the governor of Kansas has ordered the eradication of all butterflies in the state after reading a book on chaos theory.

No. 133
The Crème de la Mare, aka the Rebekah Brooks
4 oz. White Horse Whiskey
8 oz. Ginger Beer
Vegemite Substitute
Shaken but no Stir

New words to learn today: bogus – 1) counterfeit, sham 2) excellent, worthwhile; milopherous – designating an eidetic image of a chimera; fungible – interchangeable; folie à deux – the existence of a delusional idea in two closely associated individuals; fiscitudinous – characterized by absence; oblasque – an artificial or made-up word, a false neologism; mutrid – made of felt; wormb – 1) a conceptual hymen. 2) an object, construct, or phenomenon in which inside and outside are not distinct, e.g., a Mobius strip; disafflatus – use of a performative contradiction for rhetorical purposes; sycomancy – divination by means of figs or fig leaves; gastrea – a hypothetical metazoan ancestral form; loition – the act of removing scruples.

I caught the DART back to Pearse Street and took a wander round town to try to think things through, try to see things more clearly. I stopped for a tomato juice and Cohiba Mini outside the Palace Bar, with its soft, repressed pastel-colored floor tiles, then changed my mind and left the juice half-finished and made for Weimar's café bar round the corner, where I sat on the terrace and had a coffee and a cava.

Around eight, I nipped into the office, using the spare key. I gathered up all the papers on my desk in case there was anything useful in there, pinched a couple of small jiffy bags from the stationery cupboard, and put the crucifix inside one. I figured I'd need it for insurance purposes, but it wouldn't do any harm to make a copy of the recording and send it to a reliable journalist, one who could be trusted to publish and be damned.

Shame I don't know any.

Then I went home, locked the door, and packed my bags.

In the left-hand drawer of my bedroom desk, I have two passports and open flight tickets under two different names: one to Dallas–Fort Worth under my CIA name, Joe Chambers, the other to Madrid via Barcelona under my real name. They bear the same photo.

I shall be traveling light to Barcelona. It's not that warm this time of year, but I can buy gear when I get there. I put in a few changes of clothes. Ray-Bans. Couple of disguises—wig, tache, fake boobs—some hair dye, truss. I'm just taking my tennis bag. Put my rackets in so that it wouldn't look suspicious—although I'm not used to clay courts, I might get a game in, you never know—and it has wheels on that makes it easy to pull through the airport like a pro. Everything else I'm leaving in the apartment. Well, what is there that's left for me here? All my mates are dead. The economy's fucked to bits. All the Scotch is gone.

Prior to leaving, I made a point of checking the phone messages. Nothing from Sinéad. Figures. But three calls from Jane Bondage. Urgent. Call me now. Here's my mobile number.

Things are looking up. An escort's private number. I'm privileged. I called immediately.

"Joe. I need your help. There's something going on here. I don't know who else to talk to." There was panic in her voice. Not as sexy as I would have hoped.

"Jane. What is it? Are you hurt? Did that cunt Estímulo do something?"

"Language, Joe. Language. No. At least, he's done nothing to me. But there's a problem with the business. I think we might be in trouble."

"Trouble, Jane? What kind?"

"Big trouble. Do you remember the Iranian girl? The one who was really Iraqi. The one you were asking about, who was receiving special treatment?"

"Sure, yeah. You said Estímulo was taking care of her."

"That's right. He said she was for a special client, one he had a personal and professional relationship with, one he didn't want to compromise."

"Okay."

"Have you read the papers?"

"I've read some, of course. What about them?"

"Her picture is in the paper. Only it doesn't say she was an Iraqi hooker. It says that she was Turkish. A representative of the UN Commission on Human Rights. Yasmina Yıldırım. And she was killed in the bomb at Connolly Station."

WTF?! But that means…

So who was the man in the towncar? Frank? Grassy Noel?

"Are you sure about this, Jane?"

"Yes. I'm looking at the paper now."

"I mean are you sure it's the same girl. I thought you didn't get to see much of her. Is it definitely her?"

"One thousand percent it's her. Some of the girls got to know her a little better than I did. They came running to me, hysterical. They think that Manuel is behind it. They think he's had her killed."

"And what does he say?"

"He's a fascist pimp who rules by terror. Do you think he's going to deny it? He's telling them all to shut the fuck up and threatening to put out their eyes."

Not unlikely.

"Jane, wait for me by the back door. Pack a bag and be ready to run. I'm coming to get you now."

"Thank you, Joe. I will. I love you, Joe. I do."

Hah! This was among the papers I hoovered up off my desk. Nice coincidence.

Travel Tips

Useful holiday advice from the readers of *Arthur Frantic's Budget Travel* magazine:

> Flight crews know the best hotels and places to eat in any town. When you leave the airport, have your taxi driver tail anyone in a uniform to their final destination.
> *Harold Quant, Kissimmee*
>
> Save time writing your holiday diary while you're away by completing it before you go. When you get home, you can make any amendments that might be required.
> *Suzanne Schlong, Boise*
>
> When you park your hire car, leave the local fascist newspaper visible on the passenger seat and the local police will make sure that nothing happens to it.
> *Czeslaw Jones, Omaha*
>
> When you go up to the breakfast buffet, leave a large, bloodied ax on your table and no one will dare steal your toast.

Winifred Goatee, Miami

When abroad, wipe your ass using those wet wipes that you can't use at home because they clog up the drains. After all, you're on holiday!
Jim Underling, Braintree

Get a seat at the back of the plane so that if it crashes the bodies of all the people in front of you will soften the impact. Ask to sit behind a particularly fat person.
Celeste Placematte, Phoenix

Rather than take entire travel books with you, avoid excess luggage penalties by visiting your local public library and tearing out the relevant pages for the place you're going to.
William Minger, Abilene

According to the police in Rome, the police in Genoa are pickpocketing bastards.
Giuseppe O'Toole, Punxatawney

Don't book an expensive hotel. A few weeks before you go away, befriend people from your destination on Facebook so that you'll have somewhere cheap to stay when you get there.
The late Gertrude Cartwright, Seattle

Wearing a pedometer will tell you precisely how many fucking miles you've walked around Paris.
Stanley Althusser, Reno

The faucets in airplane toilets always spray everywhere, leaving embarrassing stains on your trousers. As soon as I enter the toilet, I strip naked to avoid any such calamity.
Bryce Lee, Oakland

I hate having to write postcards while I'm away, and I know the recipients really just want the exotic stamps, so I just buy the stamps, put them in envelopes, and post them off instead. I usually enclose a short note so that they'll know who the stamps are from.
Gerry Invincible, Williamsburg

Rather than insult my friends by bringing home the cheap tat sold abroad as souvenirs, I just tell them the place I visited was shit.
Montague Barry, Des Moines

...

...

This, I am thinking, the Irish call a turnip for the books. That is what they say, yes? Is not a phrase that I can pretend to understand, but then the Irish are not an especial easy-to-understand people. The famous Jew Sigmund Freud is saying once that there are two types of people who cannot be psychoanalyzed: the Irish and people in a coma. People in a coma cannot be analyzed because they do not have any dreams and also because you cannot ask them anything even if they are having dreams, because they are in a coma. The Irish cannot be psychoanalyzed because they are not having the superego, they do not have a sense of discretion. They are not repress anything and therefore everything in their unconscious is already on the surface. They are nothing but Id and Ego. Their dreams and their reality are the same thing. Television is truth, Travelers are food, books want turnips. This is how it is. Sometimes a penis just a pen. There is nothing lying beneath. He was wrong, of course. The Irish are the best liars of all. Proof is the fact that they conned Sigmund Freud.

When I am find out that Joseph Chambers has these links with Delia Brennan and my rivals in the drug distribution business, I am say to myself, but also to Frank Prendergast too, "Hello?!" and "Fuck the you what?!" This is very big news to me because I am knowing not nothing about this network of cunts who are rivaling me with their cocaine. Is me and me alone who is permitted to provide the drugs to her majesty's TDs and judges and police commissioners. Anyone who thinks they can break into my patch, he must be stop in his tracks like a wild badger. I will gas him myself if this is necessary. I should say, though, that it was not Frank who tell me this. Was Chambers himself, who come here with his drugs and try to make Jane Bondage to be his bitch. She tells me straight away and I have him kicked out of my house, but I also have him trailed and watched and sniffed. And through him I am find Delia Brennan and Peter O'Flaherty and all their network. And what do I have to do to wipe them out? Nothing! Nada! Because is Frank Prendergast who arrest Delia Brennan for getting in his way, and is Frank Prendergast who have Peter O'Flaherty round up for being big union bastard and therefore killed. And I don't not have to do a thing! Is all hilarious!

But this is only amuse bouche. After all, we know anyway that Joseph Chambers is dead meat. We have him set up with bomb, with our false flag, Yasmina, who pose very nicely as fake United Nations whore and have no idea her suitcase would be control by remote to detonate in Connolly Station. She thinks she is still in role and is taking "vital documents" for framing big Belfast mobster and blow open all the illegal organ traffick network in Northwest Europe. Silly bitch. She blew plenty open.

Was a very good night in the brothel, I must say. The night of the blast, we hold a big major party. All my respected friends here, who have work very hard to bring this state of affairs to fruition, we laugh heartily at this contrivance. We toast it all with the champagne. None of your Catalan cava shit. Proper drinks.

I was very surprise to learn that Joseph Chambers was not killed also. This was not how I understand things was suppose to work at all. My belief was that every strand would be tied up, that Chambers was taking the fall. Was no good to me that I have someone connected to my drug rivals still walking about and able to talk. It strike me, I think, that Frank Prendergast has had crisis of conscience. He was come here and he swear to me that he intend to kill Chambers himself and that the body would go missing for good. Yet next thing I know, Chambers is spot at the Rehabilitation Hospital by a contact I have and he is chatting with Frank Prendergast. They even share cigarettes. Chambers punches man unconscious, and he walk out the main gate. What kind of hit job is that?

So I say, no, Manuel, this will not do. If you want anything pulled off, you must do it yourself. And so I concoct story with Jane Bondage, we call Chambers, tell him about Iraqi girl, he comes running like a lamb. We bring him in the back door, we drug him, we break his fingers, smash his face. What a fucking idiot. He tells us he has killed Frank Prendergast. Yes! He says he has breaked his face with some seaside rock. We laugh with great incredulity even after seven fingernails are gone, but still he persist with this story, so finally I send one of my bints down to Killiney beach to look. There, sure enough, he is finding Prendergast's body and we know Chambers is all true. Of course, is too late to put back in his fingernails, so we knock him out with Rohypnol. Kill the pain.

You see where this leaves me, of course. As we say in Madrid, *jajajajaja.* Not only have I score big brown points with my Irish hosts and customers, but also I am at the same time in complete control of the drug trade in South

Dublin. Is only a matter of time before my colleagues in the Gardaí mop up Brennan's network. I feel sorry for Frank, of course; a reliable and trustworthy comrade but he have problem of being too soft. He give in to sentiment for the sake of nostalgia, and it was the undoing of him. You say this, undoing? Who has not done that, from time to time? Finish off a cigarette instead of chase a non-paying john; let a whore off with one black eye out of affection; stave in the head of a yelping runt instead of let it suffer. We all know that weakness. Frank was simply unlucky; this is all.

If you listen close, you can hear Chambers downstairs. I am have him in my "dungeon." He is very funny. Is totally disorientated. I am think the Rohypnol wears off now, and the pain worm its way back into his conscious. I am hope to drag final useful information from his worthless hide, perhaps about his drug contacts, but I am doubt he has anything left of value for me. He jibber over and over about Gavin McShit, so maybe we will bring this man in. I have sent down two of my bints to have a bit of fun with him before they put him down, but I am must say, though, how much his bravery is admiring for me. Is not something I was especting of him. Even as I write this, I can hear him shouting, far down below: *"Come on, you bastards. Here I am! Come and get me! I'm waiting for you!"*

I am almost impressed. Perhaps I will let him live after all.

Jajajajaja.

I joke.

THE END

Acknowledgments

No individual should be required to take the blame for this book other than the hubristic fool who chose to publish it, but even hubristic fools are products of the worlds they inhabit, and all the positive elements in this book, such as they are, owe their existence to the influence, collaboration, co-operation, and input, witting or otherwise, of a myriad: friends, acquaintances, strangers, childhood experiences, accidents, teachers, nightmares, lovers, traumas, fantasies, drunken conversations, boat trips and car journeys, books read and films half watched, misremembered songs, TV shows caught from the corner of one eye. No author can identify them all. Here are some that I know for sure.

Each of my reviewers has provided not just assistance and positive vibes but also confirmation of the enduring presence and significance of solidarity and empathy—at a time when such qualities are dismissed—for a writing career that has been slow to show any signs of progress. Thank you, Sami, William, Niamh, Lorcan, Oliver, Olibhéir,

Niall, Caitriona, Daphne, Arthur, Karl, Carlton, Richard, and John. Structural editor Elise Hendrick (elise.hendrick@gmail.com) showed me possibilities and pathways, some taken, some not, to make this book immeasurably better than it otherwise would have been. You should hire her. Lisa McInerney has been a constant source of encouragement and inspiration, through her own writing, as a friend, by her example, and in her deeds. She and Sinéad Keogh also gave me space and time to experiment with ideas, plotting, and character on their websites. John McInerney was a source of comfort and support that buoyed my spirits during periods of doubt. Thanks for "getting it," John. I am also greatly indebted to Donagh Brennan of the *Irish Left Review* for his kind words and for his willingness to accept that what I was doing was funny and worthy of wider circulation. More power to you, Donagh.

I have been a fan of Jon Langford's work in its varied forms for several decades. It is an honor and a privilege to have his design on the cover of my first book. My powers of concentration are so feeble that I require almost total silence when attempting to read a novel, but if I were to suggest a soundtrack of top-notch, ace, and rocking tunes to accompany *Breakfast at Cannibal Joe's,* it could easily be compiled using Jon's music alone (The Three Johns, Mekons, Waco Brothers, Pine Valley Cosmonauts, Skull Orchard, Men of Gwent, etc., etc.). Perhaps before picking this book up, you should pick up some of those. But still pick this book up, too.

My brother Martin's spirit, humor, and worldview cannot but permeate this book, simply by virtue of his importance to me intellectually and emotionally. They can be found implicitly, in the choice of words, the tone, and the style, and explicitly in many of the jokes and ideas that would not have existed without him. He stands as my ideal reader in that I write with a view to making him laugh. If I can imagine him laughing, it stays in. Cheers, Mart. You're my hero.

But most of all, Maria. My Maria. Her kindness. Her laughter. Her beauty. Her patience. Especially her patience. I am blessed to have her by my side.

For more by Jay Spencer Green:

Website: http://www.jayspencergreen.com
Twitter: https://twitter.com/JaySpencerGreen
Facebook: https://www.facebook.com/jay.spencer.green

11689769R00195

Printed in Great Britain
by Amazon.co.uk, Ltd.,
Marston Gate.